P9-DMG-425

7009993320611

ALSO BY ROSEMARIE ROBOTHAM

COAUTHOR
Spirits of the Passage:
The Transatlantic Slave Trade in the Seventeenth Century

EDITOR
The Bluelight Corner:
Black Women Writing on Passion, Sex and Romantic Love

Zachary's Wings

Rosemarie Robotham

SCRIBNER

SCRIBNER
1230 Avenue of the Americas
New York, NY 10020

This book is a work of fiction. Names, characters, places, and
incidents either are products of the author's imagination or are used
fictitiously. Any resemblance to actual events or locales or persons,
living or dead, is entirely coincidental.

Copyright © 1998 by Rosemarie Robotham

All rights reserved, including the right of reproduction
in whole or in part in any form.

SCRIBNER and design are trademarks of Simon & Schuster Inc.

Designed by Brooke Zimmer
Set in Columbus Monotype
Manufactured in the United States of America

1   3   5   7   9   10   8   6   4   2

Library of Congress Cataloging-in-Publication Data

Robotham, Rosemarie, date
Zachary's wings/Rosemarie Robotham
p.   cm.
I. Title.
PS3568.03177ffl24   1998   97–23802
813 .54—dc21   CIP

ISBN 0-684-84726-4

"Redemption Song" written by Bob Marley. Copyright © 1980
Fifty-Six Hope Road Music, Ltd. and Odnil Music, Ltd.
Used by permission. All rights reserved.

Line from *Parable of the Sower* © 1993 by Octavia E. Butler, published
by Seven Stories Press. Reprinted by permission of the publisher.

To Lascelles and Gloria Robotham,
my mom and dad,
and my big brother, Gordon.
You keep me grounded.

To Radford Arrindell,
my life partner and love,
and our children, Radford and Kai.
You give me flight.

Acknowledgments

A book is truly a collective endeavor, and I am grateful to everyone who contributed to this one.

Among those without whom this book would not be: My agent Michael Carlisle, who believed in the possibilities and shepherded the first draft of my novel into the hands of a wonderful editor at Scribner, Jane Rosenman. Jane patiently explored with me what still needed to be done, helping to transform a tentative, questing first draft into a more personally satisfying work. Her talented assistant, Caroline Kim, contributed her own sensitive editing suggestions, and was scrupulous with the details.

My cousin (so like a sister) Karen Panton Walking Eagle, my friends and writing cohorts Sherrill Clarke, Sharon Fitzgerald, Robert Fleming, Tina McElroy Ansa, Robert McNamara, Lisa Redd and Martha Southgate, and my husband, Radford Arrindell, read various drafts and offered me criticism in ways I could grasp. Sharon Fitzgerald, more than once, suspended time to obsess with me over a single word, while Lisa Redd made sure I had the geography right. Valerie Wilson Wesley had faith in me from the start, and set a fine example. Eleta Greene shared her worlds of understanding, LaVon Leak-Wilks lent her infallible eye, while my colleagues at *Essence* magazine, led by Susan L. Taylor, provided a rich creative atmosphere away from the novel, and much sisterly support.

I also give thanks to my amazing family, all the loving, energetic, opinionated, colorful characters who make my life such an interesting place to be. In particular: My father, Lascelles Robotham, who blessed, and still blesses, my efforts; my mother, Gloria Robotham, who encourages me even when I venture beyond the bounds of her own comfort; and my brother, Gordon Robotham, childhood partner in outrageous fiction, who challenges and champions me, welcoming with sweet pride whatever I produce.

And especially to those who nourish me daily: My husband, Radford Arrindell, who knew my heart's desire before I knew it myself, and our children, Radford Arthur and Kai Angela, who with their dad remind me always that I am part of something magical and alive. This family. This love.

Contents

PROLOGUE 1983
The Seduction 15

PART ONE 1973–1983
1: *Rebel Dreams* 31
2: *Quincy Street* 49
3: *Black Power* 68
4: *The Seduction (Reprise)* 83

PART TWO 1983–1985
5: *True Love* 93
6: *Modigliani's Girl* 113
7: *Nomads* 137
8: *Smoke Signals* 157

PART THREE 1985–1986
9: *Going Home* 181
10: *The Carpenter's Shadow* 203
11: *The Rooms* 219
12: *The Secret Savior* 239

EPILOGUE 1987
Rest 263

Zachary's Wings

Prologue
1983

"For a raindrop,
Joy is in entering the river."
—Ghālib

The Seduction

11026847269

AFTERWARDS, THEY WOULD AGREE THAT SOME INSTINCT had angled them in each other's direction from the start. They had been like two wayward streams of energy, originating at vastly opposite poles and spilling in apparently random directions, when in fact, all along their internal compasses had been sure. For when, finally, they stood before each other on the broken asphalt of a Philadelphia parking lot on that gentle October afternoon, the moment had held a peculiar organic force, as if some deep quiescent memory had flashed suddenly to the fore.

Neither Zachary nor Korie had suspected that this day might be any different from the hundreds that preceded it. Zach had certainly not expected a woman the color of roasted cashews to pull into the Carson Agency parking lot at the same moment he did. "I thought you'd be an earnest white girl," he told Korie much later. "It never crossed my mind you'd be black." There had been that spark of recognition between them the moment their eyes met. But Zach ransacked his memory and couldn't recall ever encountering the corkscrew-haired, sultry-eyed young woman who was opening the door of a generic blue Chrysler, clearly a rental. The young woman was dressed, on this warm Friday afternoon, in a loose denim dress belted neatly at the waist and falling to her ankles in a curtain of pleats. In one hand she held a notebook and two pens. She was rummaging inside a huge black leather tote bag with her other hand, all the while keeping her thick-lashed, rude-girl eyes unwaveringly on Zach.

Mechanically, still holding the young woman's gaze, Zach exited his car. The slam of his car door jerked him out of his trance. He crossed the parking lot to introduce himself. Not quite handsome, he was still a fine-looking man, tall as the pro-basketball player he had once dreamed of becoming, smooth and brown as sweet chocolate, his movements graceful and lithe. Although in his khaki trousers and loose short-sleeved shirt he appeared slender, his arms were ropy and muscular, and his wide shoulders strained at the material of his shirt. His greeting was friendly, but aloof.

"You're the writer from New York," he said rather than asked. "I'm the caseworker for the Paleys."

"Korie Morgan," she confirmed, extending her hand. "You must be Zachary Piper. Irv Ryan mentioned you."

Zach thought he caught a hint of an accent, or not an accent exactly, but a peculiar lack of any regional intonation. It was one of Zach's more useless skills, the ability to match an African-American accent to a specific region of the country, and often to a specific state. He had practiced it during six academically uninspired years at Howard University in Washington, D.C., from which he had graduated, just barely, with a sociology degree. If the landscape of his life had been different, he reflected now, he might have made a good linguist. He had the ear for it, and a keenness of observation that allowed him to pick up on subtle clues like gesture and demeanor. But this Korie Morgan didn't seem to fit any of his familiar categories. She didn't even sound African or West Indian. Her accent seemed—he searched for the right words—faintly lilting, yet somehow scrubbed.

He found himself trying to estimate the young woman's age as he led the way into Carson Agency's offices.

Close up, her skin had a sallow undercast in the mid-afternoon sun, so that pale greenish tracings showed at her temples. Her lips were full, unpainted; at the moment they were curved into a quizzical shape, as if a question suffered, unasked, on the crest of those lips. But it was the eyes that fascinated Zachary: Rusty brown, with a faint upward slant, they held a kind of secret radiance, a playful, even flirtatious, quality that was somehow at odds with the seriousness of her demeanor.

Early twenties, Zachary decided, but a moment later changed his mind. She was greeting Irv Ryan, Carson's hulking executive director, with a clipped, professional assurance that made her seem much older. There was no hint of uncertainty in her manner. She was all cool business, ladylike as hell, expertly controlling the entire exchange. She had been at this a while, Zach realized.

Grant and Margie Paley were waiting for them in the agency's small conference room. Grant, dark and walleyed, huddled against Margie's reassuring girth. She was the more self-possessed of the pair, and she rose to greet Korie and Zach as they entered the room.

"Hey, Zach Man!" she said, punching his shoulder. "Afternoon, ma'am," she said, turning to Korie. Grant remained slumped in his molded plastic chair, his eyes darting from his wife to Zach, to Irv Ryan, to Korie. Korie shook Margie's hand and nodded to Grant, then concentrated on testing her tape recorder. Irv Ryan had told Zach that she would do only a preliminary interview, more to decide whether she would build her story around the Paleys than to gather actual grist for the writing of it. She had been assigned by her magazine to do a feature on mental patients who were managing their lives outside of an institution. When, on the morning of October 13, 1983, she had called the Carson Agency inquiring about subjects she might interview, Ryan, eager to promote his agency's good works in a prestigious national magazine, had thought immediately of the Paleys.

The director had made the appointment with the writer from New York for later that day, praying he'd be able to track down the Paley's caseworker at such short notice. Zach Piper was, if truth be told, Ryan's best caseworker, but Christ, he was a pain to supervise. He refused to punch a clock, declaring after only three days on the job that crises didn't conveniently happen between nine and five. It was never a case of Zach sloughing off. He racked up more total hours than any other caseworker and could be counted on to find a rapport with even the most violent or enigmatic "clients," as Ryan insisted Carson's mental patients be called. But Ryan never knew where Piper was, what he was up to, or when, and for those reasons he didn't quite trust him.

Ryan had dialed Piper's desk, cursing when voice mail intercepted the first ring. At the beep, the director barked into the phone: "Four o'clock this afternoon, at the agency. We got a reporter coming in wants to interview the Paleys. If you're late for this one, so help me, Piper, you're fired."

Throughout the afternoon, as she probed the Paleys' history, Korie grew more aware of Zach to her left, chain-smoking cigarettes, watching her. He'd pitched his chair backwards onto two legs so that his shoulders rested against the sand-colored wall where the handprints of several generations of staff and clients clapped in chorus about his head.

Korie drew a deep breath and tried to erase Zach from her peripheral vision. She needed to focus on Grant and Margie. She was struck by the naive gentleness with which they treated each other, by the selfless efforts of each to promote the other's successes. As she drew their stories from them with the reporter's practiced accommodation of curiosity and care, Zach said little. He might have said nothing at all, but Grant and Margie incessantly solicited his agreement: "Ain't that so, Zach?" one or the other would say. "Just ask Zach Man. He'll tell you."

A current seemed to express itself in the small conference room. Korie realized that she did not trust herself to address the Paleys' caseworker. Zach's squinting gaze unnerved her, and she avoided meeting it. She decided she would interview him later, without an audience, and in spite of herself, felt a peculiar thrill at the prospect of seeing him alone. She weighed her chances of piercing his professional cool.

As it turned out, that would prove easier than anticipated. It was almost nightfall when Korie switched off her tape recorder, and Ryan left the room to call an orderly to escort the Paleys back to their quarters down the street. With Ryan out of the room, Korie turned to Zach and asked if they might go for a drink together; she wanted to ask him a few questions.

In the agency parking lot after the Paleys left, they settled on a blues place Zach knew on Lombard Street downtown. Zach offered to take Korie in his car—he'd be happy to bring her back to the agency after the interview so she could pick up her own vehicle. Korie was tempted, more so than she liked to admit. Everything Grant and Margie had told her suggested that Zach Piper was a man in whose care one might choose to place oneself. Standing there opposite him in the parking lot, Korie had pretended to consider his offer, but the truth was, she couldn't find her voice for a moment. She looked away from Zach, trying to release her words from the place in her throat where they had lodged. It was then she caught sight of the moon, a full yellow orb glowing palely in the dusky sky. It was the moon, she decided, that was to blame for all this, for in some deep, newly awakening part of her, she wanted nothing more than to close her eyes and put herself in Zach Piper's care. The intensity of the feeling didn't quite make sense to her.

"No," she answered finally. "I'll drive my car." Better, she thought, to travel under her own steam. She didn't quite trust herself to enter the intimacy of Zach Piper's car, wasn't ready to relinquish her increasingly tenuous control of the situation. Besides, she knew nothing at all about Zach's drinking habits. Or his driving, for that matter.

Korie drove behind Zach, trailing his car closely as he turned through the side streets of downtown Philadelphia. Finally, she pulled up next to him and parked in the deserted lot across the street from the club. A sign announced in cursive blue neon lettering: STONY's. Korie didn't speak as Zach guided her to the door of a low-slung, shingle-walled building. Inside, a bored-looking man greeted them. But for a couple at the far corner of the bar, the club was empty of customers. "It's early, yet," Zach commented, glancing around the room. Korie, walking behind him as they followed the maître d' to their table, admired the broad symmetry of his shoulders, the supple ease of his stride. As they sat down, a waitress appeared, pencil and pad ready to take their order—a Heineken for Zach, a white wine spritzer with lime for Korie.

Korie knew she would ask Zach some question about the Paleys, but she was loath to so quickly define the mood. She said nothing, just peered through the hazy, bluish light at a quintet of musicians tuning their instruments onstage. She felt Zach observing her with a small, amused smile. But he, too, kept the silence. They sat like that for a long while, allowing the coiled energy between them to dissipate slowly, letting it drift and scatter in the air around them until their silence became almost companionable. At last, Zach leaned into the space above the scarred little table that separated them and, for the first time since that afternoon, took the conversational lead.

"So, Ms. Korie Morgan from New York," he drawled with an exaggerated southern inflection, "what's this accent I hear?"

Just then the waitress arrived with their drinks. Korie, glad for the distraction, stirred her wine spritzer slowly, the thin straw creating a tiny tornado of bubbles. Her stomach felt like those bubbles. She realized her heart was racing, quickened by the humid nearness of this man, his laughing eyes, his big, calloused hands splayed openheartedly on the table.

"I'm Jamaican," she said. She even managed a touch of flippancy. "Born and raised. Went to college in New York City, though."

"No kidding." Zach whistled softly. "I'd never have guessed. You don't sound like the Jamaicans I've known."

"My accent gets stronger around other Jamaicans," Korie said. "People tell me that."

Zach picked up his beer and began pouring it into the frosted mug that the waitress had brought. A wide cap of foam bloomed at the top of his glass. "I went to college with a whole bunch of Jamaicans," he said. "Other West Indians, too. They all kinda kept to themselves, though."

Korie didn't answer. She knew how it could be between West Indians and American-born blacks. She had seen how, in a country that relegated most people of color to second-class status, the two groups could nevertheless fail to connect. Korie had been forced to maneuver within her own particular version of that schism in college. She didn't want to revisit the frustration and uneasiness of that time. Not with Zach. Not this night.

"So how did you come to choose social work?" she asked him instead.

Zach grinned, shaking the last of the beer into his glass.

"I'll tell you a secret," he said. "This job isn't hard for me. It doesn't even feel like work. Well, maybe dealing with the boss might be work"—they both laughed a little at that—"but the rest of it? It's nothing more than helping some people get through their day." He paused to take a sip of the beer, then wiped the froth from his lips with the palm of his hand, an unconscious gesture that Korie found oddly appealing. Zach looked up and caught her eyes right then, and found them quiet and attentive, so he went on.

"After I got out of college, the job at Carson was available and, well, seems crazy folk like me." He shrugged. "They sense a kinship, you know."

"You don't seem crazy." Korie smiled. She offered it as a tidbit of small talk, but Zach didn't respond at once, and when he spoke again, his mood had grown pensive.

"Who's to say who's crazy, anyway?" he mused. "With all the drugs and the violence out here, and so many kids growing up lonely and scared, it just might be that going crazy is a very sane thing to do."

"Saner than pretending it all makes sense, anyway," Korie agreed. "When you think about it, it's the perfect paradox."

Zach was silent for a moment, considering. "'A paradox is a truth standing on its head,'" he said finally. "That's the way I learned it in school. Except it might be this particular truth is standing squarely on its feet. Crazy is just a word, you know."

"It's more than a word," Korie argued. "Once it's been officially applied, it can define a person's horizons."

"That's what's sad," Zach murmured, his expression darkening. But just as it seemed that he might veer into gloom, a mischievous light came into his eyes. "You know what?" he said. "We won't solve the world's problems this evening. And the fact is, Ms. Morgan, at this precise moment, there are a few other things I can think of that I'd prefer to do."

Korie couldn't help laughing as she met his frankly flirtatious eyes. She was impressed by his range, by the ease with which he could skip from contemplative to playful, from serious to seductive, and carry her along. As Zach laughed with her, he reached across the table and put his palm over her hand. It felt, to Korie, perfectly natural and spontaneous, and she turned her palm upwards to meet his, liking the bigness of his hand and the warm flush of his skin against her own.

What a curious man, she thought as the laughter died down, and they stared into each other's eyes. But then Zachary Piper, sitting wordlessly in the conference room while she'd interviewed the Paleys, had been a curious figure from the start. He'd seemed markedly indifferent to her reporter's perception of him, unconcerned with how she might portray him in whatever story she might write. And yet the way he leaned in to her now, the teasing intimacy of his voice, the naked fascination in his eyes—all of it told her that Zach was clearly interested in being here with her, in this tiny blues bar sipping wine spritzer and beer, and he wasn't about to pretend it was all just business. Korie had to admit she was having a hard time remembering the Paleys herself.

"What about you?" Zach asked her now. "How did you get to be a big shot journalist?"

"Oh, please," Korie said lightly, but she had the uncomfortable sense that he'd been following her thoughts.

"Hey, don't be modest. You write for a national magazine. That's a pretty big deal."

"Well," Korie said, stalling. She felt suddenly self-conscious.

What she wouldn't say to Zach, at least not right now, was that part of her attraction to journalism had to do with a deep vein of shyness in her nature, which she had learned to cover by throwing the spotlight away from herself, asking the questions rather than answering them. Whether this was fostered more by a thirst for details or merely the desire to hide, the fact was, when she couldn't take refuge behind her questions, her confidence, her bravado tended to flag. But now, in spite of her old shyness, she found herself strangely grateful for Zach's interest, and felt herself opening up to him, her natural reserve falling easily away.

"I just always wanted to write," she heard herself say. "At first, I wasn't sure how to do it and still make a living. And then I discovered journalism."

"Bet you're good, too," Zach said as he reached into his shirt pocket for a cigarette. He struck a match and held the fire to the tip of the cigarette.

"Why do you do it like that?" Korie asked him suddenly.

"What—?" Zach stared at her, the cigarette halfway to his lips.

"The way you light your cigarettes," she said, "holding them to the fire without inhaling. I noticed it at the agency. You handle them like joints."

Zach seemed to take his time absorbing this. He drew deeply on his cigarette, then blew the smoke to one side, his slow grin as he looked back at Korie letting her know that he was on to her, that he had not mistaken her comment for something other than it was—a bold, intentional departure from safe ground.

"Well you see," he drawled finally, "I was what my mama liked to call 'precocious.' Started smoking way too young. And when I started, this was the way I saw my big brother light his sticks. I just thought it was cool. What did I know? And now, it's just a habit, I guess."

"I see." Korie nodded with mock seriousness. She could tell he was toying with her.

"So that's the story of *my* misguided youth," Zach quipped. "Your turn."

"Nothing to tell." Korie laughed. "I was the original good girl."

"I believe that," Zach said softly, but he wasn't teasing her now. His eyes ranged over her face, drinking in details he hadn't noticed before—the fleeting dimple in her cheek, the pale brown mole at the edge of one eye, the tiny forcep mark on her temple. Korie, uncomfortable, shifted in her chair, unable right then to summon a whimsical comeback that would keep the mood light. She decided to say nothing at all. She just sipped her white wine spritzer and looked towards the stage, where the musicians, five fiftyish black men, seemed finally ready to play.

After another moment, Zach leaned all the way across the table and put his lips to Korie's ear.

"Let's go to my house," he proposed over the sudden, haunting wail of a trumpet. "Let's be a little bit naughty."

Korie smiled slowly and held his eyes.

Suddenly, she didn't want to pretend anymore that Grant and Margie Paley had anything to do with this meeting. Had that been true, she could have interviewed Zach back at the agency. She could have sat with him right there in Irv Ryan's conference room and gotten all she needed for her file. But this Zachary Piper intrigued her far more than any story she was investigating. *He* was the reason she'd come to this funky little blues bar on Lombard Street in downtown Philly, where she now sat with her face so close to his that her hair brushed his cheek.

"Why not?" she said evenly.

A fidgety doberman named Ringo greeted them at Zach's front door. His apartment, the top floor of an otherwise uninhabited two-family house, was on the bare side, functional and neat except for streamers of toilet paper that Ringo had spread all over the living room. "My brother Ben's dog," Zach said, moving around the living room, gathering up the paper. "Ben used to live downstairs, but he moved to Atlanta last month. Got a good construction job. I said I'd keep Ringo till he found an apartment. He finally did, thank God. He's sending for his mongrel this week."

At last, the yards of paper crumpled to his chest, Zach bowed gallantly. "My humble abode," he said. "Make yourself comfortable. I'm going to feed Ringo and then I'm going to change. If I'd known I'd be meeting you today, Korie Morgan, I might have worn a necktie."

"And I some lipstick," she bantered. "Some heels, maybe."

Zach spooned cornmeal mash into a dish and took it and Ringo to the basement. Then he went into his bedroom and half-closed the door. Korie wandered into the kitchen while Zach changed. She saw that it looked more inhabited than his other rooms. A medley of overripe fruit spilled from a basket next to the window; brown earthenware jars labeled FLOUR, COFFEE, PASTA, and RICE were aligned on the windowsill, along with a plethora of seasonings; grease-blackened pots and several different sizes of frying and sautéing pans hung from hooks in the walls.

"So you cook," she remarked lightly. Zach had come in behind her, his fresh, white cotton shirt unbuttoned. Korie noticed the way his jeans were slung low on the hard rippled slope of his stomach.

"I'm very domesticated," he said, moving behind her and pulling her gently against him. "Does that interest you?"

Korie leaned back into him as he embraced her. His arms circled her loosely, his hips pressed forward ever so slightly, and Korie could sense more than feel the rhythmic beating of his heart against her shoulder blade. They said nothing for a while, but just stood like that, allowing the now almost familiar electricity to course through their bodies, to flow back and forth between them, charging the very air.

Zach's kitchen window looked onto a distant highway overpass, and in the gathering night the lights of cars seemed to merge on one side in a stream of receding red neon, and on the other, in a continuous flow of quicksilver white. Above this surging yet strangely tranquil scene the full moon glistened, unmoving, suspended in the very center of Zach's kitchen window, balancing the flow of light within its frame.

"They say that's a hunter's moon," Zach murmured, his face in Korie's hair. Korie pretended to study the moon, suddenly unsure how to act. They had arrived at this moment so quickly, and yet nothing had seemed rushed, unnatural, contrived. Right then, she decided the symmetry was perfect. She marveled at it and marveled, too, at the symbolic rightness of their meeting on a Friday the thirteenth by this shimmering moon.

All the same, she was astonished to wake the next morning in Zach Piper's arms. She realized that they were lonely, kindred types, and that in each other's company they laughed effortlessly. The most intimate confidences had risen easily from her lips, and Zach had gathered all her secrets, her stories of events that had left their imprint, and filed them with the care of one whose gift is to nurture and whose task, therefore, is to understand.

Part One
1973–1983

*"Emancipate yourself from mental slavery,
None but ourselves can free our minds."*
—Bob Marley

I
Rebel Dreams

*K*ORIE SLIPPED THE BLACK SCHOOL LOAFERS OFF HER feet and bent to remove her socks. Closing her eyes for a moment, she scrunched her toes through the wet new grass into the cool mud beneath it. Then barefoot, her shoes and socks in one hand, her book bag in the other, she picked her way through the trees to a spot beside the lake. She had come here often in the last year. In the fall, she had skipped stones along the water and scribbled poems and stories in her notebooks. When the frost came, she had used a twig or sharp stone to carve pictures into the soft ice crust that capped the lake. After the spring thaw, Korie often found herself lying in the grass with her head on her book bag, not writing or drawing at all, but daydreaming about what the next period of her life would be like.

It was Korie's last month at Kendall Girls, an old-line boarding school tucked into a green valley in rural Connecticut. Though of faded reputation, the school still attracted the promising girl children of wealthy New England families. Korie was from another world entirely. She had been bred against the hot, noisy, colorful Caribbean tapestry of Kingston, Jamaica, and found the hushed, damp atmosphere and tight-lipped reserve of the Kendall girls a bit of a culture shock. She had nobody but herself to blame, though, because it was she who had lobbied her parents to send her to Kendall for her final year of high school, convincing them that there could be no better preparation for an American college than to attend an American school.

In September, she would be entering Barnard College in New York City. The long-dreamed-of brass ring was almost in her hand.

For as long as she could remember, Korie had had this yen for America—New York City in particular. She had decided, the summer she visited there with her parents when she was nine, that she would live in New York when she grew up. Even as a small child, that northern city had been the glittering metropolis she had dreamed of escaping to, the place where she might finally live free of the claustrophobia of other people's expectations.

Now that her year at Kendall was nearly over, Korie was almost sad that it had flown by so quickly. Her melancholy surprised her, because the year hadn't exactly been flush with friendships and good times. It had been, in fact, the loneliest year of her life, but she had found, for the first time, a degree of comfort in her loneliness, an opportunity to sink into this aspect of herself and claim it as an intrinsic part of her nature.

This small lake on the other side of the woods was where she had done most of her thinking. None of the other girls ever came here. There were deer and rodents and other animals in the woods, and sometimes boys from the surrounding hill towns came there to poach. Though she kept a keen eye out for the animals, and hid the only time she ever saw a poacher,

Korie didn't worry much about the hill town boys. What would they want with a skinny black girl who had somehow wandered into their lily-white enclave? Most of the tow-headed, pink-cheeked boys were day students at The St. Francis School nearby; Korie had seen them at Kendall's bimonthly socials, but not one of them had seemed to truly see *her*. She realized she was a mere shadow to them, standing with her back to the wall, gazing longingly towards the door, alternatively wishing to disappear through it and praying that some-one, anyone, would save her from humiliation by asking her to dance.

Finally, at the pre-Thanksgiving party, someone *had* asked her to dance. Korie had been braced against the wall as usual, silently vowing that no matter how much her absence was frowned on, no matter what the house monitor said, she'd stay in her room the next time one of these ridiculous socials rolled around. Just then, a tall, cinnamon-colored girl had walked up to her and held out her hands. The Kendall girls often danced together at the socials while the St. Francis boys, swaggering to cover their shyness, circled the dance floor and ogled them. So it didn't matter to Korie that she'd been chosen by a girl. Relieved just to be noticed, she followed the tall girl onto the dance floor and faced her in the rose-colored light.

"Simona Jones," the girl had smiled in an apathetic sort of way. "I'm in Mr. Welch's homeroom. A senior like you. I've seen you walking over near the woods."

"Korie Morgan," Korie said.

She recognized the girl. She'd seen her a few times at sup-per and in study hall, and had made the mental note that there was another nonwhite student in the twelfth grade. Simona was athletically built. She wore a short black skirt and a tight black sweater and had long smooth muscles in her bare brown legs. On her feet she wore big-heeled platform sandals and no socks, even though there was snow on the grass outside. Her hair was cropped short like a boy's and parted to one side, its curls subdued by some shiny wet substance. Her eyes were heavy-lidded and bored, her lips full, cupidlike, sulky. On them, she was wearing fire-engine red lipstick—a grave infraction of Kendall's rules, even at socials. If any of the teachers or monitors who chaperoned the dance caught sight of those lips, Simona would be in detention for a week.

It was the lipstick that won Korie over. She was suddenly enthralled by Simona, thrilled by what the lipstick revealed about her—that she was a rebel, fundamentally and decisively, and that she didn't belong at Kendall any more than a skinny, brown-skinned Jamaican girl did. But if Korie survived her awkwardness, her sense of being perpetually a stranger, by shrinking into the background, Simona wore her outsider status proudly, defiantly. The night of the pre-Thanksgiving social, her long arms snaking through the air, her hips moving in sultry circles, Simona's "otherness" was as plain to Korie and everyone else as the fire-engine red lipstick on her full pouty lips.

They became fast friends. Simona's single (all seniors were granted singles) was in the residence cottage diagonally across the main quadrangle from Korie's, and they had no classes together, but they met often in study hall, ate all their meals together, and spent their recess and evening free periods together. Simona was from Brooklyn, New York, where she'd been raised by an elderly aunt in a tiny apartment on Flatbush Avenue. Her mother had deposited her there when she was six, then went off to drink herself into oblivion. Simona didn't have a clue where her mother might have gotten to in the intervening years. She might be dead in some nameless town for all she knew. Most of the time, Simona acted like she didn't give a damn, but sometimes late at night, after lights out when Simona and Korie would sneak out of their dorm rooms and meet for a smoke in the cobblestone alley beside the north wall, Simona would break down and cry. The school's groundskeeper kept Simona and a host of other Kendall girls well supplied with hand-rolled hashish joints, and Simona always brought a couple of them. Korie didn't really like the taste of the makeshift cigarettes, so she'd take a draw and let the joint burn down in her fingers while Simona drew deeply on her cigarette, and turned moody in the dark. Korie learned to sit silently by without touching her. Once when Korie had tried to hug her, Simona shook off her arm fiercely and snarled: "Don't you pity me!" So now, Korie just sat next to her while she cried, until at last, Simona's cigarette would be done and they'd make their secret handshake and scurry back to their rooms.

Korie's heart ached for Simona on those nights by the wall. It was impossible for her not to notice that while her parents had been busy inventing a rich and flourishing childhood for her—holiday house parties with a rainbow-hued army of relatives and friends; Sunday afternoon picnics with the flamingoes in Hope Gardens; weekends with her grandparents in the cool hills of Malvern; summers at her parents' north coast beach condo—while Korie had been experiencing all this, Simona had spent her childhood in a two-room walk-up with the bathtub in the kitchen, yearning for a mother who was never coming back.

And yet, in one sense, Simona's mother had blessed her by leaving her with the old aunt. It was the aunt who first noticed the child's native intelligence, and pushed for her to be tested. It was the aunt who had agitated and schemed for scholarships to Brooklyn's best private schools, then, as Simona approached puberty and the streets began to beckon, had arranged for her to attend Kendall Girls on a scholarship for disadvantaged inner-city kids. In those early days of affirmative action, Simona was a critical statistic at Kendall; the presence of girls like her secured a measure of federal funding for the school.

And now Simona had been accepted on a full scholarship to the University of California at Berkeley, and would be heading across the country to stir up the other coast's famed gold dust come fall.

A bell sounded in the distance—five minutes till afternoon study hall. Classes at Kendall were over for the year, and students were expected to spend the next week and a half studying and writing papers for finals. Korie rinsed her feet in the icy lake and pulled on her socks and shoes quickly. Then she slipped her book bag over one shoulder and retraced her steps through the woods to the wide green lawn on the other side of the trees. Girls in blue plaid skirts and crisp white blouses with Peter Pan collars were milling around outside, strolling in small groups or lounging on benches under the broad trees. A few were already walking towards the massive cut-stone school building, not willing to risk a demerit for being late. Korie hurried across the grass. She'd received her share of demerits for being late to study hall this year. One more would cost her a whole point on her grade point average. Not that it really mattered. She'd already been accepted early decision at Barnard. Still, Korie prided herself on being a good student, and so she wanted the 4.0 grade point average she was carrying to remain intact.

Simona was already in study hall, a long, high-ceilinged room with towering windows that cast their misty light across highly polished, mahogany tables. She had saved the seat beside her for Korie and when her friend appeared at the door, she let out a sharp whistle to alert her. The hall monitor glared at Simona, who stared back at her with wide-eyed innocence. The monitor turned back to her books, apparently deciding to let Simona's violation of the silence rule pass—one more month and the tall black girl with her smartass attitude would be gone for good.

Korie slipped into the chair next to Simona, took out her books, and settled down to study. She was a fierce studier. Her habit was to cram furiously before exams, a studying style that had netted her top grades throughout her school career. The trick, Korie had learned, was to not know the material *too* thoroughly. Years earlier, she had discovered that if she studied a text too closely, she did less well in the exam, because she became consumed with trying to get down all she knew. But when there were gaps in her knowledge, Korie was forced to go more deeply into those points she had full grasp of, and to make creative extrapolations on the points of which she was less sure. The result was invariably more original, and seemed to please examiners far more than a faithful regurgitation of the facts. So Korie was always careful not to study a subject in depth too soon, which meant that come study week, she had to get serious.

Now, as she riffled through the pages of her physical geography book, looking for the chapter on water erosion, she reflected on the irony of her studying approach: How absurd that she should choose cursory knowledge of a subject over more solid learning for the sake of a higher grade. Growing up in Jamaica, she had always envied those classmates who didn't feel such pressure to achieve top marks. By virtue of who she was, the family she came from, Korie had never felt that she had that luxury. She had always felt the need to justify her blessings.

She was, after all, the cherished and freely indulged only child of Osgood Morgan, a respected surgeon, and his wife, the painter Alice Mathurin. People flew from all over the Caribbean to be operated on by her father at the University Hospital. People flew from all over to consult with her mother, too, though for more aesthetic reasons. Alice Mathurin had a way of drawing people to her; everyone seemed to want to bask in her reflected light. Indeed, she was a dazzling presence, a slender, half-Chinese woman partial to flowing caftans and hand-painted gowns, whose rich black hair, now threaded with silver, was worn tightly swept back from her temples, showing off her sculpted cheekbones and long, thick-lashed black eyes. Alice Mathurin was known throughout the region for her large, abstract canvasses, and for the fact that she had discovered and made the careers of many a struggling West Indian artist, simply by showing their work at her north coast art gallery, The Sugar Mill. She had located her gallery in the beach resort town of Ocho Rios, in the renovated ruins of a sugar plantation. And since she counted many Caribbean and North American collectors among her regular patrons, the works exhibited at The Sugar Mill had a very good chance of finding their way into highly reputable collections.

Alice drove from Kingston to Ocho Rios several times a month to supervise showings at her gallery, and Korie had often made the hour-long trip with her, sometimes even prevailing on Alice to let her skip school in favor of helping to hang paintings for a show. Korie adored her mother, but she had always been a little in awe of her, too. In Alice's presence, Korie felt singularly undistinguished. She was medium brown like her father, and appeared almost mousy against her mother's luminous black and gold coloring, her light brown eyes almost colorless next to Alice's laser black stare. To make matters worse, Korie had inherited her father's intense myopia, and so had spent the latter part of her childhood peering through thick lenses set in pearly white frames. Her father insisted the glasses looked just darling on her, but Korie, even at seven, knew better. Her appearance improved somewhat when wire-rims became trendy, and she was able to swap her pearly frames for less intrusive gold wire ovals. But her lenses were still very thick, and distorted the appearance of her eyes, making them seem weak and distant and sleepy. At fifteen, Korie had graduated to contact lenses, which freed her lovely almond-shaped eyes from their funhouse-glass prison and gave her the promise of beauty. But by then, Korie's vision of herself as a lackluster, bespectacled girl had become a personal fact, and she was never quite able to believe it when her mother took her face between her palms and told her softly that the duckling had become a swan.

In the shadow of her mother's poise, her near perfection, Korie had grown up shy. She'd always felt like something of an impostor in her parents' world, an urchin who had wandered into a very fine gathering, her presence so forgettable, her radiance so dim, that nobody had bothered to notice that she really didn't belong there. As she approached puberty, and bursts of contradictory emotion rocketed around inside her, her notebooks had become her refuge. In them, she drew idealized self-portraits and scribbled stories of young women who were the stars of their firmament, sirens of dramatic bearing who inspired undying passion in both women and men, confident, self-possessed creatures who could enter into any setting on earth and simply *know* that they belonged.

It was in Ocho Rios, helping Alice mount a one-man show of work by her newest discovery, a young Kingstonian named David Gilchrist, that Korie had first voiced her wish to go abroad. David Gilchrist had been working across the large stone-walled exhibition room, sorting his small, exquisitely painted collages into several groupings on the floor.

David was twenty-five, a wiry, dark-skinned man with a wispy goatee and dark, sunken eyes. He had the look of a man who had often chosen paints over food. Korie had liked him from the first, more because she liked the survivalist spirit of his work and the kindness in his eyes than because of any real knowledge of his character. And she admired his perseverance. Alice had told her how she'd found him in a two-room shanty in Western Kingston, where he had painted on any material available to him—pieces of cardboard, discarded wooden planks, zinc scraps scavenged from the dirt around his makeshift house. He'd used found materials like shells, tree bark, rusty springs, and bits of rubber to build up layers of collage on his paintings. Alice Mathurin had first encountered his creations in a craft market stall, and was immediately mesmerized. She found his approach entirely original and saw in his work the mark of an artist who created from sheer love of the medium, as if to live without his art would have been to relinquish his life.

So Alice had sought him out, even going into Western Kingston herself, a dangerous neighborhood for a woman who wore her sense of entitlement so plainly. But Alice also had about her a palpable sense of mission, and no one harmed her as she walked through the dusty streets to David's two-room shack. She went there three times before she finally found him at home. Bemused, he came out to greet her, shirtless, in paint-stained shorts, his feet bare. Alice told him right then that he'd soon be the toast of the art world, and peeled off several one hundred dollar bills to help him buy canvas and paint and food.

"Mom," Korie said now as she helped her mother assemble a wooden easel. "I don't want to go to university here. I want to study art in New York."

Alice looked at her daughter, her expression careful.

"You can study art here," she said. "We have a thriving program at the School of the Arts. Why not enrich your own culture?"

"I'll still be of this culture, Mom. I just want to go abroad, that's all. I got some brochures from Cooper Union. It's an art school in New York."

Alice didn't respond immediately. She turned back to the easel.

"Pass the screwdriver, Korie."

"Mom!" Korie voice was plaintive. She knew her mother's impassiveness was a form of opposition, and she knew she needed Alice's support if she was ever going to convince Osgood.

"Pass the screwdriver, Korie. We'll discuss it later with your father."

Across the room, David Gilchrist cleared his throat. Alice and Korie looked up and noticed he had stopped sorting his work. He stood perfectly still amid the stacks of his creations, looking at mother and daughter thoughtfully.

"Miss Mat'urin," he said at last, "let de chile go a foreign."

"She's only sixteen—" Alice began.

Korie started to protest, but David broke in.

"If to go to New York is what she want," he said, "mek de chile go. Don't stan' in her way." David paused for a moment, as if trying to find the best way to make Alice Mathurin understand. He stroked his straggly beard with two bony fingers as mother and daughter stared at him. Eventually he sighed, a resigned sound.

"Is like dis, Miss Mat'urin. You right here makin' all my dreams come true. So many years I hear about you, an' how you help so many Jamaican artists find a way. I never dream you would one day be here helping me, too. But now is your daughter's turn. Don't stan' in her way, Miss Mat'urin. Let her go. You just have to trus' she will find her way back."

Alice didn't answer right away. She studied David coolly, trying to decide whether to take his interjection as impertinence or care. They had developed an easy association over the last several months, with David advising Alice with absolute confidence on such things as which of his art pieces to include in the show, how they should be grouped for an observer walking through the gallery, what the lighting should be. Alice had to admit that for a man who had never shown his work in a gallery, much less been the author of a one-man show, he had infallible instincts. On the other hand, he woefully undervalued his collages, and Alice had had to argue with him for several weeks to get him to raise his prices. Overall, theirs had been one of the more satisfying artistic collaborations that Alice could remember, and her respect for David Gilchrist had only deepened as she'd got to know him better. Still, their relationship had never extended beyond discussions about his work and preparations for his show. Certainly Alice had never discussed her own family with him, even though he had met them several times.

Now Alice looked over at her daughter, whose hungry, questioning eyes were fixed on her face like searchlights. Oh, the fierce ardor of youth, Alice thought wearily. She gave Korie a small smile and turned back to David. She nodded her head. "Okay, David," she said quietly. "I'll bear that in mind."

"I've always loved this part of Jamaica, Mom."

Korie was leaning out the car window, her chin resting on her crossed arms as she gazed up at the softly hump-backed hills of Walkers' Wood, where thick carpets of razor grass rippled over the hillsides like waves in the breeze. Low stone walls and barbed-wire fences meandered through the undulating landscape, carving out pastures where cows browsed and seagulls, circling inland from the coast, alighted for a few moments in the cool trees. Here and there, white farmhouses with wrap-around porches and intricately carved wooden gables graced the very tops of hills. Elsewhere, abandoned sugar mills were falling into picturesque ruin, grass sprouting from between their stones, twisted trees poking through their crumbling window spaces.

Alice and Korie were headed back to Kingston from Ocho Rios, Alice at the steering wheel, Korie across from her in the front seat of the silver-gray Volvo. They had just left David Gilchrist in Ocho Rios, where he was now living, and were driving over the winding roads that led to Fern Gully—Alice's favorite part of the trip—where tall bamboo stands laced with thick ferns arched overhead, forming a dark green canopy over the rock-walled road. Fern Gully had always made Alice feel cozy, sheltered. She had never known that it was the broad, temperate, soft-bellied hills of Walker's Wood that had beckoned her daughter. Alice noticed that Korie's voice had sounded almost wistful, as if, in her mind, she was already saying good-bye to these hills.

"I've always wondered who lives in those farmhouses," Korie said now. "When I was little, Mom, I wanted to live in one of those houses."

"I never knew that," Alice said, smiling. There was so much about her daughter that she didn't know.

"Isn't it funny how we never seem to see anybody walking through here?" Korie mused. "Everything is so serene. Even the trees sway in slow motion, like the whole place is a mirage from another time."

To Alice, this dreaminess, at least, was familiar. Korie had always been a dreamy child, content in her own world, the loner in the schoolyard, twirling in solitary circles, her face to the sky. Yet despite her solitary habit, other children had always seemed to like Korie. They surrounded her, pawed at her, trying to include her in their playground formations. Korie would smile back at them sweetly and then simply drift away, so that the children were left staring after her, confused, bewildered, wondering in some not-quite-verbal way why she always seemed so approachable yet couldn't be grasped at all.

Alice had known, watching her wander off from other children, that Korie was a child who would grow into a woman destined to make her way alone. Some women birthed children who cleaved to them, became extensions of them, and Alice had occasionally wished that her only daughter had been that kind of child. Instead, Korie had been an inscrutable little girl, unfailingly pleasant and obedient, scrupulous in her attention to other people's needs, and yet, Alice had always had the sense that a part of her was not quite present, that she was holding herself in reserve. Alice didn't know where she had learned it, but Korie had always been selfish with her joy. She hoarded it; she was not spontaneous with it at all, as if to express it—to let it gush out of her the way other children's enjoyment gushed out of them—was a guilty thing.

Then in the summer of 1963, when Korie was nine, the family had visited New York City, and out of curiosity Alice and Korie, returning from a morning museum tour, had stopped by a rally that was being held in the ballroom of their downtown hotel. The room was packed with people: solemn gray-suited professionals, fur-hatted church ladies, grease-stained workers from nearby construction crews, intense young students, both black and white, and, over in one corner, a cluster of quiet black women in maid service uniforms who were obviously part of the hotel's cleaning staff. The speaker, a slender black man in a preacher's black suit, was exhorting people to support a march on Washington planned for the following week. He thundered words like *duty* and *justice* and *equal rights*. He told the people gathered that the Right Reverend Dr. Martin Luther King Jr. would meet them in the nation's capital if they just came out to support him. He told of buses which would line the streets of Harlem at six o'clock sharp the following Wednesday morning, ready to transport anyone who needed free passage to the day-long march.

"Yes, indeed!" the speaker had shouted. "You have an appointment with *truth*, brothers and sisters! You have an appointment with *God*! It is your responsibility to serve *God* by giving your footsteps to the cause!"

"Hallelujah!" somebody had called out. Around the room, Alice heard low murmurs of "Praise the Lord!" She remembered thinking that this North American ballroom felt like nothing so much as a Jamaican tent revival.

Then, as the speaker left the podium, he lifted his open palms to the audience. "We shall overcome!" he yelled, and all around Alice and Korie, answering calls filled the air. A roar rolled through the room. Even the quiet women in maid service uniforms erupted into cheers. Alice sensed that she was watching something historic, that she was witnessing the prelude to a momentous divide in modern history. She looked down at her daughter, expecting to find her usual good-natured composure. What she saw startled her; she was so unused to that expression of frank joy on Korie's face, in her furiously clapping hands, in the way she turned to her mother again and again, her eyes gleaming as she grasped her arm: *Did you see, Mommy? Did you hear?*

"Can we go, Mom? Can we go to Washington?" she had urged that night in their hotel room. Alice had been tempted by the excitement bubbling out of her daughter. She was hungry for more of it. She wanted to feed this new urgency in Korie, draw it out. But Osgood insisted they had to get home. He had patients waiting, and Alice herself had to supervise the installation of a new show. Besides, Korie's new school year would begin the following Monday. She would be entering grade five, and it made no sense for her to start by falling behind.

Now as Alice steered their car through the halflight of Fern Gully, the sunlight every now and then piercing the foliage and collecting on the roadway in sudden pools, Alice couldn't help wondering whether attending that march in Washington so long ago might have quenched the thirst in Korie. It had been only a little thirst then, but over the years it had quietly grown, and Alice saw how, inexorably, it would draw Korie back to the place where she had first dared to express her need for a higher purpose, indeed, for joy.

The good doctor had been harder to convince. It wasn't that he was so opposed to the idea of his daughter studying abroad, but Osgood Morgan wouldn't hear of Korie going to America to attend an institution called Cooper Union.

"It's quite a good art school," Alice told him, but Osgood was adamant.

"She's not going to study anywhere abroad that won't equip her to make a living," he declared. "What is Cooper Union, anyway? It doesn't even have 'university' in its name. It doesn't even have 'school'!"

"Daddy!" Korie almost screamed in her desperation to reach him, "those are just words! And this is *my* life!"

"You are *my* daughter," Osgood countered. "And you're asking to go to America on *my* dollar. You can sit on a street corner and paint for the rest of your life for all I care, but by God, you'll have a choice! The day you decide you're tired of that street corner, you are *going* to have a legitimate piece of paper that will get you *a job!*" He was silent for a moment, breathing hard. Finally he said, "Find a reputable school and we'll consider it."

So Korie had found Barnard College, one of the prestigious Seven Sister schools—her father couldn't argue with that. Barnard, like Cooper Union, was in New York City, it had a program in the arts that included studio painting, and it encouraged young women to apply under its early decision plan. That meant she didn't have to wait till next year to apply, even though she was two years away from finishing high school.

Better yet, Barnard's program in the arts included a creative writing section. That was Korie's true quarry. Writing was what she really wanted to do; it was just that she hadn't been able to imagine how she might sustain herself with it. Art, on the other hand, had been so much a part of the Mathurin-Morgan household it was like breathing to her. Art seemed a sure thing. She wrote in her application that she wanted to be an art critic.

The following April, a letter came welcoming her to Barnard as a member of the class of 1978. She'd been accepted! No one but Korie was really surprised, though. She was a straight-A student, after all, and her teachers fell over themselves to write her glowing recommendations, thrilled at the idea of one of their own attending an Ivy League school. But Korie didn't want to wait a whole year and a half to matriculate. She wanted to go to America *this year*. And so she had found herself back in front of the Educational Opportunities Abroad shelf of the Kingston Public Library, poring through boarding school catalogs. The closest school she could find to New York City had been Kendall Girls.

Now, sitting next to Simona in study hall, Korie understood at least a part of why she had wanted to come here. She realized that, in her year at Kendall, despite the loneliness, she'd begun to embrace her independence in a way that was impossible in a close-knit place like Jamaica. It was as if her life was finally her own. Not that she wasn't grateful for all that had been given her. She thought of David Gilchrist and his years spent painting inspired collages amid the squalor of the shantytown where he'd lived. He had toiled so faithfully, with little hope of ever finding an audience that might support his work. Alice had facilitated a different ending to his story than the one that was more typical. Still, when Korie compared her own life to David's hardscrabble existence—and to Simona's, for that matter—she knew she had no right to feel so burdened by her privileges. And yet, she had wanted nothing more than to leave it all behind her, to go to a place where she might become more than Osgood and Alice's well-mannered daughter, a place where she might finally discover who exactly Korie Morgan aspired to be.

2
Quincy Street

*F*LORIDA PIPER LOOKED DOWN AT HER THIRD CHILD. THE boy lay with his face pressed into the frayed cushions of the couch that sat in an oval of shadow under the stairs. Zachary had been home from school for six days now, and he had, each morning, curled his lanky sixteen-year-old body into the old couch, forcing sleep for as many hours as he could. The week before, he'd been suspended from Academy High. In a roiling exuberance of adolescence, he had acted the fool before too many teachers, cut too many classes in favor of shooting hoops at the playground, and finally, was caught smoking a marijuana cigarette in the girls' locker room. Worse, a quartet of girls had been sampling the cigarette with him.

Now, Florida Piper nudged him with a broom handle. "If you're going to be housebound for so many days, you might as well be useful," she said.

The boy turned his head and peered up at his mother. Ribs of raised fabric had left ghosts on his face.

"Get up now," Florida repeated.

Zach unfurled his long limbs, brought his feet to the floor, and sat hunched over steepled knees, his elbows sharply triangled.

Like wings, Florida thought randomly.

"Here," Florida said, offering him the broom. "This room needs sweeping. After that, the laundry needs doing." The last she flung over her shoulder. She was already on her way to the kitchen where the smell of bacon frying didn't quite cut the garlicky aroma of the soup they would eat for dinner that night—Florida's special brew, thick with ham hocks, potatoes, and a stew of vegetables. The Piper kids, all four of them, had been weaned on it.

Zachary Emmanuel was the third child among Florida Piper's three sons and one daughter. He came right after the girl, Annie, already a wilful and passionate young woman, much like her mother had been. The interval of years had gentled Florida some, but she was still an irreverent sort of mother, never one to insist on homework or bedtimes or curfews or chores. Or, she might suggest these things, but invariably she'd neglect to follow up, leaving her children to discover for themselves the wisdom of her suggestions. And come late afternoon, whether homework was done or not, whether beds from the morning had ever been made, Florida would take a seat on the front porch and call her children to sit with her. She'd sip beer from a glass and wave to her neighbors and hold meandering conversations with her children, one at a time or all at once, depending on who happened to join her.

Growing up, Zach had liked the long lethargic afternoons of summer best of all, because with school out and the air warm, Florida let the kids taste her beer and giggled with them at the froth moustache it left above their lips. Then, slightly tipsy, they would settle themselves against the wooden porch banister, in the weather-beaten chairs and on the cool stone steps of the stoop. Sprawled like this, they could entertain one another for hours, their voices weaving and rising, dipping and vying with one another in a chaos of sound. Only Hanson, the children's father whom Florida had never divorced, was absent from these spontaneous family gatherings.

The neighborhood women, whom Florida had often called on to sit for her kids, clucked among themselves that it was just scandalous the way Florida let those babies sip her beer. Their chatter simmered more gently as the years slipped by and Florida became their friend, for they found that she had a generous spirit mixed in with the recklessness. Still, the women who tended their families within identical brick row houses up and down Quincy Street had never ceased to murmur at the haphazard manner in which Florida was raising her chattering brood.

And yet, the women of Quincy Street, though it seemed they worked harder at mothering than Florida, were not having noticeably more satisfying results. So often in their lives a husband had strayed, a daughter had been obscenely touched, a son was mixed up in drugs. And it was to Florida's kitchen the women came, knowing that she would offer them coffee—brandy if they preferred—and listen to their woes for as long as it took for the angst of living to ease a little.

"Sit down," Florida said as Zach came into the kitchen, trailing the broom. His wiry body, clothed only in jeans, curved inward at the torso, each rib utterly defined.

"Eat," Florida ordered.

Obediently, Zach sat, taking for granted the plate heaped with bacon, fried eggs, and grits that his mother slid before him. Florida wiped her hands on the skirt of her faded, flower-patterned house dress, then settled into the chair opposite her child.

"You're my boy, that's for sure," she said, cradling her chin in her palms, "always in trouble over some damned thing." Suddenly, she grinned. "What the hell!" she declared, slapping the table. Zach looked up at his mother warily. She laughed— a short, ironic burst of sound. "Well, son, I turned out okay. And I know you'll be okay, because you're like me, a survivor."

What, Zach wondered, would he be called on to survive? He concentrated on eating, aware that his mother was regarding him closely, as if taking a measure of her third child. Zach registered the affection in her eyes, and something rueful and amused. If there had been no censure from her when his school had called to recite the litany of his offenses, now, in her knitted brows, her pursed lips, he perceived something else: worry.

He polished off the last morsel, picked up his plate, and scraped back his chair. "Delicious, Ma!" he announced, bending to peck his mother's cheek on the way to the sink. Florida wiped the spot he had kissed.

"Don't you try to sweeten me, Zachary Emmanuel. By the time you get through all the chores I have lined up for you, you'll wish you'd paid a little more attention to your school books."

"Ma," Zach groaned, but then he remembered that his boys wouldn't be around till the afternoon anyway, and daytime TV was already numbing his brain. He changed tack. "Of course I'll help out, Ma." He turned on the sink faucet. "Just tell me what you want done."

Zach rinsed his fork and plate and put them, still beaded with water, on the shelf above the sink. He crossed the room to the refrigerator and disappeared behind its open door for a long rummaging moment. Finally, he came up with a half-empty can of beer.

Of all her children, Florida decided, watching him, Zach had always offered her the most companionship. He'd always been the most sensitive of her children, the one who, even as a young child, had been able to sense the gradations of shadow or light in her mood. She wanted to tell him, suddenly, that when things got hard, he might turn his empathy into a release of sorts. It had worked that way for Florida. When her own pain grew to such a ludicrous size, the women who were her neighbors along Quincy Street had helped her exorcise a little of it.

Their stories helped Florida Piper maintain a sense of proportion. Look at what Dessie Andrews, Lottie Jones, and Etta Mae Timmens had to cope with. Etta Mae Timmens had cried her heart out in Florida's kitchen just last evening, her two oldest boys sentenced to jail that morning for a simple-minded holdup with a toy gun. But to the Korean grocer on the other end of it, the pistol had seemed menacingly real, and when the boys were picked up (shoppers from the neighborhood identified Joe and Alvin Timmens with no difficulty, despite the bandannas they wore cowboy-style across the lower portions of their faces), the grocer pressed charges with a righteousness that convinced the judge to give the boys the maximum, fifteen years each, though both were first offenders.

And there were other tragic stories up and down the street. The week before, Dessie Andrews's little girl had been kidnapped from nursery school by her own father. Now he was pressing for custody, and calling Dessie a whore for letting her new man sleep by the house nights.

And Lottie's boy, that Jimmy Jones, had to be using dope; Florida was sure of it from the way Lottie's money kept disappearing from her hiding places all around the house. And Lottie couldn't afford to lose a dime. She'd only just managed to get her no-count husband out the house—neighbor talk had it Lottie's husband had been feeling on their daughter Zoe since before the child had even started menstruating—and nowadays, Lottie hardly had two nickels to rub together. At least she only had the boy Jimmy to feed. But it was a mixed blessing:

Zoe wasn't too much older than Zach, still too young to move out of her mama's house as far as Florida was concerned. But move she had, and even though she'd quit school and got herself a store job, she didn't help Lottie none. Seems she thought her mother should have done something about the way her father had had the run of his daughter's body all those years.

Then there was Josie Wade's girl: Left home one evening last December and never returned. She was only fourteen, but she was filled out in all the right places and you couldn't tell she wasn't grown. The story went that a white cop down in Washington, D.C., was pimping her to his partners and paying her with drugs.

Florida listened to these women and heard, in the spaces between their words, their breaking hearts. Tenderly, she hoarded their stories and patched their hurts, sick with the certainty that the melancholy spirit of Quincy Street, of that whole desolate corner of Philadelphia, would claim some portion of each of its families—as it had her own.

Zach walked with strutting nonchalance back to the table and set down his beer. Sitting, he reached into his pants pocket for cigarettes. Leaning back, he lit one, exhaling luxuriously before squinting through the smoke at his mother. He had never smoked in her presence before, and so he expected some sort of comment. But Florida chose not to remark on it. Nor did she mention the stale beer. "Now your sister, Annie," she said instead, "what am I going to do about Annie?"

Annie's particular problem that year, or more precisely, Florida's problem with Annie, was that her daughter seemed to count as her constant companions and closest friends the two most butch women in the neighborhood. One of them was Lottie Jones's girl, Zoe, who had shacked up with a mannish-looking woman she'd found at some girl bar downtown. It didn't surprise Florida one bit that Zoe wanted nothing to do with men, considering the way her father had done her, but that didn't mean Florida wanted the same life for Annie. But Annie was always over at Zoe and Mabel's house, and Florida couldn't figure out whether Annie, at so tender an age, had decided she was gay.

"You know your sister," Florida was saying. "You dare not tell her what to do, and God bless you if you try to tell her what to think. It just makes her contrary. So I can't tell her not to spend time with them, but Zach"—her voice was suddenly thick with an inexplicable sadness—"I don't want her fighting people's backward notions every step of the way."

"Annie will surprise you," Zach muttered through teeth clenched Bogart-style around his cigarette. He was less concerned than his mother about Annie. "She's a smart girl, Ma. She likes Zoe and Mabel and she doesn't care what people say. But they can't influence your girl. She'll make up her own mind."

"That's what I'm afraid of," Florida murmured.

She was beginning to drift, her thoughts floating unchecked to an obsessive terrain, the tender contemplation of her children's lives and temperaments. In the lengthening silence, Zach studied his mother. The wool cardigan she wore belonged to his older brother, Ben. The elbows were worn clear through, but his mother would barely have noticed. She would simply have grabbed whatever garment was close at hand when it struck her she was cold. Now, watching her, Zach was unexpectedly startled by her beauty, which was not diminished by the threadbare sweater, her unfixed hair. At that moment, Florida appeared much younger than her forty-one years, her face washed clean of makeup, her eyes shining more than any other mother's eyes Zach could imagine. He was suddenly seized by a fierce protectiveness—as if this whip of a woman were in need of his protection. A ridiculous notion to begin with! And yet, his heart swelled with infinite longing to shield her from the slightest misgiving or insidious care.

As though Florida's body had been subject to precisely regulated biological signals, she had delivered Benjamin, Annie, and Zachary at two-year intervals exactly. Neal made his appearance six years later, surprising everyone, but no one more than Hanson, who by then had taken to staying away from the house on Quincy Street for weeks at a time.

As it happened, Ben and Annie had been childhood allies, and Zach had been the odd child out. A skinny boy, always eager to go where Ben and Annie went, he was relegated more often than not to entertaining himself. There was something in the stoic manner with which Zach had endured his siblings' small rejections that had twisted Florida's heart. Oh, Annie had been willing enough to include him in their games, and sometimes Ben grudgingly let him join them. Most times, though, they wandered off without giving him a second thought. Florida carried in her indelible mother's memory the image of Zach with shoulders thrown back as he set out after the older two, determined to be included in their play. Perhaps her special feeling for Zach had been born when those five-year-old shoulders, drooping now, had returned home alone.

That was the same summer, Florida remembered, that Ben had tied Zachary to the heating pipe in the basement to stop him from following him to the playground. Zach was small and slight for his age, and nine-year-old Ben hadn't wanted the responsibility of watching him. Florida had been working the early shift at a hospital cafeteria then. Hanson wasn't working, and should have been home with the children. But he hadn't come home the night before, and Florida had been obliged to call Mrs. Greenlee next door to look in on the kids. The second time Mrs. Greenlee came over to check, seven-year-old Annie, still in her nightgown, was sprawled across her mother's bed watching soap operas. She told Mrs. Greenlee that Ben and Zach were at the Western Avenue playground shooting hoops with the Timmens boys and little Jimmy Jones.

Downstairs, Zach refused to call out, though the rope chafed his wrists. He sat wimpering and lonesome in the musty silence until four that afternoon, when his mother arrived home and discovered him. Florida was furious with Ben, and she grounded him for the remaining weeks of the summer. But it was a punishment that without Hanson's help she was powerless to enforce. Inwardly, she raged at her husband, whose absence then had already become more predictable than his presence.

Florida was working as a companion to the elderly at a nursing home over in Camden the year she finally kicked Hanson out. Her husband's drinking she could have endured, but his public displays with other women she found humiliating. One week, when Neal, her youngest, was four, Florida stayed home from work to meet Hanson at the front door. When he finally showed up at noon on Thursday, she calmly handed him a suitcase of his clothes and suggested he find other quarters. A dazed Hanson went without complaint, no doubt to the bosom of some barroom sweetheart. But had he put down the ruckus Florida had half-expected, the children were all at school, and Neal next door with Mrs. Greenlee, which was the way Florida had planned it.

As spring verged on summer, the bond between Florida and her third child grew almost psychic. Florida talked of everything as she and Zach shared breakfast, then divided the day's chores between them. Annie continued to crop up in their morning conversations, for she had stayed close to Zoe and Mabel, spending most afternoons at their house. Only Zachary remained nonplussed. As he and Florida grew plainspoken in the kindred way of friends rather than parent and child, Zach also drew closer to Annie. Her toughness fell away, he had found, when they sat together on the front porch talking late into the night.

Florida thought she smelled marijuana smoke out there one evening. She opened the screen door to them.

"You children smoking pot out here?"

"Somebody walking by on the street was smoking," Annie mumbled.

Her long, thin body was bent almost double and seemed to bristle in its stillness. She gazed fixedly at the shapeless dark beyond the horizon of neighborhood rooftops. Florida saw suddenly that her eyes were wet, that thin ribbons of tears stained the terse composure of her face. At the same moment, she registered Zach's pained, imploring look, his right hand raised in a gesture of caution. Silently, Florida backed into the house. Pulling the screen door shut behind her, she went slowly up the stairs.

Never again would she disturb them as they sat talking at evening, she vowed. Let them share their secrets. Let Annie empty her worries into Zach's care—as Florida herself had done, and would do again.

Zach was seventeen now, taller and no longer so skinny. He had sprouted and filled out quite suddenly. His height still lent him an apparent leanness, even as his thickening arms, his broadening chest belied it. One morning, Florida noted Zach's newly hairless chin and upper lip. He had begun to shave! Her son now looked to be a grown man, and he was acquiring capacities to match and deepen his manly demeanor.

One by one, each of his siblings learned to seek Zach out. Florida didn't quite understand how it had happened, but a mature compassion had opened within Zach in the months he'd stayed home from school. She thought that perhaps their mornings talks had pushed his adolescent responses towards an interaction with the world that was more measured, more adult.

Each sibling had a preferred corner. Annie would huddle with Zach on the front porch, or hole up with him in his room. "What's up Zach?" she'd say, ambling in, picking up a comic book or a baseball glove and falling against Zach on his narrow cot. There was nowhere else to sit or recline in Zach's room, which had recently been a linen closet. When the basement had become too crowded for the three boys, Zach had removed the shelves from the closet in the upstairs hallway and installed his bed. He kept his clothes in gym bags hung over nails in the walls.

Ben liked to take Zach away from the house altogether, strolling with him to the Western Avenue playground where they'd lie flat on their backs on the concrete basketball court and watch the moon through the netless rim on which, in separate seasons, each of them had honed their game. There in the dark, Ben and Zach would discuss things.

Florida soon realized that it was Neal, her youngest, who was most reticent in sharing the secrets of his heart. But sometimes, he would sidle up to Zach as he stood over the gas range cooking dinner, a task Zach now performed more often than Florida. "Hey, bro," Neal would say almost shyly, his moonface split by an angelic grin. "Can I ask you a question?"

Years later, it would pain Zach to remember that it was Neal, his slanted green eyes dead earnest under his thatch of tight red curls, who was always most tentative, yet always called him "bro."

Zach held himself perfectly still. He was sitting on the top step of the porch with his back to Florida, his expression unreadable. Florida stood at the banister to his left, looking out onto Quincy Street. Old Miss Emily Jackson—who objected to being called "old" even though she had to be pushing eighty—was mincing down the block on her way to church. A great plumed ostrich feather in her netted black hat bobbed in rhythm to the click-click of her heels.

"How y'all doing this fair Sunday morning?" she chirped as she passed by the house. "Florida, young Zachary?"

"Good day to you, too, Miss Emily," Florida smiled.

Zach seemed oblivious to her greeting. At that moment, he was conscious of nothing but the weight of Florida's sudden confession on first coming onto the porch. Zach had been idling against the banister, smoking a cigarette and watching the street when Florida, realizing that she and Zach were alone in the house, had followed him out.

"Zachary?" she had said, and Zach stiffened, recognizing at once the grave query in her tone. But he could not have expected what his mother stammered out.

"I don't know how to tell you this, son, and yet, I keep feeling it's something you should know, all of you . . . should . . . know. . . ." Her voice trailed off. Then, in a whisper, she continued, her voice almost pleading. "I can't tell the others, Zachary, only you. The others won't understand, but you, son"—she sighed deeply—"you might."

"What is it, Ma?"

Florida's next words came in a rush.

"Neal isn't your father's child."

Then she stopped.

Zach, feeling a sudden weight, bowed his head.

Florida waited for Zach to acknowledge her words, but the boy remained silent. She waited a long time for him to speak, watching old Miss Emily until she had turned the corner onto Bachelor Avenue, where Pastor Rowan's Baptist church had stood for at least as many years as Miss Emily. When Florida couldn't see her neighbor anymore, she looked down at her son.

"Zachary?"

He didn't answer.

Florida forced herself to continue. She sensed Zach's pain, but the dam of her own silence had finally been breached, and she felt its waters surging free.

"I don't know how to ask you to forgive me, son, or even why I should need your forgiveness so badly. But I do." She paused. "I'm sorry, that's all," she said at last, then added carefully, "Not for having Neal, you understand. God knows, I love him the same as I love the rest of you. And not for having found a little tenderness when your father gave me none. But I am sorry, Zach, profoundly sorry that I've deceived you all these years. I've lied to you kids. Worst of all, I've deprived Neal of his true father. And now, it's too late."

Zach turned to his mother, his face impassive.

"Does my father know?" he asked.

Florida shook her head.

"He never knew? Even now, he thinks Neal is his?"

"I never told him," Florida said.

"Who is Neal's father, then?" he asked finally.

"Do you remember Mr. Hendricks?"

"The white man who fixed our stairs?"

Zach could see him immediately in his mind's eye. He had been a small boy at the time, but he remembered the carpenter who had arrived on their doorstep just after the family moved to the house on Quincy Street. Parts of the house had been in dire need of repair. Several of the stairs were broken, the floorboards splintering and plaster flaking from the walls. Florida marshaled Hanson and the two boys to redo the walls, while she and six-year-old Annie set about cleaning. Mr. Hendricks she hired from the Yellow Pages.

His address had been in the black part of town, so when he

showed up at their front door and turned out to be white, Florida had stood for several minutes staring at him, her mouth gaping. The surprise was that the old carpenter had shown up at all, because in Philadelphia in the late 1950s, white men didn't tend to do work in black people's houses. But Mr. Hendricks had been a different kind of white man. He'd been born around black people, on an island called Aruba in the Dutch West Indies. Zach vaguely remembered the stories he had told them about island life, about bathing in the sea and walking barefoot to school and picking star apples from the low branches of trees for breakfast. But there had been a sad story, too, among the idyllic ones, for Mr. Hendricks's father, a fisherman, had died early one morning in a storm at sea. His mother had moved with her young son to America soon after, and apparently, hadn't been too particular about where they lived. She eventually settled with her boy in a black neighborhood, since it looked to her a lot more like the neighborhoods she'd left in Aruba than the white neighborhoods did. So Mr. Hendricks was used to black people. To him, fixing Florida Piper's stairs was just another job.

At least, in the beginning.

Zach could still see the carpenter so clearly. From the vantage point of a small boy, he had been so reedy he seemed perpetually to sway at his great height. The underlying hue of his skin was orangish; his eyes flashed green and disappeared into slits with ready laughter; his teeth were large and yellowed, a friendly space between the front ones. The old carpenter had taken so long to fix everything, it seemed to Zach now that he'd never quite left. He just kept showing up, week after week, cutting and sawing and sanding wood in the basement, fixing whatever was broken in the house, sometimes even agreeing to watch the three older kids while Florida ran errands.

Now Zach tried to call up a look, a touch, anything that would suggest to him the relationship that must have existed between his mother and Mr. Hendricks all those years earlier. How long had it continued? Had Mr. Hendricks known that Neal was his son? Zach was somehow unwilling to know the details, but it was clear that after more than a decade of silence, Florida sought full confession.

His hands clammy, a sick feeling in his stomach, Zach obliged.

"How did it happen?"

"It didn't happen here," Florida said. "And it happened long after Rick had finished the stairs."

"Rick?"

Florida smiled almost shyly and looked away. "It was a name I had for him, a joke we shared. We used to go to the midday matinees sometimes when you kids were at school. We saw *Casablanca* a few times. We used to spin stories about how we'd run off to Morocco together someday, how we'd open a cafe, call it Rick's."

The sadness in her voice made Zach shiver.

Florida, Florida, he hungered to ask her, what would you have done about your four children? Would we have accompanied you on your Moroccan adventure? A part of him flinched at this revelation of his mother's unsuspected dream life, at her capacity for fantasy shared so exclusively with a man who was not his father. Zach understood dimly that the old carpenter had touched his mother's spirit as Hanson Piper had never been able to.

Florida had fallen silent. Now she roused herself, speaking without inflection. "So, that's why I called him Rick. He liked it better than Alphonso. His actual name was Alphonso O'Neal Hendricks."

"Neal Alphonso Piper," Zach said dully. "You named Neal for him."

Florida nodded, watching Zach closely for some response other than studied composure. Zach willed his expression to stay neutral as inside, a voice screeched, *Don't tell me! Don't tell me anymore! I don't want to know!* Why had she chosen him? he wondered wildly. Why him, on behalf of the others, to account for her lie? He would be forced to admit, finally, the utter shambles that had been his parents' marriage, the wreckage out of which their children had been born. In months, perhaps years to come, he would lie awake nights and weigh the treatment his father had meted out against his mother's search for solace, a solace that begot the love child that was only half his brother.

Zach conjured up Neal's pale round face with its sprinkle of red freckles that had gone unaccounted for until now. Neal was small for twelve years, but his hands were large and square and his feet were abnormally long. He'll probably spurt to great altitudes, Zach thought, considering the carpenter.

"You always told us Neal was a throwback," Zach said.

A note of bewildered accusation shadowed his voice.

"You said he looked just like your granddaddy. Why did you say that, Ma? Why'd you *lie?*"

"Oh baby," Florida whispered, lowering her eyes. She clasped her palms and brought them to her lips, so much hurt in the bony curve of her shoulders it made Zach wince. Suddenly, Zach realized he felt no differently towards his youngest brother, even knowing Florida's secret.

Florida was speaking again. He tried to focus on the words.

". . . the morning your father came home after he'd been gone a week. He was stink with liquor and women and I was furious with him. You all were just kids. Your father should have been home with you. That was the week that your brother tied you to the pipe in the basement. I came home and heard you sobbing down there . . ."

"Sobbing? Ma, come on."

"You were crying your eyes out, trying not to make a sound, but it seemed that all day your little heart was breaking in the dark, and there was no one there to hear it. Your brother was young. I don't know if he understood what he'd done. I remember all I could think of was that Hanson should have been home with you kids."

"I was all right, Ma, really," Zach protested, horrified that he might be assigned some role in the unfolding drama. "I didn't blame Ben. I didn't blame Pop for not being home. I wasn't hurt, no harm done."

"You were tethered in the basement like a wild animal," Florida insisted, her face dark with pain. "That night I called Rick. He had known for a while what was going on with Hanson and me. He spent a lot of time in our house. He'd arrive early for work and know Hanson hadn't been home the night before. He'd know I was upset. He used to talk to me, not about your father, about other things."

Again, she paused. Her eyes searched the distance. When she resumed speaking, her voice was soft.

"He'd talk to me about making furniture, and the feel of sanded wood under his palm. He said if you sanded it right, it felt like velvet. He'd tell me about Lake Winslow in the fall when the leaves start to change. Later, we used to go fishing there. He knew so much that I didn't, and he enjoyed his life so. I began to lean on him, to need his simplicity, to want his love.

"So I called him that night when you all were asleep and he drove over. He parked across the street and I sat with him in his van. We just sat there and talked about everything. Zach, it was the first time in my life a man had listened to me like that! I cried and he just held me. But up to the day I found you roped up to that pipe, he hadn't tried a thing, though we'd been for coffee quite a few times. The ball was always in my court, and after that night"—Florida paused, then said simply—"I started seeing him more."

They met mostly in the afternoons after work, Florida told Zach, stealing a couple of hours two or three days each week.

Later, after Neal came, and Hanson's absences from the house on Quincy stretched to weeks at a time, Florida had concocted reasons for Rick to be in their home—parts of the house that needed fixing, rooms that could use some renovation, carpentry jobs that were never quite finished, just abandoned when Hanson found his way home, then resumed when Hanson left again. "And I never stopped seeing Rick, either, not until he died seven years ago," Florida finished.

The two of them were quiet for a long time. Zach heard the Johnson boys down the street waging war over who would get the pickup that night. Around the corner, the bells of the Baptist church began to toll, announcing Communion for the absolution of souls.

"So did he want Neal?" Zach asked at length.

Florida nodded. "Neal was just three when Rick died," Florida said. "He was a good twenty years older than me, and he had a bad heart. But, yes, he wanted him. I remember he was so happy he cried when he found out he was having a baby. Neal was his only child."

Zach put the numbers together and calculated that Florida hadn't asked Hanson to leave until a full year after Alphonso O'Neal Hendricks was dead and committed to the black earth. But now, it made no difference. Neal was certainly no less his brother—it didn't matter that the carpenter had fathered him. All the same, Zach was troubled by the sense that his place in the world had shifted, and in a flash of clarity, he understood why:

Things had never been as they seemed.

How very hidden was the pulse of his mother's life, Zach realized with a pang. He had fathomed so little of his mother's inner nature, for it had been her secret life with the carpenter that had sustained her all along. Even her marriage to Hanson had remained tolerable only so long as she could escape into the seclusion of her love affair.

Zach had no idea what was required of him now. After a while, he rose from the steps and went to where his mother stood. Because he could think of nothing else to do, he circled her with his long arms and held her close.

"It happened so long ago," he whispered. "No one else has to know."

But Florida barely heard him. Zachary's arms, she was thinking, cover me like wings.

3

Black Power

KORIE

HERE IS HOW SAMSON DOUGLASS MARSHALL CAME TO be my husband. I go to college in the fall of 1974, and he's there, tall and gaunt, gleaming like new copper wire, but with somber eyes and hollow cheeks and the tragic air of a martyr, and so of course I notice him. I notice him the first day of orientation, strolling up College Walk alone, his arms loosely swinging, his body sloping forward, his stride long and loping. I see him from the back at first. He is walking ahead of me, a prematurely stooped figure in black corduroy overalls and a thin white T-shirt with sleeves rolled up to the shoulders, a young man with an old man's mien. I like that old soul aura he has, and I like his walk, lazy, bowlegged, and deeply sensual— all the more so because he is obviously a man used to traveling alone. Fresh from my year at Kendall, and missing the compelling isolation of my friendship with Simona, this boy's lonely air attracts me at once.

After that, I notice him everywhere, walking alone most of the time, books in his hand, his haunted gaze looking inward, as if perpetually tangled in his thoughts. Wherever I go, he is there: in the stacks at the library, ahead of me in the bank line on Friday afternoons, browsing an aisle away in the dusty recesses of the campus bookstore, sitting alone in the corner of the falafel place when I go there for dinner with my new college friends.

Whenever I see him, this man so recently a boy, his surroundings seem to recede into misty pastels while he shimmers with vibrant, intensified color. This, I think, is why I keep noticing him. There are other people I run into as often as I run into him, but none seems to float out of his environment the way Sam does, none inhabits my imagination the way he has.

He is what my mother Alice would call "a brooder." Even in the midst of his friends, a cluster of black upperclassmen and women who gather at lunchtime in a particular booth in McIntosh Center, even in the midst of that animated, laughing crowd, there is some separate, *separated*, about him, an invisible field that keeps him intriguingly apart. He is handsome in a scruffy student sort of way, his hair long and unkempt, his beard untouched by any grooming tool, his clothes rough-dry and disheveled. But his hands are slender and exquisitely graceful in their movements, his fine brown head sits elegantly on his shoulders, and his speech—what I can catch as I eavesdrop on his conversations in McIntosh—is rich with soft vowels and the musical cadences of the black South. Among his friends in McIntosh Center, he actually talks quite a bit, his full lips wryly pursed, his commentary often drawing peals of laughter. And yet, as I watch him secretly from the booth across the room where I sit with my own friends, I note that the expression in his eyes is never amused so much as ironic, and sometimes even sad.

Before I ever speak to Sam Marshall, I am aware of wanting to take him in my arms and whisper that he can let his guard down now; he can relax his vigilance and take himself lightly for a minute or two.

I can never tell if he notices me noticing him, and so the night I come home and find him downstairs in my dorm, apparently waiting for someone by the pay phones, I pretend I need to make a call. I approach the phone next to him, fumble in the pocket of my dress for coins, then dial. I pretend the phone on the other end is busy, and hang up the receiver, prepared to try again. As I hang up the phone, I look boldly into Sam's face. He is smiling down at me.

"I've seen you around campus," he says. "You're a freshman, aren't you?"

He is so much taller than I'd realized, and he smells of some heady cologne (so disheveled and yet he wears cologne!) and I suddenly feel flustered and foolish. I'm not wearing my contact lenses, so I have on my wire-rimmed glasses. Their thick, Coca-Cola-bottle lenses make my eyes look like little fishes swimming in deep, refracted pools. I've also added some pounds in these first weeks of college, and the material of my dress feels tight across my breasts, and clings too closely to my buttocks, which have filled out some with the weight.

"Hi," I say nervously. "I'm Korie Morgan."

"I'm Sam Marshall. I've seen you over there with the West Indians in McIntosh. You should come on over and say hi to us *American* blacks sometime."

I'm not sure how to take that, so I ask him where he's from.

"Jacksonville, Florida," he says. "And you're Jamaican. I know. I asked around about you."

"You did?" I sputter stupidly.

"Of course I did. You're just about the prettiest freshman I ever saw, and I've been trying for weeks to figure out how I might get you to go out with a po' black southern boy."

I am stunned and thrilled at the same time. I'm not used to men showing such candid interest in me. The truth is, I've never had a boyfriend. My father made that as difficult as he possibly could. In Jamaica, if a boy had the courage to venture up to our house, which sat at the very top of a hill overlooking Kingston, Osgood would greet him sternly, pipe clenched in his teeth, and invite him to the living room to "converse." There, my father would grill the boy mercilessly, probing such aspects of his character as personal ambition, parental affiliations, and, of course, academic performance. It embarrassed me no end. None of my girlfriends had to go through this when boys came by their houses. And those boys who submitted to my father's inquiry were invariably so shaken by the time they left that they never returned.

I took to spending afternoons at my friend Marlene's house down the street. The boys I'd meet at parties sometimes visited me there, under the guise of visiting Marlene. Marlene had three older brothers and two older sisters, and her parents were too worn out to worry much about the scrawny boys with stop-sign afros and hipster bell-bottom pants who arrived on their veranda. I'd groped with a few of them in Marlene's upstairs bedroom when her parents weren't home, but apart from wet kisses and hips grinding together experimentally, my romantic education was, by my lights, way behind schedule. Marlene had already lost her virginity by the time I left home for Kendall, and even Simona, who had spent most of her teenage life at boarding school, had managed to get laid a few times during summer holidays. I admit I felt left behind. But now, with Sam Marshall smiling down at me, his eyes mysterious, I feel myself literally opening inside, swelling with all the sweetness and potential of new love.

•   •   •

The person Sam has been waiting for, a senior named LaToya whom I know by sight, arrives with a political science text-book she has for him. Sam introduces us, and when LaToya leaves, he invites me to walk with him.

"Are you a poli sci major?" I ask him, nodding towards the textbook.

"Um hm. When I graduate next year, I'm going to do civil rights law."

That night, we wander all over the campus, exchanging details of our families, which is our way then of exchanging details of ourselves. I tell Sam about growing up in Jamaica, among handsome relatives whose sleek confidence had always made me feel somehow less than they were. Sam understands. He knows what it is to feel alone. "I began as a nomad," he tells me, then explains that he was given to strangers as a baby by his confused teenaged mother. His great-aunt Corinne traveled hundreds of miles to fetch him back; she wanted him to know his family as he grew. But she was old, and too weary to pay much mind to a child, so Sam had ministered to her aches, spo-ken in whispers, and let himself be coddled on her pillowing lap. He had grown from that silent watchful little boy into this reticent yet witty young man, his nature almost feminine in its pitched sensitivity and finely honed perception. As we walk the lamplit paths of the campus on that very first night, my fas-cination with Sam deepens. More than once, I find myself gaz-ing at his scruffily elegant profile and thinking: I can love this man.

That first semester, Sam waits patiently for me to be ready for lovemaking. Five times he invites me to his room, but, inexpe-rienced and nervous, not wanting to admit to him that I'm still a virgin, I decline. Sam only smiles and says softly, "No rush. We have time." Then one night in December, in the heat of final exam week, we leave the Malcolm X Lounge where we have been studying and go to his room. Along with several other students, we had planned to pull an all-nighter, but sometime after midnight Sam comes over to me, his books stacked neatly under his arm.

"Let's split this joint," he says.

That's all he says, but I know what he's suggesting.

When we get to his room, Sam undresses me carefully and lays me down on his bed. He doesn't think to switch off the light, and I stare over his shoulder at the hairline cracks radiating outward from the base of the ceiling socket like a frail sun. I lie quietly under Sam, studying the trail of cracks in the sunbright ceiling. I don't know what to expect, really; I don't know enough to object to the perfunctory way he enters me a moment later. I squeeze my eyes shut and clench my teeth as he begins to roll in tight circles above me. I tell myself that my period's just over; I probably won't get pregnant.

Afterwards, though, I'm confused. Sam pulls out of me suddenly, going limp against my thigh. Wetness seeps from the bruised place between my legs, staining the sheets a delicate watercolor pink. Sam holds me against him, "Oh, Korie, I'm sorry, I'm sorry . . ." He says it over and over.

I peer up at him, trying to grasp what is happening.

"It's your first time," he whispers. "I didn't know."

"But I'm fine," I answer. I squirm apart from him a little bit, trying to fathom what I feel. "It went okay," I decide.

The next morning, I parade around Sam's room without clothes, for the first time unselfconscious in my nakedness. Sam reaches out constantly to touch me. Again and again he pulls me back into his arms, moves his hands over the soft swell of my stomach and slips thin probing fingers into the moist vale between my legs. At one point, as he rubs himself against me, and grows hard again, he tells me in a voice so full of pain I think I must be imagining it, that I'm the only woman who can save him. I don't know what he means.

In some ways, Sam is exactly the kind of man I dreamed about loving when I dreamed about America. His black southern childhood with its segregated lunch counters and boycotts and marches had always seemed to me dangerous, necessary, alive. When he was eleven, Sam had even helped to integrate one of Jacksonville's all-white public schools. His black elementary school wasn't all it should have been, but Sam had triumphed in the end. Applying from his white high school, he had secured admission to an Ivy League college up north, a laurel none of his white classmates had been able to garner. Stunned by this achievement by a boy who worked weekends pruning landscaped yards for their parents, his peers had grudgingly voted him "Most Likely to Succeed."

At Columbia, though, Sam faltered. It became apparent to him that his academic training, even at the white school, wasn't on par with those of his college classmates. He'd never taken a physics class, for example, and didn't know until freshman English at Columbia what an adverb was. Of course, he used adverbs all the time. He was quick-witted and articulate, even erudite in his speech, but occasionally his written grammar lapsed, and when Sam discovered such a lapse, he felt deeply ashamed. After a while, he began to hold on to his course papers indefinitely, not wanting to turn them in until he was sure the grammar in them was airtight.

He shows me some of his papers. The reasoning and analysis seem to me first rate, yet Sam can't shake the notion that a professor, finding a "was" where a "were" should have been, or some other subject-verb disagreement, will label him stupid, an affirmative-action recruit who is lowering the university's academic standard. Sam is vulnerable to such criticisms. Sometimes, as we sit in my dorm room studying, Sam gets up on his soapbox about affirmative action, stung by its applicability to him. Oh, he knows *he* isn't inferior, he tells me, but his early training was, not because his black teachers weren't dedicated, but because they could never afford the books, the degrees, the state-of-the-art science labs and gym programs they needed to give the little black children in their care an equal chance. Separate was *never* equal, Sam lectures me on such nights. Little black children knew that firsthand.

I sit there saying nothing as Sam goes on, aware that this is Sam's way of shoring himself up. He certainly doesn't need to convert me to his way of seeing things. He's preaching to the choir where I'm concerned. I already know he is bright—even with affirmative action, Columbia wouldn't have given him a second look if he weren't. But I also know that the disparity that marked his childhood has eroded his confidence more than he likes to admit. It doesn't surprise me when I discover that his transcript is littered with incompletes.

Well, I can help him with that. Language, after all, is my secret love. I tell him I'll proofread his papers before he turns them in, and he need never again be concerned that a professor will think less of him (or that he'll think less of himself, I don't add) because he didn't construct a particular sentence exactly right.

On campus, ours is an atypical alliance in that I am West Indian and Sam is a black southerner. At Columbia in those days, African-American and Caribbean students attended one another's parties and forged individual friendships, but cross-cultural romances like ours were rare, for the larger group dynamic was strangely separate. This was something I'd never wanted to believe, that American and Caribbean blacks on campus might be so estranged. Everything I had read over the years, all the issues of *Ebony* and *Life* I'd consumed as a teenager, all the weekly news magazines, all the penny-dreadfuls (as my mother referred to these novels) on Jim Crow and the South, had led me to believe that black people in America were, of necessity, a unified front.

Of course, my clear-eyed father had known this was not always true. He'd tried to tell me, too. "You just remember, young lady, this race war up there in America is not *your* war," he'd said. "Your future is *here*."

He'd made the comment after walking into my bedroom to give me my college financial aid application, which had just arrived in the mail. Osgood seldom entered my bedroom, and now he was dismayed to find Scotch-taped to my wall a prolif-erating army of Black Power posters. Malcolm X had recently joined Huey and Angela, as had a red, black, and green poster of a raised, clenched fist, the ubiquitous Black Power salute.

Deep down, I already knew that once I made it to America, I was never coming back. But I figured Osgood and Alice would need time to get used to that. So I didn't challenge my father's assumption that day. I held my tongue. "Racism is everybody's war, Daddy," was all I said. The fact was, I needed Osgood's support to get to New York. In plain terms, I needed him to finance my ambitions until I was in a position to finance them myself.

My father wasn't sure he wanted me to go, though. He wor-ried about sending me into the racial maelstrom of America. He wasn't at all convinced that he shouldn't keep an ocean between his daughter and her rebel dreams. I sympathized with his position, because I knew he loved me dearly and wanted only to preserve me. But I also knew that I was chafing in Jamaica. While men and women of color had been marching and dying up north, I'd been idling in the breezy rooms of a sprawling, split-level house, with curving wrought-iron terraces and mango trees laden with fruit kissing my bedroom window.

Yes, I'd had a protected childhood, magical even. And yet I couldn't shake the notion that I was living in a bubble, that indeed, I hadn't yet begun to *live*. Growing up in Jamaica, devouring the news from abroad, I'd longed to be part of the passion and purpose of the Black Power movement, longed for the unequivocal sense of independence and belonging I thought the movement would confer. Of course, by the time I got to college, the arc of Black Power was on its decline, and the everyday reality of race in America turned out to be much more complex than I'd imagined.

"West Indians think they're better than us," Sam tells me one evening as we stroll holding hands down Broadway. We're on our way to dinner at our favorite Spanish-Chinese place, La Bella China. "I don't mean you," he adds hastily, "but the rest of these West Indians think we have a chip on our shoulder. They think they're special just 'cause the white man gives them a job. Any little pittance job—they'll take it. They don't see it's the old, old story—divide and conquer, all the way down the line." Involuntarily, I sigh, because Sam is on a roll now, rocking his head, mimicking voices, letting go of my hand to gesture broadly. "It's like, '*This* black is better than that one. This boy is *foreign*. He works hard. Not like our *local* Negroes. They have the nerve to think they have *rights*.' West Indians, they didn't live through Jim Crow. They don't even know the details of *Brown v. Board of Ed.* How could they possibly know what we're talking about?"

As we walk down Broadway that evening, I at first fall back on habit, merely listening as Sam rails on. The truth is, I hate this script. The whole black American-West Indian division seems absurd to me. I am so much a part of both worlds, so unquestionably West Indian and so unquestionably a black person in America, that I remain mystified as to the logic of the schism.

And then, all of a sudden, I can't help it. I get on my own soapbox. "West Indians get called nigger, too," I remind Sam with more heat than I'd been aware of feeling. I point out that the same slave ship that stopped here also stopped in the islands, and we're all connected anyway, plucked from the same continent, united by bonds of race and suffering and the will to survive. I'm getting really stirred up now; I want so passionately to prove how intricately woven our two groups are, how much we are the same, but as I pause for breath, Sam grunts skeptically and mutters, "Try telling your West Indian friends that," and all of a sudden my shoulders droop, and I catch myself thinking, Oh, what's the use?

We walk in silence until we arrive at the florescent-lit, storefront restaurant, which sits on the corner of 109th Street. As we turn into its door, Sam says quietly, "You need to wake up and stop romanticizing this U S of A, Korie. You need to get real clear on the way things *are*."

The summer after Sam graduates from college with his political science degree, he goes to work for a huge bookstore chain. His job is to make the orders. He says he'll apply to law school the next year, but he doesn't. Nor does he apply the following year. After a while, he hardly mentions law school anymore. I suspect that deep down he's afraid he won't get into a top-flight school, which would force him to adjust the way he views his life.

Two years later, I graduate from Barnard summa cum laude, Phi Beta Kappa, an English major with a minor in art history. That same year, a new picture magazine is launched in New York City, and I apply there for a job. They hire me as a reporter, the only nonwhite on the staff. I'm an affirmative-action recruit, which makes Sam mad, but I don't care. I know I'm equal to the job. But although I'm the only Phi-Beta-Kappa-summa-cum-laude-Ivy-League graduate among the reporters, I'm being paid less than the others, and I have to go through a year of probation while the white reporters are hired outright. This, I do care about. It pisses me off. But I take the job and determine to play the game. I don't even tell Sam about the pay differential. I console myself that the magazine will be a rock-solid credential someday.

Sam has left the bookstore by then, and is working sporadically, mostly office temp jobs. He isn't coming close to making a living. We discuss pooling our resources. We discuss the fact that my foreign student work permit will expire soon, and I may have to get the magazine to sponsor me. Finally, we get around to discussing marriage.

I don't doubt that I want to stay in New York, and I don't doubt my love for Sam. Still, if not for his financial circumstances and my immigration status, we might never have walked into City Hall that breezy spring morning and applied for a marriage license. The next week, with no fanfare, just a justice of the peace and a law clerk for a witness, we get married.

I call my parents that night. My father grunts and sniffles surreptitiously and mutters, "Well, good luck I suppose," before turning me over to my mother. Alice cries on the telephone, mourning the lovely artistic wedding she will not now be able to create for me. They know Sam quite well by then. He'd visited Jamaica with me the summer after my sophomore year, and shepherded Osgood and Alice around New York when they visited me the following winter. They were together again at my graduation, after which we all went out to dinner. They've always liked Sam. They can easily grow to love him, Alice tells me now, because they trust his intentions towards me. No, it is not my choice of a partner that makes them so ambivalent about my marriage. It is not even the fact that Sam isn't the most steady of workers (they're confident that's a passing phase). It is simply that we had not deemed their presence important enough to wait until they could be there. This, for my parents, is the ultimate violation of familial closeness, and it doesn't auger well for our union.

There's a strain in our relationship after that night. Osgood and Alice adopt a new hands-off policy with me. No longer do they presume to advise me on matters of my life. No longer do they call each week and ask if I'm set for money. I tell myself that they've finally appreciated my self-sufficiency, but I miss their hovering concern more than I thought I would. They still call me every other month or so, but sensing their continuing disapproval of my marriage, I am stiff and reserved on the phone. They scold me gently for neglecting to keep in touch. I promise to do better, but I don't. I'm traveling a lot for my job as a reporter now, and sometimes two or three months pass before Osgood and Alice can catch up with more than my answering machine. Eventually, I become so caught up in my New York life, I no longer dwell on what we have lost.

Sam and I move soon after our marriage into a small West Side apartment, its wall of windows giving onto a serene Hudson River view. But our life is hardly serene. Sam's jealous rages have begun; he cannot endure the parade of new people, particularly new men, who pass in and out of our lives. His jealous interrogations multiply and intensify, wrenching us apart. There is the night Craig, a fellow reporter whom I consider a friend, visits our home. We end up smoking reefer and laughing over the foibles of our workmates, while Sam watches us moodily. At one point in the evening, Craig puts his arm around my shoulders in a comradely fashion, and I know instantly that Sam will be seething. Later, he berates me for being too flirtatious, for encouraging Craig to put his hands on me. Patiently, I explain to him that Craig, with his curly brown hair and ocean blue eyes and soft round baby face, is gay. Sam refuses to believe me. He declares I'm trying to throw him off the track, and demands to know what workday rendezvous Craig and I might be planning. At such moments, I am sure that Sam is a little bit mad, but I convince myself that his madness lends a measure of excitement to our lives, proving the apocalyptic fervor of the love that binds us. (God, was I ever this young?)

Sam stays out in the streets some nights. This he has always done, ever since college, but now he begins to stay out more. Before, he would call to say he'd be late, but now he just shows up the next morning with dark circles under his eyes, and makes some excuse. He's depressed, he says, disappointed in himself because he hasn't made it to law school. I try to be encouraging. I tell him that if law school will make him happy, he should just go ahead and apply. At this point, he usually shrugs his thin shoulders and turns away.

I never get used to his disappearances. I pace the floor till morning, sick with anxiety, imagining Sam mugged on some side street or dead in some garbage-strewn alley. But I don't know which is worse, because on the nights Sam does come home, he ends up haranguing me again about Craig or some other male acquaintance. At times, I think he picks these fights so he can blow out of the house in a righteous rage, and stay gone all night.

Just as I begin to wonder if there's another women, Sam accuses me of being unfaithful. He is so convinced of it, there is nothing I can say, no way I can defend myself. He sees my growing independence as a kind of abandonment, the betrayal he has always seen as the inevitable end of intimacy. He withdraws as a husband and a lover. It will be better for us both in the long run, he says, if we can become just friends. The day after our second anniversary, he moves out of our apartment. By this time, I am so exhausted by his paranoia and the intensity of his rages, that I don't even cry at first. His leaving is almost a relief.

Here the story ends and here it begins. It turns out that as friends, Sam and I thrive. Now that sexual jealousy no longer ambushes us, we become staunch allies, partners in an almost familial sense. We talk by phone several times each day, and spend most weekends exploring the city or doing nothing at all in each other's company. We grow so comfortable together that I hardly notice the months slipping by, or the fact that I seldom date other men.

But then, on a warm October afternoon in 1983, I drive to Philadelphia to interview a pair of mental patients as part of the research for a story. I find a parking space in the asphalt lot outside the agency, and open the door of my rented, nondescript blue Chrysler. As my feet touch the earth, my eyes are drawn to a tall, lean man on the other side of the parking lot. I have never met this man, and yet it seems, as I meet his gaze, that the very ground beneath my feet has shifted.

4
The Seduction (Reprise)

ZACH MADE EVERYTHING EASY. "WHY DON'T YOU SLEEP here?" he'd suggested to Korie at midnight. "You can have the bed. I'll take the couch." He hadn't wanted to assume too much, hadn't wanted to take the slightest risk that Korie might suddenly become skittish. They were knee-to-knee on Zach's bed, where for the past several hours they had sat, talking intently, gazing from time to time at the fabulous moon. Sometimes, mid-sentence, the current between them had become too much, and they fell upon each other hungrily, their mouths pressed together with ardor and searching. Through it all, Zach had forced himself to go slowly, to not rush the seduction. But the sense of holding himself back only heightened his desire.

"I'm going to take a shower," Zach announced once the sleeping arrangements had been decided. Then, with sudden inspiration, he added, "Would you like to go first?"

He found Korie a clean towel and a large T-shirt to sleep in, and she disappeared into the bathroom, closing the door securely behind her. Zach heard the shower start. He stared at his reflection in the mirror opposite his bed: His mother's flashing dark eyes; his father's deep velvet brown skin; square chin, clean shaven; a smile more like a grin, crooked at that, making him seem boyish. At that moment, Zachary felt every bit the unformed adolescent, all prurient desire and knotted anticipation. He reminded himself that they'd only just met, that she wouldn't want to seem easy. He knew all the reasons why it might not happen this night, why it was more likely that he'd curl up on the sticky green vinyl of the living room couch and get blue balls by morning.

Korie emerged from the bathroom. The T-shirt came down to her knees. She was holding the material to her waist in an almost defensive gesture.

"Now my turn," Zachary said.

He went into the bathroom but didn't close the door. His deceptive bulk miniaturized the checkerboard-tiled bathroom and blocked all view of the cream porcelain fixtures. A bare lightbulb swayed an inch above his head, casting shadows down the wells of his eyes, cloaking his powerful shoulders in beatific light as he shrugged off his shirt. He unbuttoned his jeans, bunched his fists around denim and underwear, and pushed them deliberately down his legs. Stepping out of the wreath of clothes, he turned, completely naked, to Korie.

All Korie had to do was look away, but she continued to stare. She thought: How beautifully carved his body is, like deeply polished wood, dangerous and hard.

Her gaze fell lower.

"You didn't invite me to your party," Zach said in as light a tone as he could muster, "but I'm inviting you to mine."

Korie didn't answer. She turned away from him instead, and

stared through the window at the swollen moon. Still silent, she moved towards the window.

When he had finished showering, Zach dried himself and wrapped the towel around his waist.

He stepped from the bathroom to find Korie already in bed, the lights turned low. Zach flicked off the bathroom light and walked to where Korie lay. He lifted the covers and, letting his towel slide to the floor, slipped in beside her. Her naked back was to him, rigid, awake. The heat of her skin pulled him like a suction. He fitted himself along her, and she raised herself up a little and settled her perfect round buttocks in the cups of his palms.

Zach, kneading her flesh slowly, considered reaching into his sidetable drawer for a gold-foil-wrapped condom, but he didn't want Korie to think he took women to his bed like this as a matter of course. He could explain, he supposed, that the box of condoms was still sealed because he hadn't been with a woman in close to six months. But the right words wouldn't present themselves. Zach feared he might dissipate the spell, feared that Korie would start thinking practically, and then she would see that this was all happening too fast.

Zach wavered for another moment, closing his eyes against the painful pitch of his desire for the woman in his bed. He breathed the clean Ivory soap scent of her skin, brushed his face against the ticklish frizz of her hair.

"What will we use?" he whispered finally.

"Do you have a condom?" Korie asked softly.

So Zach had reached into his bedside table drawer after all. Then, moaning, he stroked her with his shaking fingers, and lowered her onto him, all the way down, with such aching slowness he thought he just might explode. Zach winced at the hot rush of sensation as he entered her. A strangled cry escaped him, and he crushed his lips against the silky depths of her throat as their bodies arched backwards together into a quivering bow.

Korie stirred against Zach, leaning her weight on one elbow so that she could look down at his face. Morning sun haloed her screwy red-brown hair, wilder now after their couplings of the night before. Zach felt his groin slip, tighten, remembering how in the throes of pleasuring her, of pleasuring them both, his hands had been lost in the forests of her hair.

Korie seemed to be mulling something over.

"What's on your mind, pretty lady?"

"I suppose I can't write about the Paleys now," she said, and sighed. "They were great, as perfect a couple as I could hope to find. It's a shame." Mischief flickered in her eyes. "Now I'll have to find another agency, other subjects." She tweaked one of his nipples playfully. "Maybe another caseworker."

Zach tried, and failed, to feel her mirth. Would she, after all, be leaving so soon?

"Why can't you still write about them?" he asked. A hoarseness in his voice betrayed him.

She rolled onto her back, serious once more. "Because Zach Man, here I am with you. I've lost my independence before I've even begun."

"No one has to know that," Zach tried.

"But I'll know," Korie said. "*We'll* know."

She stared at the ceiling for a long time.

"You know," she said at length, "Margie and Grant love you. They trust you completely. It was their patent worship of the ground you walk on that made me curious about you."

Zach called up his best Bogart grin. "You mean all my scheming was for nothing?"

"What scheming?" Korie teased. "It was them. You didn't

have a thing to do with it. You just sat in that tilted chair looking ridiculously sexy and didn't say a word!"

"No!" Zach almost shouted, suddenly laughing with an
exhilaration he couldn't explain. He dove across Korie, pinning
her hands beneath his big, knotted ones. "Say it was me!" he
insisted. "Admit you were powerless in the face of my charm."
She struggled under him, squealing and fighting his hands as
he tickled her ribs mercilessly.

"You didn't have a thing to do with it!" she insisted between
gasps. She caught his wrists finally, and he let her hold them.
"You just sat there and didn't say anything. How could I know
you? It was Grant and Margie who told me what you might be
like."

Then they were holding on to each other, and tumbling
over and over on the wide bed, limbs thrashing wildly as they
cascaded to the floor in a giggling heap. In the midst of it all, it
occurred to Zachary that the seduction was over, yet the cus-
tomary claustrophobia had not yet fingered him; he was as yet
untouched by any desire to flee. God, what had happened to
the bachelor of last evening? Suddenly he wished Korie *would*
want to snare him, would want to hold him in the unflinching
intelligence of her eyes, which were dancing now, the radiating
webs of her irises lit from within by her ringing laughter. He
pulled her close against him, wanting his body to be jolted by
the spasms of her joy.

"How old are you, anyway?" he asked, suddenly aware he
didn't know.

"Twenty-nine last March. And you, Zach Man?"

"Twenty-seven. Next month. Cradle-snatcher!"

Still tangled together on the bare wood floor, they were
slipping back into sleep when Zach thought to murmur, "So
tell me, Korie Morgan, what planet did you fall to earth from,
and what do you want with li'l ole me?"

•   •   •

At four that afternoon, they still lay entwined amid soaked sheets. Korie was on her side, her head on Zach's chest, her body furled along his. They had been speaking softly of heartfelt things.

"I always figured I'd never get married," Zach said as the thought made itself known.

"Why?" Korie asked him.

"I don't know, it just never seemed in the cards for me." He shrugged, shifting onto his side so that he could see her face. "But if I were the marrying kind, you'd be in deep trouble now, Korie Morgan. Just so you know."

"Well, that's not a problem," Korie shot back. But her voice had become suddenly brittle, its brightness forced. "You see, Zach Man, I've never been divorced."

Married. Zach swallowed hard. In one motion, he propelled himself from the bed and was across the room. Not knowing what else to do, he picked up his jeans and busied himself putting them on. Late afternoon sun stole through the blinds, casting thin blades of light on the room's bare walls. The blades bent around Zach's body, rippled across the tossed sheets, dusted frail patterns of hair on Korie's naked arms.

Zach let his hands fall to his sides. He stared at the woman in his bed for a long time. She didn't speak. How was it, Zach wondered, that already she had such power—to wound, to betray?

"You know," he said finally, "I didn't ask."

"A mistake," Korie said. "I mean, there's a question you surely should ask."

It seemed to Zach now that Korie had been altogether too bold, too uncaring of the outcome to have had much stake in what had passed between them. She was a woman already spoken for, and not by him.

Not by him.

"So," he said, finding an airier tone, more fitting, he coldly reminded himself, to a one-night stand. "What other goodies do you have in the grab bag?"

"It's not quite what you think," she said after a while. "I'm separated. We've been separated for going on three years, but neither one of us ever mentions divorce."

"Do you have a hankering for this guy," Zach asked softly. He fingered the belt loops of his jeans.

"I guess not," Korie smiled. "I haven't hankered after anyone for a very long time. At least, not like this. So come back over here, Zach Man." She was kneeling, bare ass on her heels, one hand stretched toward him, the other patting the sheets. "Over here, Zach Man," she whispered. "Next to me."

Zach wanted to resist her but found he couldn't.

Still, he hesitated a few more moments, trying to decide just how he should act, what he should do. At last, he sighed under his breath and unbuttoned his jeans, laying them carefully back down across the seat of the chair. He crossed the room toward Korie.

She fell slowly back as he straddled her, but instead of moving inside her, he held himself perfectly still, studying her anew in the fading light. He decided she was more breathtaking like this—her face too etched for true beauty, dark half-circles beneath her pale brown eyes. But those pale eyes glistened with a fever equal to his own, and her full lips were parted in reckless invitation.

Part Two
1983–1985

"Drowning people
Sometimes die
Fighting their rescuers."
—Octavia E. Butler

5
True Love

ALL THAT WEEKEND, THEY STAYED INSIDE ZACH'S APART-
ment, hardly fathoming that they had met barely forty-eight
hours before. They made love everywhere in the house—on
the hallway floor, straddling the couch in the living room, up
against the kitchen door, on the crumpled mat next to Zach's
bed. Sometimes, hearts humming, they floated into sleep with
Zach still inside Korie, and later, they would wake to a fresh
throbbing in their genitals, which would cause them, even
before they were fully awake, to press themselves into each
other like famished souls, and make love again.

They took baths together, rubbing soap over each other's
bodies in slow, circular strokes, massaging the brown circles of
their nipples, the upper reaches of their thighs, the creases of
their buttocks with particular care. They paused often in their
explorations to parry with their tongues and trace patterns
with their fingers in the soap.

On Sunday evening, still naked, their bodies freshly showered and skin glistening with almond oil, they moved around the kitchen preparing their first formal meal. They sautéed vegetables in bouillon broth, poached fish with butter and herbs, and tossed a fruit salad for dessert. Zach found a pack of candles in a drawer. He lit one and let some of its wax drip onto a saucer, then secured its base to the plate. He brought the candle to the table where he ceremoniously placed it in the center of his one good tablecloth, a blue plaid. The candle was industrial white, the kind people in Jamaica used when the local power station was overtaxed and the lights tripped out. But Korie knew that here, such power outages were rare.

Zach pulled out a chair and held it for Korie, motioning her to sit.

"Your lights get cut off sometimes?" Korie asked as she took her seat.

"Hey," Zach shrugged. "On my salary, sometimes you have to pay this bill instead of that one, you know?"

Watching him as he placed the plates of food around the candle, and slid into the chair opposite her, Korie again admired his ease, his unapologetic way of being just who he was.

Naked, they ate. Their richly oiled bodies caught and reflected the candlelight, and their eyes caressed each other hungrily as they picked at their food. Though carefully prepared, the fish, the vegetables, the fruit salad were all nearly tasteless, their flavor dampened by the ripe scent of sex in the air. Still, they tried to eat. Almost twenty-four hours had passed since their last meal of dry bread, cheese, and apple cider, which they had scavenged from the refrigerator, only to abandon the larger portion of it on the counter. They were so firmly in the thrall of desire, so captivated by the astonishing speed of their connection, that they moved in a kind of dream, a state of unreality that rendered such considerations as food unimportant and mundane. And so, they left this meal, too, unfinished.

Glasses of cider in hand, they retired again to the bedroom where they placed their drinks on the floor next to the bed, and pretzeled themselves along the length of each other, their hands touching roaming exploring as they rode the slowly escalating sensations of the most exquisite intimacy either one had yet known.

After they'd made love for the last time on Sunday night, Zach threw his arms wide on the bed and declared, "God put you on this earth for *me*, Korie Morgan. There's no escaping me now." He mugged, De Niro-like, as he said it, but he was more serious than he'd ever been about anything. Korie was across the room shaking the creases out of her denim dress, which had spent the better part of the weekend draped over the chair in Zach's room. She smiled at Zach's teasing tone, but said nothing.

Zach was aware, now, of a nascent ache in the region of his heart. Korie would be going soon. She was due back at the magazine the next morning, and already she was moving about the bedroom, reaching under the bed for her low-heeled shoes, rifling through her tote bag for mascara and a comb—she didn't find either; both were in her overnight bag, which they had never bothered to retrieve from the trunk of her rented car.

It was already close to midnight. Korie felt too tired to make the drive back to New York, so she had decided to take the train. Fortunately, Amtrak ran all night, and she didn't mind the idea of sitting on the train for an hour, dozing and dreaming about her weekend with Zachary. They'd agreed that Zach would take her to the train station in her car before returning it to the airport rental lot. Then he'd grab a cab home.

Zach watched as Korie pulled on her white cotton panties with lace trim, which he had carefully washed for her that morning. On Friday night, before she'd discarded her underwear for good, the crotch had become soaked with the quiet evidence of her desire, and the lace trim had stiffened as it dried. "Umm, lace," Zach had commented as he sat in the bathtub and soaped and gently scrubbed the fabric between his palms. Korie sat opposite him in the water, her legs wrapped around his hips. "Give me a woman who wears lace under denim any day of the week," Zach had murmured.

Watching Korie get dressed now, Zach understood that this was a ritual he wanted to observe again and again in the weeks to come. As she stood before the mirror, pulling her blunt-tipped brown fingers through the soft corkscrews of her hair to comb it, Zach felt suddenly forlorn. He had the sense that he was losing her, losing this mesmerizing woman who had never been his. He wanted nothing more than to pull her against him once more, to halt her preparations to leave, but he could see that she was already reconnecting with the world beyond his door, her thoughts returning to the dictates of train schedules and job responsibilities and her life in New York.

Zach got up and went to his dresser. He pulled out a clean pair of jeans and a plain black sweatshirt. Dressing quickly, he sat down on the edge of the bed to put on his sneakers, not bothering with socks. Then, he just sat, his eyes following Korie as she gathered up her bag, slipped on her shoes, and turned expectantly towards him.

How would he live without her now? Now that he knew she existed, how would he go back to the way life had been?

They hadn't yet spoken of when or where they would meet again, and now Zach felt a desperation to establish the shape of their future, to secure from Korie the assurance that this weekend had touched her life as profoundly as it had touched his.

"So when do I see you again?" he asked, trying to sound casual.

Korie came over to him and entered the circle of his arms, slipping her own arms around his neck. She kissed him softly at the point where his close-cropped black hair made the tiniest V at the center of his forehead.

"Next weekend?" she asked. "I can come back down."

Zach only nodded, his throat full. He rested his cheek against her shoulder and, closing his eyes for a moment, sent up a grateful prayer.

Lightly, he said: "Okay, Ms. Morgan. Let's get you on that train."

Back in New York on Monday morning, with barely an hour's sleep in her own bed, Korie felt like she was floating. Her body remembered Zach's touch, remembered it so keenly she felt random pangs and twinges, like little bubbles skipping through her insides. Recalling their weekend of lovemaking, she had even grown wet on the subway as she traveled to work.

She had to get control of herself. Okay. So she'd just about lost her mind. Slept with a man only hours after meeting him, then went ahead and spent the whole weekend at his house. In his bed. Who was Zachary Piper, anyway? What did she really know about him beyond what he had told her? Yet for two-and-a-half days in his company, she had given herself up to the strange alchemy that had overtaken them. And now, trying to fathom just how it had happened, what madness had consumed her, she couldn't keep the smile off her face, couldn't shake the sense that it had all been exactly right, and Zach would turn out to be just who he seemed. She'd never met a man so devoid of the need to impress, so gentle in his humor, so simple and straightforward in his approach. How could such a man be dangerous?

Even now, as she stepped from the elevator and walked down the beige carpet to her cubicle at the magazine, the questions that presented themselves were more from lifelong conditioning than from true concern. In one sense, Zach Piper was a stranger to her. She wasn't used to his type. He had none of her ex-husband's angry intensity, none of her father's starched elitism, none of the urgent, lofty ambition of the boys she knew from college. Zach was different, a more easygoing sort. He didn't spend his time designing how he'd make his mark on the world—how he would benefit black folks or poor folks or sick folks as he stuffed his bank account with the profits of a well-plotted career. Instead, Zach Piper simply rolled up his sleeves and did what needed doing for whomever needed it done. As far as Korie could tell, he merely performed his job at the agency each day with as much imagination as he could muster—anticipating no glory, expecting no praise.

No, she'd never known a man quite like Zach Piper, and yet he felt as familiar to her as breathing. Indeed, she had to fight the odd notion that their sudden chemistry had been a kind of magic, that their relationship—could it be called a relationship after only three days?—had existed even before they laid eyes on each other. They seemed to have skipped right over the getting-to-know-you part and landed right in the middle of the script.

How had Zach felt about that in the cold light of Monday morning, Korie suddenly wondered. As she put away her bag and settled herself at her desk in the white, plasterboard cubicle, she began to worry that Zach, in her absence, would think back on their weekend and grow uncomfortable with the speed at which things had progressed.

Just then, Simona Jones stuck her head into the cubicle.

"You're here!" she said, coming in and flopping down in the chair next to Korie's bookcase. She fingered the waxy green leaves of the bonsai that Korie had placed on a brightly woven cloth atop the low bookcase. "Jack Somers was calling you all weekend. Says you never checked in at your hotel. So where were you, sweet pea?"

Korie grinned at her friend's endearment. The other

reporters, used to Simona's tough, streetwise manner, would never dream her capable of such affection. But Korie had known Simona a long time, and though they'd never mentioned that fact to their fellow reporters, the experience they had shared at Kendall was a kind of touchstone for each of them, a secret refuge.

Simona was even taller than she had been at Kendall, and she had become a strikingly beautiful woman, though with a demeanor more sullen than sultry, her steady brown eyes cool and unsurprised. She still wore her hair short and sported the reddest lipstick of anyone Korie knew, and she still preferred short skirts and tight sweaters to the loose, flowing, layered look that was currently in vogue. Simona had moved back to New York from San Francisco only nine months before, to take a job at the magazine. She'd graduated from Berkeley the same year Korie left Barnard. Her major had been media studies and she'd been working as a copy girl at the San Francisco *Chronicle*, trying to break into bigger leagues. She and Korie had maintained a close phone friendship during their college years, and had even visited each other on their respective coasts once they got "real" jobs. So when a friend at the Newspaper Guild confided to Korie that her magazine was looking to hire another minority reporter rather than lose some of its affirmative-action funding, Korie had called Simona.

Simona hadn't really planned on moving back to New York—her aunt had passed away the summer after her junior year, and the city held mostly painful memories for her, for it would always be the place where she had lost her mother. But the idea of working with Korie was appealing, and reporting for a picture magazine did sound intriguing. So Simona had flown east to be interviewed by a phalanx of editors and human resources administrators, and then had flown east again after she was offered the job.

Now Simona propped shiny black boots on Korie's bookshelf and repeated, "So what's going on, girl? Where you been all weekend?"

"What did Jack Somers want?" Korie asked, avoiding her question.

"They scheduled your plea-bargaining story for January. You need to get the file in."

"Shit," Korie muttered, her mind trying to calculate how long it would take her to sift through her notes, transcribe her interview tapes, and write the file. Making it back to Philly this weekend had just started to look iffy. The plea-bargaining story was a complicated one, about a double murder case in Springfield, Illinois, and Korie knew it would easily take the better part of the week to write the file, if in fact, she could get it all done in a week.

"Did Saul get his pictures in?" Korie asked.

"Dunno."

Simona hunched down in the chair and studied her half-inch-long nails, waiting for Korie to get over her panic attack about the deadline she'd just sprung on her. She wanted to hear about her weekend.

But Korie's mind was racing now. She didn't think the photos were in house yet. The photographer she'd worked with on the story, Saul Matthis, had often been paired with her for assignments. Korie knew his pattern. He'd snapped well over two hundred rolls of film during the two-week trial, and he was most likely still sorting through his contact sheets and making print selections. Korie didn't want to write the file until she'd been able to go through the selections. That way, she could build the story around the images. But if she waited till she saw the sheets, she wouldn't be able to get started till the end of the week, and then she'd be writing all weekend.

That would mean no Zach.

There was another way, she decided. She had been Saul's

shadow the whole time he had been photographing; she knew which situations had excited him. She'd just write the story around them. She could do it even before looking at the selects, she assured herself. After all, she'd taken copious notes on the physical surroundings, snatches of conversation, people's gestures and facial expressions, even the quality of light in a room. In between the picture-taking, she had engaged the players—the judge and the lawyers and the defendants, the relatives milling in the hallway and the courtroom hangers-on—and they'd all been forthcoming with their answers, for Korie was a disarming interviewer. Her receptiveness was not fake. It was her journalistic gift, the willingness to step into another person's reality, to imagine the shape and feel of other people's shoes, and it encouraged subjects to let down their guard with her. But it was the time spent observing the scene while the photographer worked that, for Korie, yielded the richest, most telling details—the kind of detail Korie wanted to deliver on this story.

It was particularly important to her that she not fail on this one, for the story had been the brainchild of the magazine's editor emeritus, Randall Wright, a large, shambling, snow-haired man who rumor had it was part Native American. Korie had never had the courage to ask him if it was true. He didn't look Native. He looked like a regular white man, with powdery white skin and raincloud gray eyes. But, Native American or not, Wright's thick, sun-spotted hand had turned out some of the most searing yet delicately constructed prose about race relations in America. Korie had long admired his work. As a teenager in Jamaica, she'd faithfully followed his civil rights coverage in the weekly news magazines during the late sixties. Later, when she met him at the magazine, she'd been surprised by his bashful, self-deprecating manner. But if Randall's reticence baffled her, it also made her want to engage his attention, to win his professional esteem. That was why she'd been so excited when he'd chosen her to work on the plea-bargaining story. It was the first evidence of his confidence in her.

Her mind skipped over the highlights of the case they'd chosen to focus on: The two murders had been committed one liquor-soaked weekend by three accomplices, and one of them, despite having pumped five bullets into a girl on her knees pleading "Oh my God," had been given a sweetheart deal to turn state's evidence against his two friends. "I'm not dealing with precious boys and sweet little old grandmothers here," Korie recalled the state attorney telling her when she'd asked him how come. "Sweet little old grandmothers aren't drinking by the lake and murdering people over a drug deal gone wrong at three o'clock in the morning. Fact is, sometimes I have to make deals with sinners to catch devils."

Deals with Sinners, she scribbled on a yellow legal pad. Perhaps there was a title in there somewhere. She even thought she knew the first sentence of her file ("William Hicks, Billy to his friends, is a murderer . . .") and as any journalist knew, once you found the lead sentence, it was like a map you could follow into the thick of the story. Maybe she'd get through the file this week after all.

She looked back at Simona, who still sitting in her chair, watching her with a hint of impatience.

"You finished?" Simona said.

"Finished what?"

"Your little worry snit. Are you finished? If so, I'm waiting to hear about your lost weekend? So fess up, Korie girl."

So Korie did.

Around noon, her phone rang. Jack Somers wanted her to come into his office. She picked up her notebook and walked down the corridor to see her editor, a tall, patrician-looking

Bostonian. All the reporters were assigned to a particular editor. The science editor and the news editor each had three reporters, but everyone else, including Jack Somers, had one. Jack and Korie were primarily in charge of the human interest stories, although they also tended to cover such "soft" features as anniversaries, collectibles, and the arts. In addition, editors could tap any reporter they thought would be well suited to a particular story. That was how Randall Wright had brought Korie into the plea-bargaining story.

Jack Somers was sitting at his computer, tapping keys. As Korie entered, he swiveled his chair to face her.

"Tried to reach you," he said with typical brevity.

"I have a cousin who lives in Philly," Korie lied. "I ended up staying with her."

"Ah," Jack said. Then, "How *was* Philadelphia?" Meaning, had she found a story.

Korie chose her words carefully. "Well, there was one couple that was interesting, but the situation wasn't very visual."

"Will it work?"

"Not sure. The setting was very institutional. Florescent lighting, cream walls, plastic chairs, fake wood desks. Maybe as a black-and-white story it could work."

"What about the couple?"

"The genuine article," Korie admitted.

"The caseworker?"

The crux of the matter, Korie thought. The caseworker.

"He was interesting, too," she said noncommittally. "Young black man, dedicated, kind of quiet, though." It was true that Zach had been mostly silent during the interview with Grant and Margie Paley. Later, though, he'd spoken volumes, with his lips, his hands, the rhythm of his hips.

Afraid she might betray herself, Korie quickly steered the exchange away from Zach. "The director was kind of photogenic. Lots of bushy red hair, big guy. He wants this story."

"So? Why not?"

"It's just a feeling I have," Korie finally said, not lying at all. "I think we should check out the other agency in Chicago before we decide."

"Okay," Jack agreed. He had grown used to trusting Korie's judgment, so he didn't press. "But you can't go until the plea-bargaining story closes. It's up for January. You better get cracking on that file."

"Already started, Jack. I'm aiming for Friday."

"Good," Jack said, adding wryly, "now we just have to coax our Saul Matthis to get his masterpieces in."

That evening, at just past seven, Simona stopped by Korie's cubicle. Korie glanced up from her computer.

"Craig and Gina and me are heading over to Black Rock," she said. Black Rock was their favorite after-work watering hole. It had a nice private bathroom with a large stall that was perfect for a quick joint or sniff of cocaine. "You coming?"

"No," Korie said, gesturing towards her computer screen. "I have to finish this."

Simona moved closer to Korie and lowered her voice. "Care for a little powdered encouragement?"

Korie was tempted, not for the first time, by the idea of coke. She had a long night ahead of her, wrestling with her file—she had so far managed three paltry paragraphs. Simona and Craig had told her how they would sometimes take a sniff of the white stuff right there in their cubicles, doors closed of course, and then tap out a story in a blaze of inspiration. Korie had never tried cocaine, but sitting there at her computer, thinking more about Zachary than about that sad, ugly murder case in Springfield, she could have used a little inspiration.

But she didn't dare. Not on this story.

"No, you go ahead," she told Simona. "I think I'll do this one the old-fashioned way."

"Suit yourself." Simona shrugged. She trilled her fingers and sauntered off to find Craig. Korie watched her go, then sighed and resumed typing. God, it was going to be a long week.

Korie hadn't known till the last minute that she would make it to Philadelphia on Friday. The evening before, she and Zach had spoken by phone, as they had every night that week, and Zach had whispered into her receiver, "Come see me this weekend, baby. I need to know I didn't dream you." Korie wanted to go, but she didn't know yet if she'd be finished with the file. There were a couple of details she still had to track down, and the whole last section, which included the verdict and the denouement of the case, still to write. As it turned out, she had worked, writing feverishly, right up until that afternoon, and had finally put the finished manuscript on Jack Somers's desk at something to six. Then, with a growing sense of anticipation, she'd caught the subway home, not fully understanding until she blew through her front door and began throwing clothes into an overnight bag that she was on her way to Philadelphia. She got back on the subway and arrived at Penn Station in plenty of time for the seven-fifteen Metroliner.

Standing on the platform, waiting to board her train, Korie suddenly remembered that Zach didn't know she was coming! She dialed him hastily from a pay phone, praying he'd be home. He was, and judging by the commotion in the background, a lot of other people were there with him. "Friday night dominoes," he explained, apologizing for the noise. When she told him she was at the train station, bound for Philadelphia, his excitement had crackled through the line.

Now, getting off the train, she saw him before he noticed her. Standing by the stairs at the end of the long platform, scanning the straggles of people for a sign of her, he was more attractive than she remembered, his body lean and well made, his brown leather windbreaker open over a plain white T-shirt, his close-fitting blue jeans brushing the insteps of clean white sneakers. And his unabashed grin once he saw her—it made her heart turn over in her chest, and she felt herself smiling foolishly in return, her feet unsteady, impatient to cover the distance between them.

"Hello again," she said as she arrived in front of him, and he embraced her tightly, his whole body meeting hers.

"I missed you, pretty lady," he murmured, looking down at her. "It seemed your train just wouldn't get here."

Korie kept grinning, unsure what to say, then sure that there was nothing she needed to say. What they'd experienced last weekend had been real after all, and seeing him now felt like nourishment.

Zach took her bag. "Car's this way," he said, leading her up the stairs, through the wooden doors, out into the night. He opened the passenger door of his ancient navy blue Rambler, and Korie realized that this was the first time she would actually be traveling in his car. How could everything feel so *known*, and yet there was so much they had not yet done? she wondered. She slid into the front seat, and reached across to open the door on the driver's side. But it wasn't locked.

Zach chuckled. "No one wants this rusty old trap," he said, throwing her overnight bag into the backseat and slipping in next to her. "But thank you anyway."

As he pulled out of the parking lot and steered towards the highway, he thought to mention, "By the way, there are a whole bunch of Negroes at my house. Waiting to meet you."

●　　●　　●

His mother Florida was there, and his sister, Annie, although they were both getting ready to leave when Zach and Korie walked in.

"So this is Korie," Florida said when Zach introduced her, his pride pushing through his chest. "You're the one giving my boy sheep eyes." Her voice was deep and generous, and she patted Korie's hand as she spoke, but her words made Korie self-conscious.

Annie, boyish-looking in khaki chinos, combat boots, and a green rollneck sweater, stood to the side, her eyes narrowed as she observed Korie.

"And this is my big sister," Zach said. Korie put out her hand to shake Annie's. Annie grasped her hand, but instead of shaking it, pulled Korie forward and gave her a rough hug.

"Don't you hurt my brother," she whispered, her lips at Korie's ear. It came out almost like a threat.

"I won't," Korie managed.

"Well, we have to go," Annie announced brightly, pulling away. "It's way past Florida's bedtime. Mama's an early bird these days. But you take good care of my brother, Korie. I've never really seen him this smitten."

Korie searched for the right way to respond, and came up blank. She was overwhelmed by how much Zach's family already knew of her, and amazed by the openness with which he had played his hand.

"I'm glad I got to meet you," she said lamely as Florida and Annie went down the stairs.

"Pleasure's all mine," Florida said, turning back to her, smiling warmly. Korie found herself liking her, and thinking that Zach's good-heartedness must have begun with her. She wanted to like Annie, too, but hadn't quite achieved that yet. She decided she'd just appreciate how protective she was of her brother and let it go at that.

The youngest Piper, Neal, was also there. Zach pointed him

out after Florida and Annie left. Neal was sitting on the green vinyl couch across the living room. He was slender like the rest of them, but he was pale where the rest of them were richly brown, and his hair was curly and orangish. His eyes appeared transparent, almost ghostly in the low-wattage light in Zach's living room, and they were glued to the TV screen. He didn't glance up as everybody else in the room, all of them men, jostled and teased Zach and swirled around Korie, introducing themselves.

There were the two Timmens boys, Joe and Alvin, just home from ten years in the penitentiary, they informed her. "We're rehabilitated," Joe laughed, slurring his words, his breath stink with beer.

There was Micky Manning, with his huge jelly stomach and wrinkled bald head and jawline scar. "Been knowing Zach Piper from way back," he said. "Pipes is my man." Korie noticed that the scar along Micky Manning's jaw had healed with a large keloid, making him seem fierce, and yet she instinctively trusted him, trusted the note of allegiance in his voice when he spoke Zach's name.

And there was Hux, short for Huxtable, as in Bill Cosby's sitcom character. Hux was a small, corn-colored man with silver-rimmed glasses and a conceited air. "She's a pretty little West Indian gal," he told Zach, gazing at Korie, his eyes flirtatious behind his lenses. "What she want with you, man? She can do better than you." To Korie: "Girl, don't you know you a princess? This Negro don't know how to treat a princess. Now take me . . ."

"Out of my way, Hux," Zach joked. "Just 'cause you're going to be some kind of doctor don't mean she want you."

"He have to pass his tes' first," Joe Timmens slurred.

"You always been stuck on yourself, Hux," Micky Manning laughed.

Korie's head was spinning. She was flattered by all the

attention, but she'd already begun to wish that they'd all just go away. Truth be told, she had been a little disappointed at the train station when Zach had told her they were all still here. Sure she wanted to meet his friends, but not tonight, not after she'd spent the last five days aching for him, barely sustaining herself on the memory of last weekend.

She smiled stiffly at the banter, and moved through the group towards Neal. "Hi," she greeted him, sitting down on the couch. "What are you watching?"

"Just the news." Then, "I'm Neal."

"I know. Zach told me. I'm Korie."

"I know," Neal smiled. He had a sweet, guileless smile, much like Zach's, Korie thought. "Nice to meet you," he said.

Across the room, the men returned to a game of dominoes, which Zach and Korie's arrival had disrupted. Zach mixed and ferried drinks back and forth from the kitchen. Occasionally, he sat at the domino table and played a game himself, talking trash loudly with his friends as Korie slouched next to Neal on the couch and prayed for the social part of the evening to end.

At about two, Neal announced that he was leaving.

"Okay, bro," Zach said, hugging him.

"She's nice," Korie heard Neal tell Zach at the door. She didn't know on what evidence he'd decided that. They'd hardly talked, just watched the news and then the late movie together, while the rest of the men whooped it up at the domino table.

Then Neal was gone, and Korie waited for his departure to cue the other men. But they continued to sit playing dominoes, laughing and growing drunker by the minute. Finally, Korie couldn't stand it anymore. She got up and went over to Zach.

She made her voice sound pleasant. "I'm tired," she said. "I think I'm going to bed."

Zach looked at her with concern.

"You all right?"

Inwardly, she was churning with hours of repressed frustration, but she said, "I'm just tired from the train ride and work and all that. Don't worry about me. I'll just turn in."

Zach studied her closely, sensing something amiss. He excused himself from the domino game and followed her into his bedroom, closing the door.

Korie realized that Zach, too, was a little bit drunk, and her heart sank. She'd spent all week visualizing what their reunion would be like, how they'd fall into each other's arms and pick up right where they'd left off. This wasn't the way she'd imagined things at all.

"I'm going home," she said.

Zach looked confused. "You just got here."

"And now I'm leaving," she said. "Then you can play dominoes all night and drink beer with your friends."

For a man usually so perceptive, Zach had taken a long time to get it, but now, suddenly, he did.

"Hey," he said softly, "I can tell them to leave."

"Don't bother," Korie said, picking up her bag.

Zach couldn't help it; he wanted to laugh. Korie caught the quiver of a smile at the corners of his lips, but he managed to avert a full-out laugh. Later, he would admit that she'd looked so irresistible, standing there pouting and angry, yet refusing to admit she was mad, refusing to give voice to the fact that she hadn't wanted to share him just yet. His heart leapt a little as he realized that she must want him as much as he wanted her! He fought the desire to just gather her into his arms and hold her there. Instead, he took her bag from her hand for the second time that night, and rested it next to the bed. Then he touched her cheek.

"Wait here," he whispered. "I'll make this right."

Zach left the room, closing the door delicately behind him.

Fuming, Korie sat down abruptly on the bed, wondering what she'd gotten herself into. If Zach had felt like a known quantity to her, his milieu of ex-cons and scar-faced beer buddies and made-it-good boys from the 'hood was more raw than anything she was used to. In her head, she could hear her ex-husband telling her to stop romanticizing everything, to open her eyes to the way things were. Well, this was Zach's life, his world. These were his family and friends. He'd thought it important that she meet them, that she understand who he was.

So now she knew. Fine. But couldn't they all go away, now, and let her have Zach?

Zach was speaking outside, his friends laughing, protesting. ". . . all you trifling Negroes out of my house! Right now. Everybody out!" There was a lightheartedness in his voice that robbed the words of their sting. "Yes, Hux, you, too. No, forget the game. Take the goddamned game. Finish it somewhere else. I can see you freeloaders any day of the week. The rest of this night is for me and my woman!" He went on talking, hustling Joe and Alvin and Micky and Hux out of the apartment, finally slamming the door behind them.

Korie sat perfectly still on the bed, waiting for him to reappear.

My woman, he had said.

The words had pierced her anger, dissipating it, so that the little bubbles that had danced through her all week started up again, and her heart beat fast and her cheeks felt hot and she had to squeeze her thighs together to stop them from trembling.

She heard Zach in the bathroom peeing, washing up, brushing his teeth. Then the bedroom door opened, and he was standing across from her, grinning happily, his frame filling the doorway.

Korie said, "Who's your woman, Zach Man?"—squinting at him, teasing him—"Who did you say she was?"

"Korie Morgan," he answered, moving towards her. "She is most *definitely* my woman."

"Let me see," Korie said, studying the ceiling and tapping her lips with a finger. "Do I have this right? If *she's* your woman, that must mean that you're *her* man."

"Smart, too," Zach murmured, kneeling in front of her and taking her face in his hands.

6
Modigliani's Girl

IN JANUARY, JUST AS KORIE'S PLEA-BARGAINING STORY HIT the newsstands, Zach lost his job as a caseworker at the Carson Agency. It all started with Grant Paley's arrest. Grant never could seem to find his way home from the neighborhood errands he was always so eager to perform. He'd been lost several times and had finally wound up in a precinct lockup, charged with indecently exposing himself. Grant explained that he'd simply been asking directions of a woman when the desire to urinate seized him. But since his inquiry had been incomprehensible to the woman to begin with, and since she had only stopped to listen because she was afraid of riling the wiry, distinctly wild-eyed black man before her, she'd been deeply alarmed when he casually unzipped his trousers and pulled out his penis. Backing away, the woman shrilled for help. A cop had been idly watching them, and now he ambled over to lead a bemused Grant Paley away.

From the precinct house, Grant telephoned his wife,

Margie. Unlike Grant, whose umbilical cord at birth had coiled around his neck, strangling his first crucial minutes of air, Margie had been born normal, had even been an exceptional student through high school. But an early marriage to an abusive man had derailed her sanity so that by the time she turned twenty, she couldn't recall any life other than the muted routine of the state mental hospital, where she'd been sent after killing her husband. Life hadn't begun again for Margie, in fact, until the day Grant had shuffled up to her in the hospital corridor and offered her a crudely sewn rag doll that he'd made for her in needlecraft.

"Oh, Grant," Margie wailed now, "how could you be in *jail*?"

"I don't know, Margie," Grant said, his voice winnowed with fear. "You have to get me out of here. The guys in here look mean, Margie. Real mean. I smell the *evil* on them, you know. And it's real dark in here, Margie, dark in here, dark in here . . ." Grant's speech sometimes got caught at some neurological impasse, causing him to repeat himself like a scratched gramophone record. He was stuck now, and kept whispering to Margie, " . . . dark in here, dark in here, dark in here . . ."

Margie interrupted in her most soothing tone. "Grant, honey, nobody's going to hurt you."

"Dark in here," he whined.

They were both silent for a long while, so that the police officer standing next to Grant at the precinct house thought he'd ended the call, and moved to take the phone from his hands. Grant pushed him roughly away, then crouched whimpering against the wall, the phone still at his ear. On the other end of the line, Margie spoke up.

"I'll tell you what, Grant honey, I'll hang up now and think about this."

"Sure, Margie."

Grant allowed himself to be led back to the lockup, where

he settled himself against the urine stink of the brick wall and let his cares flow from him. Margie would handle everything, he told himself. Margie always knew what to do.

Margie had been twenty when her case came to court. Now she was thirty-three, and had only a dreamlike recollection of killing her first husband. The husband—Bertram Hadley, according to the court records—had raped and battered Margie one night too many. When he'd left the house the following morning, Margie had crawled naked from their bedroom to crouch by the kitchen door, a carving knife in her hands. All day, her resolve wavering, she waited there. When evening crept in and made the kitchen shadows dense, Margie looked at the silver blade gleaming in her hands and decided to rest it on the floor. She was moments away from returning the knife to the drawer, and herself to the bedroom, when her husband walked through the door, calling her name in a manner so diffident she might well have hallucinated the evening before.

Right then, Margie's hands took on a will of their own. Her fingers clasped around the knife handle and raised it in the air. Bertram Hadley barely glimpsed Margie's cold, crazed eyes as the blade slid to the hilt into his neck. As he collapsed, a fine red stream spurting from his paste white throat, Margie lurched out the kitchen door and stumbled to the street. Clothed only in the satiny wetness of her dead husband's blood, she ran towards the highway, brandishing the killing knife, screaming without sound.

The pretrial judge, surveying the hollow-cheeked girl in plastic slippers and falling-down socks before him, had dismissed the murder charge on the grounds of diminished capacity—a sort of not guilty by reason of insanity. And Margie was clearly insane by then, dull-eyed and listless, what the psychiatrists called "lacking in affect." So the judge, because he could think of nothing else to do with her, remanded her to the custody of the state psychiatric hospital indefinitely.

Margie had lived at the state hospital for eleven years. As she'd told that reporter from New York who Mr. Ryan had brought in, she hadn't really minded her time in the crazy house. The planned activities, the unvarying routine, the regular and insipid meals in green-painted common rooms with long tables all reminded her of the orphanages in which she had been raised. She found solace in the memory of the other orphans who had been her siblings, and the muttering, meandering characters who peopled the dim corridors and windowless rooms of the hospital's psychiatric wing were as close an approximation of family as Margie had ever known.

She had, in fact, been quite happy at the hospital, at least until her thirty-first birthday. And then, quite unexpectedly, her world expanded. A patient named Grant Paley, with whom she had had until then no more than a relationship of timorous smiles, approached her shyly one day and offered her a gift— the brown-skinned rag doll with wistful button eyes that he'd sewed for her himself. Margie cradled the floppy thing in her arms and rocked it as if it were a live baby. In the depths of her cat green eyes, an idea flickered, then faded, and Margie thanked Grant with a fervor she had no explanation for.

Margie always said after that Grant was her first true friend. He was the first human being she trusted not to hurt her. As this understanding grew, she settled on a plan, and when it was all figured out in her mind, she found Grant Paley in the corridor, handed him the doll, and asked him to marry her. Holding the rag baby against his shoulder the way he'd seen Margie do, Grant had accepted her proposal.

At first, the state hospital officials brushed aside their talk of getting married, but when it became clear that the two were quite resolved, there followed a flurry of legal queries. It was finally determined that by law, Grant and Margie were perfectly entitled to be married and so the hospital officials, claiming they were not set up to handle such special circumstances, referred the couple to a social agency that might be better able to smooth the way.

Zach, a three-year veteran of the Carson Agency by then, was not actually surprised when his superiors, anticipating the same supervision headaches that the state hospital had wanted to avoid, tried to discourage the two from marrying. Carson's director, Irv Ryan, had suggested they set up house together with four other mentally impaired adults in a monitored group home. It was Zach who at each obstacle had encouraged Grant and Margie to persevere. Their wedding *would* take place, he promised them. They just had to get all the paperwork squared away.

Finally, almost two years from the day Grant had first shuffled up to Margie and handed her the rag doll, they stood together in the county courthouse and made their vows. Their caseworker, Zachary Piper, stood tall at Grant's side.

Now, after Grant's call from the precinct house, Margie pondered for just a minute before it occurred to her that she must call Zach. This afternoon, a Saturday, Margie found him at home.

After he put down the phone, Zach changed from jeans to more businesslike slacks. He put on a tie, shrugged into a navy blue blazer, and went down to the precinct house where he used his own money to post Grant's fifty-dollar bail. Zach decided against filing an incident report with the agency. Instead, he approached the woman Grant had accosted himself, calling on her in person after escorting Grant Paley home. Her name and address he'd found in the police record of charges.

An hour later, he left the woman's home feeling gratified, having finally prevailed upon the indignant Mrs. Elsie Maddux to drop the charges against so harmless a person as Grant. But Elsie Maddux, thinking it over after Zach left, found it appalling all over again that a disturbed indigent like Grant Paley should be wandering the streets alone. Why, he might have pulled out a weapon with the same nonchalance with which he pulled out his *thing.* Or he might have had an *attack* of some sort. Who knew with such people? And so she had called up the precinct and reinstated charges. A few days later, when a notice arrived at the agency stating the date Grant was scheduled to appear in court, it came as a complete surprise to Zach.

And to Irv Ryan, who summoned Zach to his office at once. The director stood at the window, his huge frame blocking the sparse winter light. His expression, in profile, seemed merely disgruntled, but his arms were aggressively clamped across his powerful chest, making him seem more a giant than ever. Zach seated himself, watching Ryan closely. The director turned from the window and there was no mistaking his fury. In one red fist he held Grant's court summons; the paper shook and crackled with his pent-up rage.

"Tell me about this," Irv Ryan said.

Briefly, Zach recounted the facts.

"And the incident report?" Ryan asked when he was done.

Zach shrugged. "I didn't think we needed one," he said. "I figured things were all worked out."

"How *dare* you take this authority upon yourself," Ryan said quietly, his voice trembling with the sheerest, most tenuous control. "The decision as to what should have been done was *not* solely yours, Piper."

Zach knew that even now, all it would take to appease his supervisor was a little hollow contrition, but he said nothing, and Ryan interpreted his silence as insolence. Oh, he and Piper had had their run-ins before. Long ago, after Zach had won his battle on the Paleys' behalf, they had agreed to disagree. Ryan knew Piper had little patience for his devotion to conventional bureaucratic procedure. But he, not Zachary Piper, understood the politics involved in making so few waves that the program's state and federal funding would not be cut. But Ryan also understood that it was Piper's very commitment to the special community he served that made him valuable.

So Ryan didn't fire Zach that time, just put him on warning for the umpteenth time. Mrs. Elsie Maddux was once again persuaded to drop the charges, after Ryan had accorded her the official recognition she felt her grievance deserved.

Then Margie became pregnant.

And Zach, knowing the agency would insist on an abortion, decided to keep her condition quiet for as long as he could. But Margie, so delighted with the prospect of motherhood, had blurted the news to another caseworker, who went immediately to Ryan.

The director was livid.

"Who the *hell* do you think you are?" he demanded as Zach sat stone-faced before him. "Margie could have miscarried. There might have been medical complications. What *could* you be thinking?"

"She's been seeing a doctor from the beginning—" Zach began.

Ryan cut him off. "And who may I ask selected this doctor?"

"I did," Zach said. "He's on our roster."

"*You* did," Irv mocked, his tone scathing. "*You* did. So now you're usurping the medical staff. You're not a doctor, Piper! You have no *idea* what we're dealing with here. My God, you have no concept of how this child could turn out, how this could affect their mental state. Goddamn you, Piper, there are legalities involved here! What are you trying to do to me?"

"To you?" Zach said, his tone cool. "Frankly Irv, I never gave you a thought. I was trying to do something for Margie and Grant. You might not believe your crazies have the capacity, Irv, but they love each other and they *want* this child." He paused, and there was silence for a moment between the two men. Ryan looked balefully at his caseworker. When Zach spoke again, his tone was more conciliatory.

"It would have killed Margie to give up this child," Zach said. "I work with them, I *know*. Think about it, Irv, what that raggedy old doll meant to them, what it did for them. To have this child could be the most healing thing."

"Wasn't she taking her birth control pills?"

"I thought she was."

"That's not good enough, Piper. You should have made sure."

Zach only shrugged. The truth was he found Margie's pregnancy thrilling. Further, he thought it sickening that the very bureaucracies set up to enhance the quality of life for Grant and Margie should, in the end, frustrate their efforts to lead as normal an existence as possible. Ryan saw this disdain for his position pass over Zach's face, saw the expression harden into obstinacy and at that moment, the director relinquished his last vestige of control.

"Get out!" he thundered. "And I mean *now*, Piper. You clear out your desk today!" Ryan struggled to regain some composure. Almost formally, he added, "You're fired, Zachary Piper. And while you're packing up your things, just think about this: Some other poor fool is going to have to carry this. You just piss and move right along, leaving your mess for some other sucker to clean up."

"I'm perfectly willing to carry my own weight," Zach muttered, rising to his feet. "Irv."

"Go," Ryan said. "Just go. This community living thing isn't working anyway. I'm recommending that the Paleys be returned to the hospital."

Zach was stunned. For a moment, he couldn't move. He hadn't ever anticipated that things would come to this. It struck him that he *had* been irresponsible, though not quite in the manner Irv thought. What use could he be to the Paleys, to any of the others, if Ryan fired him? His departure would be nothing less than a betrayal of his clients, for he had become a constant in their lives, a familiar trusted ally in a befuddling world.

"Irv, let's talk about this—"

"Go," Ryan repeated weakly, then sank heavily into his chair. One thick hand supporting his brow, the director laughed without mirth. "It isn't that I don't like you, man, it's just that I can't control you. *I'm* the head honcho here," he stabbed his chest, "but you just waltz in here and do as you darn well please!"

"But don't send them back to the hospital." Zach felt suddenly desperate. He had to win this point. "Not the state hospital, Irv! Team them with foster parents who can help them raise the child! The state hospital would take that baby away from them! That's just taking too much, Irv. You'd be leaving them no hope—"

"It's not your concern anymore, Piper."

"Irv—"

Ryan knew Zach was right. And his foster parent idea wasn't bad. "Not the hospital," he agreed finally. "Now go. Get out of here."

"I'll call to see how they're doing."

Ryan didn't respond. Zach hesitated another moment, then moved towards the door. Hovering in the doorway, he swallowed his pride enough to say, "The baby might not be retarded, Irv. Margie was born normal, and Grant's only messed up because of complications at birth. It's not genetic. This kid could be fine." He realized he was backpedaling for all he was worth. But for Ryan, it was too little, too late.

"And what kind of life will a normal kid have with the Paleys for parents?" he said, almost sadly. The two men stared at each other. Finally, Ryan said, "Just go, man."

"And I don't want to see you back here," he added as Zach stepped into the hall. "And so help me God," he continued, raising his voice yet delivering the words devoid of their rancor, "if I catch you inciting our clients to *anything*, if you meddle in any way in their affairs, I promise I'll call the cops. I'm sick of you, Piper, do you hear me? Sick and tired of your goddamned moral superiority!"

Zach didn't turn back as Ryan spoke. Instead, he continued down the hall, stopping in his office only long enough to collect the button-eyed rag doll that Margie had given him the morning her pregnancy was confirmed.

Korie's apartment was in the shadow of the university, on the margin of Harlem. It was a quirky railroad affair, with three matchbox-size rooms stacked to one side of an endless stretch of hallway. The hallway, with its double-height domed ceilings and its ornately molded but disintegrating walls, gave the apartment a stately character, which Korie had tried to enhance by hanging framed art prints along the length of the hall.

The apartment forced compensations for its old-world charm. It was cramped for one thing, in spite of the illusion of space that the sweep of the hallway bestowed. There was an alcove for a kitchen, a mere dip in the living room wall that contained a sink, wall shelves, and an ancient gas-burning stove. The refrigerator was tucked into one corner of the living room, which left space enough for a couch, a television set, an overgrown ficus plant, a butcher block table, and two slatted folding chairs that Korie had found in the hall closet when she'd first moved in.

She had been newly separated from her husband then, and embarking on solo tenancy for the first time. She had taken the apartment because of the amazing wash of painter's light that poured through its enormous northern-facing windows. Korie imagined her quarters as the sort of place that her mother might have occupied had marriage to her father not coaxed her artistic spirit along a less bohemian path. Not that Alice Mathurin ever seemed to regret choosing the loving fetters of family life. Still, she had romanticized the other road for her daughter incessantly: The movies she would choose to see with Korie were invariably about hollow-eyed artists in unheated lofts, starving with resolute dignity. On birthdays, Alice Mathurin had often surprised her daughter with a biography of some gifted author or artist bent on poetic self-destruction. And when Korie was fifteen, Alice had turned over a cherished first edition monograph about the painter Modigliani, whose restless, debauched life in Paris during the century's first decades belied the renown he would posthumously achieve. Racked by tuberculosis, gripped by a mad fever of unrequited love, the painter had hurled himself from a friend's balcony at the age of thirty-four.

Modigliani's drive for sensual stimulation and his impulsive suicide had disturbed the adolescent Korie, particularly when she compared his dead-eyed, mannequinlike portraits to the seething rush of emotion that had drowned his life. And yet his was the sort of hellbent existence that Alice Mathurin found worth noting, if only because it was marked by such passion. *Passion* was Alice Mathurin's watchword. Fierce passion directed every impecunious historical or fictitious life that ever fired her imagination, and Korie came to understand this extreme of emotion that her mother glorified as the first requirement of true art.

And yet, in blind contradiction, Alice, with Osgood by her side, had managed to convey that she expected of her daughter a more conventional life—a sensible marriage, well-mannered kids, a career that moved ever forward. As a result, when Korie had dared to test her mother's more romantic notions by basking in the haughty gloom of teenage Modigliani-like boys, and then going off to America and marrying Sam Marshall without ever consulting them, it was taken by Osgood and Alice as a clear rejection of all that they had sacrificed to give and to teach.

So it was entirely in keeping with Korie's pattern that Zach won unencumbered access to her life after he lost his job. For one thing, he was free to hop the train or drive to New York whenever Korie's schedule could accommodate him. But his savings were minimal, and the commuting back and forth between Philadelphia and New York soon exhausted his funds.

"Why don't you stay here with me," Korie whispered one Friday night after lovemaking. "If you move in, I'll even go on the pill."

"No job," Zach murmured, his lips traveling between Korie's shoulders blades. "Mmm, you smell ripe."

"So what?" Korie said.

"Huh?"

"So what, you don't have a job? You don't need a job. I make a good living."

Zach pulled away from her, a quizzical smile on his lips. "That ain't right, Ms. Morgan. A man's got to work."

"Says who?" Korie pushed herself up in the bed so that her back was against the scrolled hardwood headboard. She thrust her chin forward, planted her palms in the sheets. "I mean, if you were me, if you were the one with the good income, no one would have anything to say about you supporting me. It's okay for a man to support a woman. Why not the other way around?"

"You know what, baby, it sounds nice. And don't get me wrong, now. I like that you're open-minded. But it's not real. How long would it be before you got sick of me living off you? Besides what would your folks say?"

"It's none of their business," Korie said, almost petulantly. The stiffness of her back gave a little.

Zach wasn't really in the mood to argue. He was swamped by the scent of her, sitting naked at his head. He appreciated the correctness of her sentiment, but right now, he wanted to kiss her ripe-smelling lips and draw her tongue towards his own.

But Korie wasn't having it. "Well?" she said.

"Well, what?"

"Is it just about the job?"

"What? Is what just about the job?" Zach was having trouble concentrating. She smelled musky, damp, sweet. Zach closed his eyes, wanting only to taste her skin, wanting to part her smooth brown thighs and search out her secrets.

"Come live with me, Zach Man," Korie said, her voice suddenly cajoling. She traced the closed crescents of his eyelashes, then ran her forefinger down his cheek to his slightly parted lips. Her touch was light, feathery. "Just think," she teased, drawing circles on his skin, "all this sugar, all the time."

"Mmm," he said, pulling her towards him.

"Who cares about a stupid ole job?"

"Me," he murmured, lightly kissing her navel. "I care about a stupid ole job." His fingers dipped between her legs.

"Chauvinist," she groaned, her body beginning to arch.

"Oh, no, it's called *responsibility*, Ms. Morgan. A little Jamaican princess like you, surely your mama and papa taught you that."

"They also taught me good girls don't do this with wickedly sexy men." Korie giggled. "Especially not wickedly sexy, *un*employed men."

"Lots of jobs in New York," Zach whispered, his voice dreamy and blurred.

The following Monday, Zach rode the Amtrak to Philadelphia one last time. He sublet his apartment, left his car with his brother, Neal, and stored his things at his mother's. Four months after their meeting in the Carson Agency parking lot, Zach and Korie were living together.

At first, Sam Marshall was an unseen presence in Zach's cozy life with Korie. Zach knew that Sam had lunch with Korie several times each week, and he called her almost daily at the office, but he never came to the apartment when he knew Zach would be there, and that suited Zach perfectly. He'd seen photographs of Korie's husband. They were all over the apartment, sheafs of loose Polaroid snaps that waylaid him wherever he turned. He was tall and gaunt and brooding, this Sam, his eyes deep-set and bright with emotional fire. But Zach noted that when, in the photographs, Sam's eyes rested on Korie, the fire in them abated somewhat and a tenderness touched his features.

What had torn these two apart? Zach wondered, poring through the snapshots for some unwitting clue.

"Why didn't you stay married?" he asked Korie one night. "You and Sam seem so close. Why'd you break up?"

Korie was sprawled on the rug, writing notes on a yellow legal pad. She was working on a story about a seventeenth-century sailing ship that had been discovered beneath the city's waterfront. The ship had been a Dutch merchant vessel, ferrying iron bars and barrels of grain to the New World. At the end of its life, it had been gutted and used as landfill to support the South Street docks. Now its excavated cabins, its unearthed decks represented an archaeological treasure that Korie hoped to give life to in her article.

At Zach's question, she paused, considering. "We quarreled all the time," she said at length.

"About what?" Zach had been scanning want ads in the *Village Voice*, circling anything that looked promising. Korie had urged him to take his time, but Zach had resolved to make good on his earlier insistence that he *would* find a job. It didn't have to be a social work job, he'd decided. Security guard, shoe salesman, anything with a paycheck would do just fine.

Now, he marked one more listing, then folded the paper and put it aside. "What did you and Sam fight about?" he repeated.

"Why do you want to know, all of a sudden?" Korie asked, squinting at him.

"Scoping out the competition," Zach teased.

Korie swiveled to a sitting position, her eyes roaming the ceiling. "What did we argue about," she said. "This and that, you know, petty stuff." She shrugged. "My tendency to be late. His habit of absenting himself at all hours of the night. A lot of the time, other men."

"You saw other men?"

"No, but Sammy thought so. He always thought I was on the verge of cheating on him. Especially after we got married. He was ridiculously jealous. Mindlessly, crazily jealous. And he never had any reason. I got tired of having to keep all my friendships with men a secret. Which is what I'd have had to keep doing if I wanted peace. He didn't trust me, I guess. Or he didn't trust men, maybe both. It was pathetic and unfair. I used to yell at him that he couldn't keep me in a box, that I had to live in a two-sexed world. Eventually, I just rebelled. I stopped hiding lunch appointments with innocent folk who happened to be men. I told some of my men friends they could visit me at home. I took their phone calls. That drove Sammy wild. We just fought and fought all the time. I couldn't stand it anymore. I felt as if I was suffocating. In the end, he left. He was sure I'd violated our marriage, slept with somebody—he never could decide who. He moved into the Y on Sixty-third Street for a while. It was supposed to be just temporary so we could both cool down, see reason, miss each other a little bit. But we got on so well living apart. He didn't have to wonder about me and other men, and I didn't have to imagine what he was doing when he'd disappear nights."

"Where would he go?"

"Hell, I don't know." Korie didn't speak for a moment, weighing her memories. "Sometimes he'd call me from some street corner to say he was feeling low, that he wanted to walk for a while and think. Next morning, he'd turn up bleary-eyed and tell me something like he'd been just wandering the streets all night, thinking things through. Or that he'd been sitting in a twenty-four-hour McDonald's, watching the derelicts, reflecting on his life. At first, I thought there was another woman, an affair or something, but now I don't think so. It was as if Sammy was consumed by this loneliness he just couldn't shake. He really was a very tragic boy. It might even have been part of his attraction."

"So that's why you split?"

"I suppose so. Yet it doesn't seem so simple. Maybe we just weren't meant to be married. We were meant to meet and love each other and be each other's champion, but perhaps God intended friendship for us, not the husband and wife thing. We messed that up from day one. But living apart, like this, we're thick as thieves."

They fell silent for a while. Soon, Korie pushed her legal pad aside and moved against Zach, nestling her head in the curve of his neck. His arms opened to accommodate her.

"So tell me," Zach said softly, "is this the honeymoon or what? I don't see why Sam couldn't hack this."

"You wait," Korie threatened.

But Zach meant what he'd said. On a day-to-day basis,

Korie was wonderfully easy to live with. And she stirred Zach deeply: He was intoxicated by the smell, the feel, the taste of her. Their days together began with lovemaking, an almost instinctive act on waking, Korie curled spoonlike into Zach's body, Zach entering her sleepily. When they fell apart, breathless, Korie would lie for a few minutes before heading down the hall for her shower. Zach, after another minute, would force himself to rise, too. He'd stumble to the kitchen and rustle up some breakfast for them both. Afterwards, hoping for another round, he'd climb back into bed.

Korie left for work around eight. She was often late. More than once, fully dressed, she had caught that look in Zach's eye, caught his hand working beneath the sheets, and she had thrown back the covers and lifted her skirts. Other times, she smiled wickedly as she disappeared through the door, but she just might come home that evening and undress him slowly, and then herself, and open herself to him right there on the living room floor. Zach had never met as richly erotic a woman. Sam was crazy to have given her up.

Or had he?

It was this nagging qualm that made Zach so curious about Sam. What really bound this woman he hadn't been able to help loving and the ex-husband he never saw? Like an animal sensing a lurking threat, he resolved to watch, to be wary of potential assaults on the security of his heart.

"Simona's looking forward to meeting you Saturday," Korie told Zach. They were hip-to-hip in Korie's tiny kitchen, Zach washing dishes, Korie drying them after dinner. In two days, they would attend a formal gala affair to celebrate the magazine's fifth anniversary. It would be their first social outing together, at least in New York City.

Zach didn't say anything for a few moments, then he said,

"Simona wants to give me the once over, I guess. See if I'm good enough for you." He said it like he was joking, but he really wasn't.

"That's nobody's call but mine," Korie declared, emptying the dish rack to make space for the glasses. "And I already made that call."

Zach said, "Yeah, but now I'm being presented to your key spar." *Key spar* was Jamaican lingo for best friend; it was the phrase Korie herself had used when she'd described her relationship with Simona.

Zach continued: "I'm in social work, you know, and I've seen it a million times. Peer judgement can be a mother."

Korie looked at Zach, who was shirtless as usual, his skin smooth and invitingly warm. "You worried, Zach Man?" she teased, putting her arms around his waist.

"Hell, no," he grinned. "Just you try to get rid of me!"

"Why would I do that?" Korie grinned back. She kissed his flat brown nipples and rested her cheek against the shallow dip at the center of his chest. "I'm no fool," she said.

The anniversary party was held in a glass-walled private room at the back of an exclusive restaurant on the edge of Central Park. The entire staff of the magazine was there, so were a good number of freelancers and assorted media types. Above them, a glass-paneled cathedral roof framed winter trees studded with tiny white lights. The lights created a cozy haloing effect as inside the room, a jazz band, big-band era, played ballroom dance tunes. Partygoers crowded around the buffet tables, which were piled high with hors d'oeuvres, entrees, and desserts. Across the room, the bar was free, the drinks flowing.

Korie, wearing a sleeveless, red silk pajama pantsuit, stood next to the hors d'oeuvres, pushing one deviled egg after another into her mouth. Simona stood next to her, stunning in a body-shaping, strapless black gown.

"You better go easy on those eggs, Korie girl."

Korie looked at her ruefully. "Oh, God, Sim, why am I so nervous? What does it matter what these people think?"

"What anyone thinks," Simona snorted. "All that matters is what *you* think, Korie." Simona was being serious; as long as she'd known her, Korie had been self-conscious in large crowds. And the fact that her date tonight was a shade over-dressed in a black rented tux, while all the other men wore regular suits or sports jackets, didn't really help her feel any more comfortable.

"Of course," she pointed out to Korie now, "your Zachary looks a damned sight better in his rented suit than all the other men here."

Korie laughed at that, because it was true: Zach *did* look good, even in his too-formal suit, the sleeves of which fell a good two inches short. Zach had insisted on renting the suit. He didn't own another one, and had been worried he'd embarrass Korie if he wore his frayed navy blue blazer, the only jacket he owned. Korie had been dismayed when he'd pulled the black tuxedo from its garment box earlier that afternoon, but she hadn't wanted to make a fuss, especially as it was way too late for Zach to get another suit. So she'd smiled gamely and told him he looked dashing. In fact, she thought he looked more like a waiter. Silently, Korie lectured herself about the folly of getting too caught up in appearances. Besides, it wasn't just Zach's appearance that bothered her. It was more that she wasn't used to revealing so much of who she was. Worse than that, she wasn't exactly sure what she was revealing.

She tried to tell herself that she didn't really care what her coworkers thought about Zach. After all, why should it matter that everyone now knew she was in love with a man who licked his fingers as he ate hors d'oeuvres, couldn't find a rented suit to fit the length of his arms, and was perfectly happy to stand alone in a corner of the room and watch the proceedings with a drink in his hand. Zach was doing that now, standing alone over near the band, nodding his head slightly to the beat and looking like it was the most natural thing in the world to stand apart like that when everyone else was mingling.

"You go ahead," he'd said to Korie when she'd wanted to go over and greet one of the photographers. "I'll wait for you here."

"Come with me," Korie had said. "I'll introduce you."

"Baby," Zach answered, "they don't want to see me. They want to talk shop with you. I'll wait here. I'm okay. Honest."

Korie sensed that underneath his projected ease, Zach probably felt as much like a fish out of water as he ever had. She had to admit this was definitely not his scene, but he was handling it bravely. It was Korie who was turning out to be the coward, Korie who wasn't managing to take things in stride.

Joel Crandon, the entertainment reporter stopped by the hors d'oeuvres table. "Hello, girls," he greeted Korie and Simona. "Tell me, who's that young black man over there? Tall, dark, and handsome, isn't he?"

"Forget it," Simona said, "he's straight."

"Girls have all the fun," Joel teased, taking a deviled egg from Korie's fingers and sailing into the crowd with it.

Korie smiled weakly after him, then looked at Simona. "My sense of humor is missing in action," she observed dryly.

"You're an isolationist, sweetie. You don't do well at parties. That's how we met, remember. Just relax." Simona picked up a piece of shrimp and dipped it in wasabe mustard. "Whew, spicy," she said. Next, she sampled a pig in a blanket, grimacing as she chewed. "Awful," she said. "Who made this garbage?"

"Four-star chefs." Korie chuckled. "You should try the eggs."

Simona made an expression of distaste. "No thank you," she said. "I think I'll take a walk. Coming?"

"No, you go ahead," Korie answered, glancing back at Zach.

Simona followed her gaze. "Don't *worry* so much," she admonished. "He's doing just fine."

Leaving Korie, Simona strolled lazily across the dance floor, the men in the room following the slow swish of her dress with their eyes. Korie's heart jumped into her throat as, across the room the magazine's editor emeritus, Randall Wright, walked up to Zach, and the two of them began chatting. She stood for a moment, trying to decide what to do, then she carefully picked her way through the crowd, exchanging greetings with familiars as she made her way over to Zach and the old editor. But as she approached them, she heard Zach say, "Well, strictly speaking, I'm unemployed. But my last job was in social work."

She decided to stay where she was, close enough to hear them, far enough away for them not to notice her amid the crowd of people casually waiting their turn at the bar.

"I started in social work, too," Randall Wright said now. "On a reservation in New Mexico."

"Reservation?" Zach said.

"Grew up near there," Wright shared. "My old man was three-quarters Apache. I was in social work trying to place Native American kids in stable foster homes." Wright sighed. "So much alcohol on the reservations, you know."

"It's a crime what America's done to the Indians," Zach said, neglecting, Korie noted with horror, to use the politically correct Native Americans.

Randall Wright didn't seem to care, though. "It's a crime what America's done to *all* people of color," he declared. "And it's getting worse. Kids these days growing up with no idealism, no sense that they can change things. Sometimes, it seems to me that social workers are the only idealists left."

"Oh, I'd say you writers have a pretty deep streak of ideal-ism." Zach chuckled. "Or so I've found. I live with one of your reporters, Korie Morgan. Now there's a stubborn idealist. But God bless her, you gotta love her."

Korie cringed at his candor, at his lack of subtlety. But Ran-dall Wright laughed richly.

"Ain't love grand," he said delightedly, with more warmth than Korie had ever seen the old man display. Amazed, she realized that Zach had performed his usual magic; he had been so open with Randall Wright, so devoid of awe, he had put him entirely at ease. She saw suddenly that Wright was so used to being treated as the revered editor emeritus, he hadn't been able to express who he truly was, a simple man, with simple delights.

"Come let me introduce you to my wife," Randall said. "She's right over there. She used to be in social work, too."

Korie stepped back into the crowd at the bar as they passed, marveling at the fact that Zach had found his way into this gathering of mostly white journalists without her assis-tance. Osgood and Alice, she found herself thinking, might not have thought him capable of such grace.

And then, she understood the source of her discomfort, understood why she would forever be anxious about present-ing a new lover socially. In the rigidly class-conscious world of her childhood, she had grasped that deportment, clothes, speech, occupation—all the facets of external presentation—were the currency that counted. A man was first judged on these things, and if, on these counts, he was found wanting, one might never glean that underneath it all, he might be a man worth knowing. But Zach's exchange with Randall Wright had shown her that nothing was quite so clear-cut as she'd imagined, indeed, as she'd feared. She felt ashamed of herself, ashamed of the way she, more than anyone, had secretly judged Zach, even as she'd pretended not to, even as she'd professed not to care about such trivial details as his employment status and party manners and the right suit.

Korie watched now as Simona joined Randall Wright and Zach in a circle that included Wright's wife and a few other magazine people. Randall Wright was talking; Korie saw the people in the group laugh at something he said, saw Zach's Adam's apple bob up and down in his smooth brown throat as he put his head back and laughed along with them. From where Korie stood, Zach looked so elegant, so much a part of everything, that her heart began to ache. Suddenly, she didn't feel worthy of him—the irony!—didn't feel worthy of this sleek, penniless lover standing easily among her colleagues in a rented suit. In that moment, she felt keenly that she would lose him, that *she* was the one who would never belong, and he would be drawn away from her, captured by the brilliance of everyone else. Even when she told herself she was being foolish, that this was merely a phantom of her childhood coming back to woo her, she still couldn't stop the hollow feeling in her heart.

Then Simona put her hand on Zach's arm, and led him onto the dance floor. Korie fought down a pang of jealousy as her friend moved into an effortless three-step with Zach, gazing up at him with laughing, too-bright eyes. Korie thought, for a wild moment, of getting her coat and going for a walk in the park, where she could smoke a joint. That would dampen the conflicting riot of emotion inside her. But, of course, she made herself stand where she was, a smile pasted to her lips as she watched the man she loved and the woman she loved float over the dance floor with an ease and fluidity that excluded her.

Zach was having fun. Somehow, she hadn't expected that. She had expected him to experience the party through her, the way her ex-husband Sam would have done.

Simona and Zach were approaching her now, Simona swinging Zach's hand as if they were old friends.

"Your man sure can dance," she said as she delivered him back to Korie's side. "And he's charming, too. I wouldn't let him out of my sight again, if I were you."

As Simona disappeared into the milling crowd, Zach slipped an arm around Korie's shoulders. "Dance?" he smiled.

No, Korie didn't want to dance; she wanted to go home. Simona was right; she was an isolationist. It was Zach, with his gentle, unpretentious humor, who had turned out to be the more socially comfortable of the two of them. Oh, Korie could wear the mask. She could smile and make small talk on demand—Osgood and Alice had given her that—but she'd never learned to *enjoy* it. Deep down, Korie had to admit that she didn't want to share Zach with the people at this party any more than she had wanted to share him with his friends that first time she'd visited him in Philadelphia. But she knew that to act on that impulse now would be selfish, and she didn't ever want to be selfish with Zach, so she said, "Sure, let's dance."

Zach bent so that he could whisper in her ear.

"Or would you rather go home," he said.

Korie looked at him, a smile breaking across her face, her shoulders opening like a morning flower in the sunlight. "There's nowhere I'd rather be with you than home," she said. And she wasn't being selfish when she said it. She was simply stating the God's truth.

7
Nomads

SAM FELL ILL.

"He has the flu," Korie explained to Zach as she rummaged in their refrigerator for juice and leftover pasta salad, bread, green pepper, cold cuts, and a brick of cheddar—rations she planned to take to Sam at his home. "He's been fighting it all spring. Don't wait up for me, Zach. Sammy's a real baby when he's sick. I'll probably stay till he falls asleep."

Korie stuffed the foil-wrapped food into a paper bag, along with cough syrup and aspirin. She kissed Zach on his cheek and was gone before he had uttered a word. In her absence, Zach felt foolish. What kind of *chump* did these two think he was? He slumped onto the couch and turned on the television. He hadn't a clue what he was watching, but he sat there anyway, staring vacantly at the screen.

Maybe she was growing tired of him, he thought. After all, he still hadn't found a job—hadn't been looking, really. Instead of tracking down job listings, he'd busied himself taking care of Korie, cooking her meals, doing the groceries, picking up her dry cleaning, scrubbing down the bathroom and the kitchen and the hardwood floors. The apartment had never been shinier, and though Korie kept insisting that Zach didn't have to do these things, he'd continued, because it pleased him to have her arrive home each evening and oooh about how he'd placed yellow roses on the hallway table, or how good dinner smelled, or how right that Haitian carving looked positioned just there.

He had been a domestic fool.

And Korie, in her way, had encouraged him. She called him from work all through the day. The way they talked on the phone all day, you'd hardly think she came home to him nights. And yet, Zach never tired of her calls, never got past the little thrill he felt each time he heard her voice on the answering machine: "Zach, baby, it's me. Pick up the phone."

But perhaps Korie was becoming weary of all that. Perhaps she was getting ready to reclaim the familiar—her husband, her first love, the man her parents knew and respected, the one she had taken to meet them.

Zach had noticed that on the rare occasions Korie picked up the phone when it was one of her parents on the answering machine (Korie screened all calls through the answering machine), she never mentioned him, never thought to inform her folks that there was a new man in her life.

Once, half-joking, Zach had accused Korie of hiding him.

"Of course I'm not," Korie had answered a little too quickly.

"Then why the glaring omission when you talk to your folks?"

"I hardly ever talk to them. Besides, you don't know my parents."

"No," Zach agreed dryly. "I haven't had the pleasure. Could be I'll have to marry you to gain that privilege. But then, you're already married."

Korie had ignored his sarcasm. She'd just stared at him with an odd, uncertain expression in her eyes, then shrugged and walked out of the room.

Now, thinking back over the last several months, Zach kept trying to locate a clue that Sam might have reasserted himself in Korie's heart. His mind kept probing, circling, the noise of the television set a steady hum weaving between his thoughts. He could see it was going to be one of those restless, interminable nights, for, try as he might, Zach couldn't shake the notion, more than that, the *fear* that the complicated love that bound Korie and Sam together was crowding him out.

And then, for the first time since moving in with Korie, he examined his position. With a shock, he realized that if Korie and Sam *were* still lovers, for him it was already too late. Zach could no more choose to be without Korie than he could choose not to breathe. He understood it consciously now: If he were the cuckold in this triangle, if the worst were true, he'd swallow his pride, pretend not to notice, and take second best.

Korie didn't come home at all that night, but the following morning, she telephoned.

"Sammy's finally sleeping," she said in a whisper. "He's a lot sicker than I thought. This is more than just the flu."

"What's wrong with him?" Zach asked.

"He has shingles across his back and chest." Korie kept her voice low. "He can't move a muscle without pain. He could barely get to sleep because it hurts him to lie down, and I don't think he's been eating much. He's weak as a lamb. I had no idea things were so bad."

"You saw him last weekend. He was okay then."

"He seemed okay, except for a cold. But he's been home all week. He told me he was laid up with a mild case of the flu. Mild case! Christ, I've never seen him like this."

"Has he been to a doctor?"

"No," Korie sighed. "Sam hates doctors. He's like an irrational child when it comes to seeing one. His great grandmother died of a brain tumor when he was three. Then his granduncle got lung cancer and hung on for years. He died in the hospital, tubes stuck all over him, when Sammy was nine. His grandaunt raised him after that, but now she's gone, too. Throat cancer. She used to chew tobacco and smoke a corncob pipe. She was a helluva mother to Sam."

Korie had met Great Aunt Corinne a few times before she died. During Sam's college years, she had been an enormous, expressive, coal black southern woman, vigorous and full of tough-tender love. But she had shriveled to nothing at the end, punched full of holes and hooked up to tubes like her husband. Her misery and pain had frightened Sam and complicated his grief at losing her, for he'd stayed away from her during the last weeks of her life, unable to bear the sight of fierce Aunt Corinne so humbled and trapped. He always said afterwards that if he ever "became terminal," he'd rather die whole than have doctors poking and pinching and cutting him.

"You'll have to get him to a doctor, anyway," Zach was saying. "If he's that sick, there's not much else you can do."

Korie had already done plenty. The evening before, she'd traveled downtown to the all-night pharmacy to get some calamine lotion for the shingles. On the way back, she'd stopped for groceries, because Sam's refrigerator had been completely bare; Korie suspected he hadn't eaten in days. Back at his apartment, she had applied the calamine lotion with cotton balls, then sat holding Sam's hand while the lotion caked and soothed the prickly pain somewhat. Later, Sam had stood in the doorway of his kitchen and watched as Korie cooked him a meal. They hadn't talked much, but Sam couldn't bear the thought of lying down, for the bedclothes would stick to his body and the shooting pain would savage him.

When the meal—baked chicken and potatoes and broccoli—was put before him, Sammy couldn't bring himself to eat. Korie had coaxed and cajoled, even railed at him, to no avail. In the end, Sam had gone to bed with a cup of chamomile tea and a sleeping pill to dull the pain. Korie had sat in the chair beside his bed until it got light, listening as he moaned in his sleep, thinking he would wake at any moment. But he slept on, tossing and wheezing and crying out.

"All he'll take are his herb teas," Korie told Zach now. "That's all he's consumed for days. No wonder he's so feeble. I can't convince him to eat a thing. He says it's better if he fasts, that the herbs will rid his body of impurities. Sammy's so baffled and crazy. You're right. He really does have to see a doctor, and it has to be today."

Zach volunteered to accompany them. Korie thought not but she broached another idea.

"Zach, I want to bring Sammy home with me after he sees the doctor. He can't stay here alone. He'll faint away here and no one will know. I want to get him where I can make him eat. Think you can deal with that, Zach Man?"

Zach understood that her question was only a courtesy, but he appreciated it all the same.

"I'll pull out the sofa bed," he answered. "I'll spread it with sheets. Call me if you need me, sweetheart. And hurry home."

It felt so familiar, Sammy in her house again. Strange, Korie thought, that it should be this natural after all this time. Of course, this time they didn't argue so much; Sammy's illness left him too weak for discord. Besides, Zach kept in check the storms that once had raged between them. It was as if Zach's presence in her house declared to Sam that Korie had at last moved on. The marital rules had finally been voided, and love alone remained.

At the beginning, to disguise his uneasiness, Zach had stepped into his caseworker mode. That first afternoon, when Korie returned with Sam, Zach had met them at the door. Sam, dizzy from the trip to the doctor and the cab ride home, was leaning heavily on Korie. Without a word, Zach had wrapped a powerful arm around his back and taken Sam's weight unto himself.

"I'm Zach," he'd said once he got Sam to the living room couch. "I suppose Korie's mentioned me."

"Yeah." Sam had smiled weakly. "I hope the little wildcat isn't making it too rough on you."

"Give me a break, guys," Korie said, relieved at Sam's banter but a little annoyed by his proprietary air. She had anticipated, even now, a jealous sulk from her ex-husband. In their four years apart, Korie had never introduced Sam to the few men she'd dated. She'd told him about them, and laughed at his wry commentary about this one or that, but that was as far as she'd gone. Sam, for his part, offered only the vaguest remarks about his own romantic entanglements. He made Korie work for each scrap of news. There had been a woman with a nine-year-old son. The woman wanted too much of him. "She wants me to be the father her son never knew," Sam had complained. "And the boy doesn't even like me." Then, for a while there had been a dancer, beautiful and ebony-skinned, but Sam eventually tired of her as well. In fact, in the four years of their separation, Korie had, in the practical sense, remained the woman in Sam's life. It was Korie he called on weekend afternoons when he wanted to kill time, Korie who, when the temp jobs were a long time coming, often lent him money to pay his rent. And it was Korie he had called that humid July morning when he was lonely, bedridden, and racked with pain.

·　　·　　·

Korie's doctor had prescribed medication for the shingles, and Sam's rash got steadily better. But his cold seemed to linger, and he wasn't getting any stronger. For days he felt too exhausted to move from the pull-out couch where he slept. Dr. Miro explained that this was natural and warned that the shooting pains would take a long time to disappear, because shingles inhabited the delicate nerve endings, and would live there, dormant, for the rest of Sam's life. The doctor told them that he wanted to perform additional tests as soon as Sam's rash was gone. He'd penciled in an appointment for ten days later but Sam didn't show up for it. Another two weeks passed before Korie could convince him to visit the doctor again.

"Sammy," she had urged, "stop being so stubborn. Something is obviously still wrong with you. The shingles are gone but you have no appetite and you're still so weak. Let Dr. Miro do the tests and treat whatever's wrong. I swear, Sammy, I'm not going to be party to your death wish."

Korie wished later that she'd chosen any words but those, because a week later, Dr. Miro diagnosed Sam's advanced-stage lymphoma.

Sam, throughout that second meeting with the doctor, had seemed in a daze, not quite cognizant of what the physician was saying. He had insisted that Korie sit with him while Dr. Miro made his diagnosis and, throughout, had been curiously detached, as if the three of them were weighing a mortality other than his own.

"I've known patients survive months and years from the date of diagnosis," Dr. Miro had said. He had intended to reassure, but Korie heard clearly what he also meant to convey— that sooner rather than later, Sam would die.

"Your blood chemistry is completely awry," Dr. Miro told Sam somberly. "There are more tests you should definitely have done, but you'll have to check into a hospital for those. I'd suggest you do this as soon as possible. I can admit you to New York Hospital tomorrow. I just need to call and arrange a bed."

"How many days will the tests take?" Korie had asked when Sam, his expression abstract, made no response.

Then Sam broke in. "Let me think about this."

"Don't think, just do it," Dr. Miro said, his voice stern. Then, more gently he added, "You must realize that your situation is critical, Mr. Marshall. You just don't have time to think about this in a leisurely way."

Sam got up slowly and turned toward the door. He seemed confused, distracted. Over his shoulder, he said, "I'll call you tomorrow, Dr. Miro. I'll let you know."

Korie and the doctor stared helplessly at each other. Korie seemed to be waiting for more.

"Mr. Marshall's the patient," Dr. Miro told her sympathetically. "I can disclose information only in his presence."

Korie rose and followed Sam out to the front office. She paid his bill with a check, took his elbow, and ushered him to the street. Sam let her lead him. He stared up vacantly at the hazy corridor of sky, pinched on each side by skyscrapers. It seemed to Korie that all color had drained from the world; despite the summer's heat, she felt cold. Numbly, she hailed a cab and held the door as Sammy climbed into the backseat. He still showed no grasp of Dr. Miro's diagnosis, and Korie could not speak, could not find words to broach what they'd just heard. It was all too sudden. Her guts felt pummeled, her insides mush, her throat thick with phlegm and blank disbelief. Sammy couldn't be dying, she kept telling herself. Dr. Miro was wrong. In a moment, she and Sammy would wake from this lunacy. Sammy's ashen complexion would once more be a gleaming coppery brown, the whites of his eyes no longer bloodshot and streaming.

The cab let them off in front of Korie's building. She paid

the fare, took Sammy's hand, and led him into the lobby. Frank, the resident drunk, was keeping vigil in the shabby front hall. He appeared shocked by Sammy's appearance, his blank gaze, bent posture, his limp hanging wrists.

"Wha's wrong wit' your husband?" he slurred with genuine concern. "Jesus Christ a'mighty, sister, he look like he dead."

Korie shook her head and didn't answer. She couldn't even look Frank's way. The elevator arrived and she and Sammy stepped inside. As it clanked its way to the fifth floor, life suddenly stirred in Sammy's eyes. He sank slowly to his knees, his back slipping down the elevator wall till he was crouched and huddled on the floor.

"It's true, isn't it?" he whispered.

He reached blindly for Korie, his hand curled like a claw.

"God help me, Korie, it really is true."

Sam didn't say anything as they entered the apartment; he just collapsed on the sofa and gazed at the TV, nodding his head vaguely at Zach's greeting. Korie, too, seemed dazed as she kissed Zach mechanically on the cheek, then sagged against him for a moment, her face turned into the detergent scent of his moss green polo shirt.

"Hey," he said softly, his arms moving around her. "Such long faces."

Korie looked up at him with a kind of plea in her eyes, and he knew then that the news from Dr. Miro had not been good.

"We have to feed him," Korie said. She realized dimly that she was veering into an automatic mode, retreating into the safe zone of her childhood conditioning, for the instinct to feed an ailing soul was something she'd absorbed from her mother. All of a sudden, Korie yearned for the simplicity of her childhood. In her mind's eye, she was a thin brown girl with thick glasses and fat braids at her family's dinner table again, she and her father waiting patiently for Alice to come bustling from the kitchen. She could see her mother, skirts flowing in her wake. She could hear her. "Nourish the body, nourish the soul," Alice Mathurin would say crisply as she brought out one of her elaborate culinary creations. The vision was oddly comforting, and Korie thought for a wild hopeful moment of calling her mother, of placing the news of Sam's illness in her capable arms.

Alice, what now? she would ask her. *After we feed this dying man, after we nourish his soul, what then?*

But there was so much to account for, so very much to explain. She would have to account, finally, for her separation from Sam, mollify her parents' hurt at the months of unanswered phone calls, and defray judgments about this strange new man whom she had never mentioned, who was without a job and living in her home. No, she didn't feel up to Osgood and Alice just yet, didn't feel capable of weathering the force of their concern and their scrutiny.

Together, she and Zachary made a pumpkin soup thick with a puree of garden vegetables and put it before Sam. But Sam turned away from it and Korie, feeling helpless, didn't even protest as she poured it down the drain.

Zach put another bowl of soup on the table. "You need to eat, too," he told Korie.

She ate the soup without really tasting it, and afterwards washed her bowl and put it away. By then, Sam had fallen asleep on the couch. Korie decided not to wake him to pull out the sofa bed. Instead, she covered him with the green-and-blue afghan that her parents had sent them as a wedding present, and put a pillow under his head. Then she turned off the TV and switched off the light. Zach stood in the doorway watching her, a crease on his brow.

"What happened today?" he whispered as Korie turned

towards him. She put a finger to her lips and took Zach's hand. She led him into the bedroom where she let go of his hand to push open the window and climb out onto the fire escape.

Zach followed her out. He sat opposite her, his knees pulled into his chest, his eyes searching her face. For a long time, Korie didn't say anything. She stared at the deepening blues and pinks of the late summer sky, and studied the pale diaphanous moon as it skimmed the treetops of Morningside Park at the end of their street. Her eyes filled up and her throat felt tight, but she didn't cry. None of it felt real enough for her to cry.

"The doctor said Sammy's dying," she said at last. "He's in the final stages of lymphoma. The truth is, Zach, I don't think he's ever going home."

Zach lowered his head, deliberately obscuring his face. He looked down at the street through the bars of the fire escape.

"You're going to take care of him?" His voice held no expression.

Korie nodded. Zach looked back at her now.

"But you have to work, Korie. And what if you have to travel? It's too much for you. Sam's a sick, sick man. And if his disease is as far gone as you say, he needs professional round-the-clock care."

"My insurance would never cover it," Korie said. Even after her separation, she'd continued to carry Sam on her insurance. "Besides, this is a small place. We don't need a stranger in here."

They were silent a long time, each avoiding the other's eyes. At last, Zach said quietly, "What am I doing here, Korie? What are we thinking about? You're still married to that man in there, and I'm just an interloper in this little domestic scene."

"Oh Zach, don't be like that. This is hard, Zach Man. This is so hard. I wish it were different. I wish I could be here alone with you. This wasn't what I pictured when we decided to move in together."

"Correction," Zach observed dryly. "When we decided *I* would move in with *you.*"

"What do you mean?"

"Just what I said." He waved his arms, exasperated. "I mean, what am I doing here? In New York. In your house. Living *off* you if you really want to be plain about it. Getting in the way of your"—his eyes raked the sky as he sought the words—"this slow good-bye."

"I make enough for all of us," Korie said, dealing with the money part of his comment because she couldn't right then deal with the possibility of good-byes.

"That's not my point."

"What's your point, then," Korie said.

"I don't know," he sighed. "Maybe I should just go home, find a job in Philly, let you get on with your life."

Korie felt as if the air had been sucked from her lungs.

"You're right," she said bitterly. "Why should you be bothered?"

"That's not fair."

"I know," Korie said. A sob escaped her throat, but she caught the second one and swallowed hard. "It's *not* fair. This wasn't the deal you agreed to at all."

"Ain't that just like life," Zach muttered.

They were quiet again, gazing deep into each other's eyes this time, the two of them sinking into the light at the center of their irises, and wishing, wishing so fervently that they might salvage some portion of the magic that had been there before.

Zach seemed to arrive at a decision.

"I'll help you," he said.

"Oh, Zach," Korie moaned. "Why should you have to? Sam's not your problem. You didn't ask for any of this."

"I asked for you," Zach said, a sad smile touching his lips. "Any way I could have you, I wanted you.

"Besides," he continued, his voice bright with forced cheer,

"I'm free to do this. In case you haven't noticed, I don't happen to be working yet. And I seem to be good at this sort of thing."

Korie didn't know quite how to answer him. The tears were welling up in her throat again, so much relief flooding her she felt almost ashamed. Silently, she reached for Zach's hands and held them prayerlike between her own. Her fingers played over the map of veins on the back of his wrists, then she turned his hands over and brought his palms to her lips. She pressed a kiss into the hard center of each one of them, and when she found her voice again, she said softly: "Zach Man, I do love you."

And so, in the days while Korie worked, it fell to Zach to minister to Sam. When Sam grew so weak that he could no longer make it to the bathroom before his bladder gave way, Zach was there at his bedside with a plastic container to catch his urine. It was Zach who most often cleaned him when he threw up the scanty meals he was able to force down, meals invariably prepared by Zach. And at night, he and Korie would undress Sam's dwindling form, lift his almost weightless body into the bathtub, and wash him gingerly, lest he break.

In the mornings, when he heard Sam shuffling down the hall to the bathroom, Zach would dress himself and exit the apartment quietly, understanding that there were years of tender comradeship between Korie and her husband in which he had no part. It soon became a ritual. Each morning Zach would leave to get the paper, drink a cup of diner coffee, and smoke his morning cigarette—Zach no longer smoked in the apartment; in fact, other than the morning cigarette, he hardly smoked at all anymore. The smell of smoke alone was enough to send Sam into coughing spasms.

After Zach left, Sam would come to Korie's room, and she would open her arms so that he might settle himself against her. For several minutes she would hold him close and stroke his hair, her heart breaking at his emaciation, at her helplessness in the face of his slide towards darkness.

Korie became reluctant to go to sleep at night, afraid that when she awoke, Sam would have expired. But Sam remained adamant about not checking into a hospital, and he refused to take Dr. Miro's almost daily calls.

"Let me just live this out in peace," he'd say wearily when his housemates tried to press him. Korie suspected that he wanted to die in her home, if not in her arms. The very idea of him dying terrified her.

"I'm an invalid!" Sammy wailed thinly one morning. "I can't do anything for myself and I'm still a young man!" Tears washed his flaking skin and pooled at the cup of his collarbone. Korie put her face to his and their tears mingled, and their hearts pumped against each other as in the days when they had been lovers. Sammy held on tight to her, a pathetic assemblage of bones in a bag of atrophied skin. His heart beat feebly against his rib cage, every thump visible and frighteningly tentative.

And then, miraculously, five weeks after Dr. Miro's diagnosis, Sam seemed to rally. It was in the fall, two weeks after Labor Day, when his low-grade fever finally broke. The pains in his joints seemed to give some respite and he could suddenly walk more firmly, breathe more deeply. A flush came into his cheeks. The world seemed new and fresh, more brilliant than he had remembered. His heart brimmed with emotion, full to bursting with gratitude at being alive. He wanted to go outside at once, to walk in the park, hear the dry leaves rustling against their branches, watch the sun set the steel gray waters of the Hudson suddenly aflame.

He walked slowly, Korie on one side, Zach on the other, to the river. It was almost dusk. The sun would be going down soon. They went to a place in Riverside Park where there was a child-size hole in the chain-link fence, and they could squeeze through to the slick rocks on the other side. Korie and Sam had come to sit and watch the sunset from these rocks often when they were students. Lulled by the flow of the Hudson, ensconced in the intimacy of evening, they had grown to love each other, feeling the magic of two souls rising in empathy for the first wondrous time. Korie realized now that she'd felt that virginal magic, that eerie fluttering sense of romantic destiny only once since Sam. She had felt it again, with a force surpassing the first time it had happened, in the Carson Agency parking lot almost a year ago, when she'd first seen Zach.

As they settled themselves on the rocks now, Sam shifted towards Korie, turned his face up to the dying sun, and closed his eyes. It was a small, almost imperceptible gesture, but Zach noticed it and casually moved away from them. Korie glanced across at him, standing a little apart from Sam and herself, gazing out at the darkening Hudson and at the lights of New Jersey, which shimmied and danced on the far side of the river like so many jewels in the water. At such moments, Korie understood the strangeness of their triangle, understood the difficulty of balancing the distinct and separate ways in which she loved these men: Sam, her onetime partner and longtime friend, and Zach, the deeply sensual and compassionate man with whom she had recently fallen in love. She wondered for the millionth time whether she was being fair to Zach, whether his participation in the slow unraveling of her ex-husband's life hadn't been an unforgivable appropriation of his feelings for her.

Korie tried to shake off the nagging sense of guilt that had plagued her since that evening on the fire escape when Zach had told her he would stay. She imagined sometimes that a guardian spirit must have guided him to her, for she was so emotionally spent, so drained of initiative or hope, she didn't know how she'd have managed the practical aspects of Sam's care without him. Now she put an arm around her ex-husband's fragile shoulders, and supporting him against her body, motioned with her other hand towards Zach. He came and sat next to her on the rocks, and she rested her head on his shoulder, and Sam rested his head on hers, and they sat like that, three figures blending to a single outline against the fading sky.

Sam had good days and bad. He often seemed dazed, not quite aware of his surroundings or even his actions. Once, Korie arrived home to find her house keys dangling in the front door. Sam had struggled home earlier from the corner deli with three bottles of fruit juice, the only nourishment he would willingly consume. He was so easily exhausted now that it took him an hour, taking a few steps then pausing against a building for several minutes to catch his breath, to make it back from the store. He stepped into the elevator with relief, letting his grocery bag slide to the floor. He felt thwarted as the elevator defied his call for the fifth floor and descended to the basement—so many more minutes before he could collapse in the safe harbor of Korie's apartment. Wearily, he rested his head against the fake-wood linoleum of the elevator wall and closed his eyes. He felt the blood course through him, throbbing at his temples, his heart pounding in his throat. God, for how long would he be so at the mercy of a body chemistry gone haywire?

He knew that he was dying, but he could not face the possibility that it was his long-kept secret, the hidden life he had so yearned to reveal to Korie, that might be silently killing him. Lymphoma, the doctor had said. Well, that was just fine, certainly in keeping with the family tradition. Cancer had ravaged his closest relatives. Why shouldn't it fix its murderous grip on his life as well? He would go without a struggle, he had decided. He'd seen this death before. You couldn't fight its stealthy progress. You'd just wear yourself out trying, make yourself sick with the medicines, submitting to the surgeon's knife till you were only half a man. He wouldn't do it. He'd be whole until his last breath. He would spend his time appreciating life's gifts, instead of locked in a war with the inevitable.

He was grateful, at least, to be near the one person on earth he loved best. He would drink in her presence, find joy in her robust survival, and try to lessen, if he could, her grief at his going. He had been right, he reflected now, to leave their marriage bed years before, to free Korie from the deceitful web of his desires while they'd still had time.

He fumbled with the front door lock for what seemed an eternity before the tumblers gave way. He shouldered open the door and, forgetting the keys, pushed it shut behind him. He stumbled into the kitchen. Zach was there, blue jeaned and shirtless, stirring a vegetable stew.

"Hey, man. You hungry?" he asked Sam.

Sam shook his head listlessly, and sank into a chair. Zach took the bag of fruit juices from him.

"Grape juice, cranberry juice, orange juice, which one do you want?"

"Cranberry," Sam said.

Zach poured the burgundy liquid over ice and put the glass before Sam. Sam made no move to pick it up. Instead, he regarded Zach wearily.

"You love Korie, don't you?"

"She's quite a lady," Zach replied evenly.

"If I'd stayed married, like I should have four years ago, I wouldn't be in this predicament now," Sam sighed.

Zach thought he knew what Sam was getting at—he'd already guessed far more than Korie—but he didn't press.

Sam sucked in a breath. He still made no move to drink the cranberry juice but let his mind drift as he watched Zach maneuver in the tiny kitchen. He wondered at how amiable he felt towards the man who had taken his place. The fact was,

Sam had grown to admire Zach with an intensity that bordered on hero worship, though he was far too homophobic to verbalize such a sentiment. Zach didn't engage in the one-upmanship that men so often fell prey to in the company of other men. Zach had never set himself up as a rival for Korie's affections. How, Sam wondered, had he managed to make himself so nonthreatening?

Now, watching the thick vein in Zach's forearm ripple and shift as he sliced carrots for his stew, Sam felt a twinge of old envy. Zach was broad-shouldered, with muscled arms and a hard, triangular torso. Sam had yearned for that kind of physique, often cursing his thin arms and narrow chest, and blaming his slender frame for his romantic failures. While he and Korie had been together, he'd been sure that she would leave him for the next musclebound Adonis who glanced her way.

"I never could get why it didn't work for you two," Zach said suddenly, as if reading his mind. "I watch you together and I can't figure it out."

For a moment, Sam didn't speak. Should he sit here in Korie's kitchen and bare his soul to the man with whom she was now sexually intimate, when he had never confessed his closeted desires to Korie herself? Should he open his mouth and let the truth burn his lips, let his secrets roll out like hot stones? Should he tell Zach of the men he went to in the city's parks, the men he coupled with down by the river, when he had pretended to go jogging? Should he explain, after all this time, that the nights he went walking, to think, supposedly wandering the dark city in search of clarity, he had actually beat an unsentimental path to a particular males-only bar? Should he confess everything now, when it no longer mattered? He would be dead soon. What Korie didn't know wouldn't hurt her, wouldn't cause her to shrink from him in betrayal and shame.

No, of course he wouldn't tell Zach.

Then again, Zach probably *knew*.

Sam had seen the suspicion in his eyes. He had noticed how Zach quietly soaked all their dishes in soapy boiling water before washing them, scrupulously discarding the leftovers. Come to think of it, Zach now cleaned the bathroom with rubber gloves, and tried to make sure Korie used them when she cleaned it as well. Sam guessed that Zach already knew what Korie would not let her mind process—that Sam's lymphoma could really be a mask for AIDS.

But they didn't know that for sure, Sam reminded himself, a frenzied hope beating in him. They had never tested him for HIV—surely that had to count for something. If they'd thought he might have AIDS, wouldn't they have looked for it? Wasn't it just possible that the disease that had stormed his body might be simple, straightforward lymphoma after all?

"I was too jealous," he said now, pushing the troubling questions to the back of his mind. "I didn't know how to be a husband to Korie. I never saw it done. My father never stuck with my mother, never even married her. He just got her pregnant and then moved on." He paused, his eyes fierce. "He had *eighteen* kids, man. Father to the whole damned neighborhood." Sam caught his breath. He was so very tired now. "I thought I would fail Korie," he said at last, and his eyes filled up. Seemed he couldn't control his tear ducts anymore.

Suddenly, Sam was sobbing—choking, heaving, wracking sobs, his thin arms folded like a straitjacket around his ribs. "Seems in the end, I failed everyone," he whispered.

Zach stopped stirring his stew. He went to Sam and put his skull-like head against his chest and rocked him like a baby as he cried.

Zach wasn't home on the day Sam finally collapsed. He had left that afternoon to visit an employment agency. Zach had grown increasingly concerned about Korie having to support them all, and, if truth be told, the days spent shoring up a dying man's spirit were wearing him down. Besides, Sam had insisted that he was getting stronger, only the nights were bad. He could certainly take care of himself in the daytime if Zach found a job.

That night, Korie arrived home to find Sammy passed out, facedown on the hallway floor. At first, she thought he was dead, but when she rolled him over, she saw that his heart fluttered hyperactively under his thin cotton T-shirt. He must have fallen and hit his head. Fear seized her at the sight of him, deathly pale, lips parched, eyelids blue-veined over bulging sockets. Fluid of some sort must have collected behind his eyes, which had ballooned to twice their size.

"Sammy," she cried, mopping the sheen of sweat from his forehead with the sleeve of her blouse. "Oh, Sammy, you'll have to go to the hospital now."

8

Smoke Signals

SAM ENTERED THE HOSPITAL ON FEBRUARY 25, 1985. KORIE
recorded it hurriedly in her journal:

*Sammy very sick. Found him passed out on the floor. Zach came
home right afterwards and we took him to St. Luke's where they ran an
IV and admitted him at once.*

After that, Sam sank quickly. Most days, he couldn't speak at
all, and would lie curled under the starched sheets, moaning
incoherently and drooling into his pillow. Korie spent hours at
his bedside ministering to him. Each morning before work, she
stopped by the hospital so she could brush his teeth, empty his
urine container, and massage lotion into his cracked and swollen
feet. The nurses, wary of Sam's illness, were relieved to have
Korie take care of his personal hygiene, and so they allowed her
the run of the ward, even outside visiting hours, merely caution-
ing her to wear plastic gloves. But Korie, unable to entertain the
possibilities that attended Sam's illness, couldn't bear to treat
him like an untouchable. So she ignored the nurses' advice,

going about her caretaking with bare hands. Once Sam was cleaned up, Korie would sit next to him, watching his blank eyes roam through space for as long as she could before leaving for her job. After work, Korie would come back to the hospital to sit with him some more, silently holding his frail hand, the bones folding together in her palm like loose sticks.

And then, to everyone's surprise, Sam became lucid again. It happened without warning: Korie simply walked into his hospital room as usual one morning and he opened his eyes and said, clear as a bell, "I'm here."

He told Korie that he'd been "traveling" the last few weeks, that in his dreams he'd been a knobby-kneed schoolboy again, and he'd seen Aunt Corinne. He described how she'd floated towards him in a radiant nimbus of light, and held her palms out to him, as if welcoming him home. In the days after that, Sam complained that clouds of white had begun to encroach at the margins of his sight, and he couldn't ever quite seem to catch his breath. But despite the clouds and the ragged breathing, a new calm seemed to settle into him, as if his vision of Great Aunt Corinne had freed him from fear.

On his stronger days, Sam and Korie would sit and chat about the weather, Korie's job, events in the news. Sam also seemed to develop a hunger to know what life had been like for various people with whom he'd lost touch. He would lie in bed, his expression pensive, musing about how things had turned out for the gifted midwestern boy with whom he'd done that theater project as a freshman at Columbia, or the pimply-faced jock from ninth grade, who could weave and fly down a football field with the grace of a dancer. "Talent itself is unremarkable," he would sigh, sounding tired and very sad. "It takes more than talent to make your mark in this world, Korie. It takes being true to who you are."

"A regular philosopher," Korie would say, smiling. For as long as she'd known him, Sam had dispensed such tidbits of dimestore inspiration, and it was comforting to find this aspect of him unchanged.

One day, when Korie came in, Sam said, "Did you tell Osgood and Alice their son-in-law is dying?"

Korie shook her head.

"Why not?" he asked. Then, his breath catching slightly: "I guess I stopped being their son-in-law when I left the marriage."

"They missed you," Korie said simply. "They didn't understand why you just dropped out of their life."

She didn't want to remember how her impulsive marriage so many years ago had distanced her from her parents, with the result that she hadn't visited them in Jamaica for almost six years now, since before her wedding day, in fact. And always, when Osgood and Alice had tried to come and see her in New York, she'd pleaded having to be away on assignment. Once, during the second year of her marriage, her parents had refused to be put off. "We'll come and spend some time with our son-in-law, then," Alice had announced when she told them she'd be traveling. "We'll just stay with Sam till whenever you get back." And so of course Korie had changed her plans, because she wasn't about to subject Sam to her parents in the close confines of their apartment without being there herself.

Sure enough, as soon as Osgood and Alice put down their suitcases, they began quizzing Sam about his plans for the future. Law school, he told them. He still planned to go to law school when he'd saved enough money. That sent Osgood into overdrive. While Korie was at work and Sam at his temp job (he'd made sure he had a gig to go to all that week), and while Alice rearranged the furniture and shopped for pretty household accents like doilies and clay pots and sofa end tables and a good silver tea service, Osgood spent the mornings visiting neighborhood banks, gathering brochures, and calling libraries as far away as Washington, D.C., to explore Sam's financing options for law school. In the evenings, he would call Sam to his side and lay his research out on the dining table. Sam listened and nodded politely as Osgood presented his findings, but Korie could tell by the tense way he held his body that he felt trapped. Osgood even offered to cosign a bank loan, even offered to contribute some financing of his own, anything so that Sam wouldn't have to wait any longer to realize his dream of law school. Alice meanwhile took Korie aside, coaching her on how she might encourage her husband, how she might bolster his confidence.

"Mom," Korie said wearily. "I can't *make* him go to law school. He'll go when he's ready. *If* he's ready."

"He has a good education and a good mind," Alice pointed out. "It would be such a pity if he wasted his opportunities."

"Law school isn't the only road he can take," Korie tried, to which her mother responded with sincere interest: "Oh? What else does he have in mind?"

Korie shrugged, frustrated. "I don't know," she said, wanting the exchange to be over. "I don't *care*."

But Alice was unfazed. "You have to care, Korie," she chided gently. "This is your husband."

By the end of the week, Sam had gone psychologically underground. He was scrupulously polite with Korie's parents, but he didn't offer anything of himself in return, and found excuses to be away from the house as much as possible in the evenings. At last, Korie admonished her parents to lay off Sam, to not be so overpowering in their approach. Osgood and Alice were genuinely surprised, and then deeply wounded by her rebuke. They retreated, for the rest of the visit, into a tight-lipped silence, their expressions of disappointment and disapproval inspiring in Korie a familiar cocktail of resentment and shame.

Even now, Korie found her parents' expectations overpowering, their continual demand that she account for her choices inhibiting. As a result, Osgood and Alice hadn't a clue anymore about the true matrix of Korie's life. Since her separation from Sam, her contact with them had diminished to a few perfunctory phone calls a year, usually at Christmas and on birthdays, with Korie assuring them that yes, everything was fine, she was working hard, traveling the country a lot, and no, she didn't need anything, and maybe she'd come home for a visit next year. Now that Sam had brought it up, though, she realized that somewhere in the last few months, an intense longing for her parents, for their focused strength and protection, had surfaced in her. She yearned to sink into their arms and let them guide her through this slow, agonizing departure of Sam's. And yet, she knew she wouldn't call them. She still didn't feel capable of fielding her father's pointed medical queries about the exact nature of his ex-son-in-law's illness—or, for that matter, explaining Zach's presence in her life. Soon, perhaps, she'd pick up the phone and let them know about Sam. And maybe she'd share that she was in love again. But not now.

"I think you should call them." Sam broke into her thoughts.

"They'll just worry," Korie said.

"They're your parents," Sam said. "That's what they do."

"My mother will want to come."

"You may need her," Sam reflected.

"And your mother?" Korie said quietly.

"No," Sam murmured. "Don't call her yet."

Then came the day Sam's dry flaky skin bloomed suddenly fresh, his eyes sparkled like fevered glass, and his voice grew strangely resonant. "They rally like that before death," a Filipino nurse whispered, and Korie realized that whatever Sam said, she couldn't wait any longer to telephone his mother. Sam had continued to ask her not to make the call, but Korie knew that she didn't have the courage to deny them one last opportunity to forge a tentative peace.

She went to the hospital pay phones, needing for a moment

to be away from Sam, from the deceptive promise of his new glow. She dialed his mother's number, and waited for the voice of the woman who, thirty-one summers ago, had given her baby boy away to strangers.

"Sam is going soon," Korie told her.

"Going where?" Sam's mother asked, and for a moment, Korie couldn't breathe. She held the phone from her ear long enough to choke down a sob.

"He's sicker," she said finally. "He's dying. I think you should come."

Aunt Elsa, as Sam had always called his mother, made arrangements to fly north from her tiny hometown of Chickory, Georgia, a few hours north of Jacksonville. She would leave in three days and arrive at Kennedy Airport in the afternoon. She would take a cab straight to Sam's apartment.

On the Saturday before she was to arrive, Korie went to Sam's apartment to clean it. There, at the back of his closet in a neat stack, she found his journals—seven thin volumes written in that familiar hand—and the deception came to an end.

When Korie arrived at the hospital the next morning, Sam was waiting. "Did you find my journals?" he asked at once, leaning with an effort towards her.

"Yes," Korie said numbly.

"Did you read them?"

"No," she lied.

Sam fell back in the bed and stared thoughtfully at the ceiling. Korie ached to ask him about the secret life she had discovered in those journals, but she had come by the knowledge dishonorably, and so felt bound to say nothing.

After a few moments, Sam spoke.

"I know you, Korie," he said slowly. "You couldn't be alone with those journals and not read them. You're too curious."

Korie didn't answer him. Instead, she reached for his hand and held it, tears welling in her eyes.

"So now you know about me," Sam whispered. "Thank God you know."

Relief and sorrow, shame and regret, and a cauldron of other emotions filled them, overwhelmed them, and they held each other, Sam's heart fluttering feebly at his throat, Korie's heart pounding in her chest—they held each other, and said nothing more.

Alone in Sam's apartment that evening, Korie reread his journals, tears streaming from her eyes. The language he had used was deliberately vague, with "you" pronouns throughout. Every so often, though, Sam would slip, and the "you" of his laments would be revealed as "he."

There was a gorgeous one there last night, he began one entry, *but he didn't want me. Now I know how it is with the ones who want me when I don't want them.*

How could she not have known? How could Sam have deceived *even her*? Suddenly, all their years together seemed mere illusion, their love reduced to a bare-faced lie. With a jolt, she understood that the illness that had claimed Sam, the blood sickness that was whittling him by inches, was not in fact lymphoma, sometimes contracted in the days before AIDS by strapping young men. Sam's illness was a specter more terrifying, contracted in ignorance at some all-male bathhouse or bar, or at the edge of some park or jetty in a nocturnal city of men.

Of course, she had always known—she saw that now. The signs had been everywhere: Sam's nighttime disappearances; furtive smiles in the street from men he knew, whom she could never recall meeting. There had been the membership card for a gay bathhouse that she had found amid the rubble on his desk. The signature on the card was "Laurence Smith," but the hand that penned the name was unmistakably Sam's.

"Who is Laurence Smith?" she had asked, picking up the card. "Is this yours?"

"Of course it's not mine!" Sam had snapped, snatching the card from her. "I found it."

She had not dared ask, had not dared even to wonder why Sam would pick up such an artifact, prizing it enough to bring it home.

Later, walking with Sam, the card had come back to her. "If you go to those places," she had said, meeting his eyes evenly, "just please be careful. You can catch diseases there." Sam had stared back with a false bravado, and said nothing. How was it, she now wondered, that even at that moment, the knowledge that Sam craved the sexual company of men still would not show itself to her conscious mind?

Looking back, she realized that the troublesome signature had never been out of her mind. She had simply consigned it to unconscious depths, where all the other clues were piled up like bones. She had willfully ignored the heap. After all, to lose Sam to another woman would have been heartbreak enough, but to lose him to a man—that would have been a repudiation of everything about her that was female. And so she'd chosen to be blind.

Korie left Sam's apartment at midnight. She had placed his journals in a brown paper bag and tucked them at the back of the closet where she had found them. She walked the streets blindly, her brain throbbing, her feet guiding her without conscious thought until she found herself outside a storefront bar with gray-tinted windows in the West Village. Sam had mentioned this bar several times in his journal. Korie stood across the street and stared at it, stood stock still and stared, as if some understanding might be gleaned from its tattered marquee, or from the faces of the young men who came and went in pairs. She knew from Sam's journals that there were rooms in the back where men coupled anonymously in a spill of purple light. She could not picture gentle Sam in these dark pits of male flesh, could not conjure up the Sam she had encountered in his journals—predatory, prowling, using the backroom lingo, negotiating The Act.

Korie didn't know how long she stood on that street trying to reconcile the man she had married with the life he had secretly led. Hours must have passed as she stood there, her feet rooted to the spot, for the first wash of morning found her still on that street. Only when the dawn's light penetrated her thoughts did Korie turn at last towards home.

It felt, to Korie, as if she would never be whole again. It was cruel enough to contemplate the world without Sam, but to discover that everything had been so different from what she had imagined—that, more than anything, crushed her. How could she even trust Zachary? How could she dare to put faith in another man's promise after sweet Sammy's lie?

When, on June fifth of that year, Sam finally stopped breathing, Korie was numb, unable to mourn. She stood with his mother at his bedside as Dr. Miro pulled the sheet over his face and signaled the orderly to wheel his body from the room. Aunt Elsa spoke of her intention to fly Sam home to Jacksonville for burial in the family plot. The woman she did housework for back in Chickory had offered to pay the fare. As always, Sam's mother was composed and remote, so that Korie, listening to her, felt that she had to maintain a fierce composure as well.

Five days later, after prayers were said over his body at the funeral parlor, Sam was loaded onto a plane for his final flight home. Korie didn't go to the airport with Aunt Elsa. Instead, she said good-bye to her on the street outside the funeral parlor, then took the subway back to her apartment. She passed Zach in the kitchen without saying a word. He followed her into the bedroom, and found her sitting cross-legged on the bed, studying a tiny Ziploc bag of marijuana buds that she was holding in her hands.

"How did it go?"

"Okay," Korie mumbled, not looking at him.

"How are you?" His voice was quiet, solemn.

Korie shrugged. "Okay."

Zach stood for a long time watching her as she silently crushed the dried marijuana buds between her fingers, grinding them to a fine green powder inside the plastic bag. He didn't know whether to push or just walk away. He decided to push.

He said, "Sweetheart, tell me what you need. How can I help?"

"You can't," Korie answered in a small, tight voice. Still not looking at him, she leaned over and dropped the bag of weed onto the dresser, then she slipped down under the bedcovers, slowly coiling her body beneath the cool sheets as she pulled them over her head. After a while, she spoke again, her voice muffled by the bedclothes. "I promise you I'm okay, Zach Man. Don't hover so much."

But Zach knew that she wasn't "okay"; he knew that nothing right now was anything close to "okay."

As the weeks accumulated, Korie railed at Sam for lying to her, hated him for dying before she could show him that his sexual choices could not have caused her to love him less. At other moments, she cursed her female softness, and was filled with disgust for her body, which was lush and rounded where men's bodies were muscled and hard. To escape the pain of her self-loathing, she began to roll joints at all hours of the day, wanting, underneath it all, to die and join Sam, to confront him in heaven or the netherlife and make him account for his lie.

She withdrew from Zachary, imagining that all men were sharers in the secret life of nocturnal male couplings that had finally killed Sam. Zach moved around her warily. It would take time, he told himself, for her to confront the revelations about the man who had been her husband. Her grief was hard, her sorrow complicated by the secret Sam had kept from her almost till the end. Zach decided he would wait for Korie to come out of it. He still hadn't found a job, but he'd begun contributing to the rent; he'd borrowed the money from his older brother Ben, who was doing fairly well as a contractor in Atlanta. Zach hadn't wanted to become a financial burden to Korie. She had her hands full with her dead husband's medical bills.

For Zach, there was a strong possibility of employment on the horizon, a position as a counselor to delinquent boys at the Springfield Juvenile Home in the Bronx. Zach would know in a week or so if he'd got the job.

He *wanted* the job.

Even with Korie so distracted, so hurt by Sam's leaving and tormented by his lie, Zach was ready to cast his lot with her. Now wasn't the time to broach the subject of a more permanent arrangement, of course, but as long as Korie would have him, he would hold her silently in the night, clean up the house each day, prepare their meals, pay a portion of the rent—and wait.

KORIE

A curl of smoke. This is what I have become. The moment I find a sharp, bell-clear thought returning, the moment I feel that the haze over my perceptions is beginning to dissolve, I roll another joint. I tap the weed from the clear plastic Ziploc bag into the folded Bambú paper and roll it into a perfect cylinder—fat or thin depending on how raw I'm feeling. Then I light the twisted end and suck the fire hungrily, as if the bitter smoke will fill the yawning space inside me with amnesia, which is preferable to pain.

So now, I've smoked. Sat on my not-quite-daybreak bed and inhaled an entire joint of Thai weed. Zachary lies next to me, his long lean body stretched out under the covers. He is pretending to be asleep. If he were up, he would feel the pressure to smoke with me. He feels guilty when he smokes, now. Ever since he got that job at Springfield, working as a counselor for boys who've run afoul of the law, he doesn't like getting high anymore. He's even cut down on cigarettes. Something about setting an example. Most of the Springfield boys found trouble because somebody in their lives introduced them to drugs, Zach says. I suppose he's right, and I admire his principles. Yet every time I smoke and he declines to join me, I feel his reproach, his concern about what he fears is my flirtation with addiction. I have no will to fight it. I avoid his eyes and close my ears to his apprehensions. The truth is, I feel easier after I've smoked. The ache ebbs from my heart, and I can breathe again. Air can pass through my chest again.

Zach tries to be patient but he cannot fathom why, when I am wrapped in so much love—by this he means *his* love—I should still be so broken about Sam. He doesn't understand how much a part of my consciousness Sam was, how much I am the result of the years I spent with him. And so, if the Sam I knew was just a figment, only one part of the story, suddenly, I, too, am incomplete, an illusion, lost among his secret desires and deceits.

All last night, whenever I closed my eyes, I saw Sam as he was the year we were married, thin but sturdy, sitting naked on the edge of our bed, his legs apart, arms stretched easily across his knees. I am standing across the room, and he is looking up at me, saying something wry, his eyes alight with ironic humor, his smile slightly rakish in that endearing way. He is bursting with life in my vision, his hands gesturing gracefully. Each time I closed my eyes, thinking that at last I might sleep, the same vision floated back, and my chest expanded with sorrow till I thought I would suffocate from it, and when I opened my eyes they were full of tears.

At the magazine, I function. Somehow, I continue to report and write my stories, even as I shrink from meetings with my editor, afraid that he will smell the smoke on my clothes, smell the ripe musky scent of marijuana in my hair. I close the door to my cubicle more than I used to, and inside the cool white walls I type my stories and stare at the phone, letting the voice mail intercept all calls, hardly returning any of them.

But I type. I cry and I type.

I console myself that some of the other reporters at the magazine smoke as much grass as I do, and some of them even snort coke. But they do drugs as a way of unwinding and enjoying each other—or so Simona insists—whereas I smoke with a different objective: to obliterate the world. It is as if I have no skin, as if Sam ripped my protective cover from me when he died. My nerve endings lie raw and exposed to the elements. So I cannot afford to feel. I smoke so as not to feel. Because what I feel when the curtain of smoke lifts is dangerous, mind-bending, insane.

Saturday night, I go over to Simona's house. When I left Zach, saying I would be back around midnight, not saying where I was going, he looked at me without speaking, his beautiful dark eyes so sad.

Do not pity me! I wanted to scream. *Do not desire to save me!*

It is hard to have him watch my descent. I am thinner than

when he met me, as thin as the year I was at Kendall, my skin paper dry, my hair like straw. It is difficult to care. Images of Sam's stiff embalmed body fill my brain.

Simona opens the door for me, her eyes brilliant and black. She pulls me by the hand into her apartment.

"Wine, grass, cocaine, a party!" she declares. "Oh, yes, I forgot. You don't do the white stuff. The coke's all for me!" She laughs and twirls about the room as if this is a delicious joke. I can tell she's started without me.

We chitchat about the magazine as I roll myself a joint. Simona is still the only other person of color at the magazine, the only one who knows the peculiar loneliness of being different, the particular tense vigilance of having to "fit in" while not betraying your own. We choose our battles, Simona and I. We let the insulting photograph of the beaming Haitian immigrant displaying his new shoes go without a fuss, saving our fuel to protest a story that depicts Haitian boat people, thousands of them confined in Florida detention camps, as slovenly voodoo bloodletters who unleashed AIDS on America. Until Simona and I get passionate, the editors don't even realize that this is the subtext of the article.

So I love Simona. From the time she asked me to dance at that party at Kendall Girls, she's never left me on that racial battlefield alone. The editors don't really understand who they got when they hired Simona. She's a little surly in the office, but her work is unassailable, so most of the time they just leave her alone. But they don't have a clue about her and the truth is, sometimes neither do I. Simona is the original wild child. She is also my smoking partner, my get-high girl. Of course, she sniffs coke as well, and likes to have me there getting high on grass with her, especially since she can have all the coke to herself.

Tonight, we've been smoking and sniffing and sipping Chablis all evening long. Simona is a little out of it at this moment, dancing by herself in the corner of the living room, her firm, athletic arms waving smoothly up and down like a snake charmer, the music of Anita Baker flowing in her blood. I watch the shadows of her arms stroke the walls, and I think how beautiful she is, with her cinnamon skin, disinterested brown eyes, her short, naturally curly hair in wisps around her head. Her body is long and hard like an adolescent boy's, and yet, for all her surly toughness, her spirit is feminine, cushioned. I want to sink into her. I want to feel her strong, girl arms eddy around me, folding me in. I want to rest my head along the smooth curve of her shoulder. I fantasize that Simona will welcome my softness. She will understand the rise of my breasts, the curve of my hips, the round shelf of my behind. They will be familiar to her, in the same way that men's bodies must have seemed familiar and comforting to Sam.

I cannot believe that Zachary, too, does not crave the hardness of men. I am frightened of the secrets I imagine he holds, the desires I have not yet fathomed. But here in Simona's house, I feel protected. She does not watch me through narrowed eyes, silently fearing that I am an addict. Instead, as if hearing my thoughts, she moves with her eyes closed across the room and takes me into her arms. She rocks me gently to the music, her small, high breasts pressed to my chest, her swaying hips grazing mine.

Men will betray me with their secrets, I find myself thinking, but here in Simona's arms, I am safe.

Sunday morning. The worst days of my life are Sundays. I didn't go home last night, but fell asleep on Simona's bed, our intoxicated bodies stretched side by side. Simona is still asleep. Her hot breath fans my cheek, and I am grateful for how easy she always is with me.

She has boyfriends, two or three. She doesn't get too bent

out of shape by their jealousies, though, and I have wondered sometimes if she is, underneath it all, really a lesbian. The thought titillates me, and I wonder if I'm becoming a lesbian.

I climb out of Simona's bed and walk into the living room. I am wearing only my panties and a bra although I don't remember undressing last night. A little grass remains in the clear plastic bag that lies on the butcher block table. I pick up the bag and inhale the soothing bitter-green smell of Colombian weed, then I sit and roll a tight smooth joint. I suck the smoke into my chest and don't stop until I get to the end, and the resin-saturated roach begins to burn my fingers.

"You can use a needle," Simona says, coming into the room. She is wearing a white T-shirt and stringy blue drawers. The thin material of her shirt outlines her small, pointed nipples. With an effort, I draw my eyes away from them. I'm attracted to her. Perhaps I have always been. I feel a familiar throbbing sensation in my genital region and I am aware of wanting to feel her body against mine.

"A needle?" I ask to hide my confusion.

"To hold the roach," she explains. "Stick a needle through it. Here."

She takes a needle from a pin cushion on her bookshelf and hands it to me. As I push its tip through the roach and relight it, Sam's image rises before my eyes. I lock onto his hooded eyes, which begin to take on the airy, feminine nonchalance of Simona's eyes as I smoke the last little bit of Colombian and crush out the fire. High now, I become fixated on the needle, studying its wraithlike thinness, its piercing tip. I begin to wonder what it would be like to stick that thin silver thread into the skin above my heart. Would it pierce deep enough to spear the heart itself, to touch the places on that mass of bone and tissue where sorrow makes its home? I picture the tip of the needle sliding into my skin, leaving a single, red dot above my breast, a clean, pristine wound that will obliterate the violent swirl of my emotions, even for a moment, so I can hold fast to the physicality of my life. So I can go on.

I arrive home at three in the afternoon. Zachary is out on the fire escape, reading. He looks up from his book but doesn't move as I come into the room. There is a picture of Sam on the bulletin board on the wall next to the window. A needle holds it in place. The needle is like an echo and I pull it from the bulletin board, letting Sam's picture float to the floor. He lies smiling at my feet but I do not look down at him. Instead I contemplate the needle. It is fire-stained, burnt at the tip from the many times I sterilized it with a lighted match before plucking ingrown hairs from Sam's cheek. I used to pull the coiled hairs from their hiding place in his freshly shaved skin, making neat red holes on Sam's face. He would wince sometimes, but mostly he lay still, giving himself up to me, trusting me.

I bend now to pick up his picture. Holding it, I turn to Zach. He is watching me from the fire escape, but he says nothing. I shrug and turn away from him. My poor Zachary, I think as I replace the photograph. There is nothing he can say.

Sometimes, I want to die. So often, as I sat by Sammy's bed in the hospital before he died, I had to fight down the urge to climb under the covers and go to sleep forever with him. Better that than the hollowness in the pit of my soul; better that than the queasiness in my stomach that signals that the frail threads that hold me are slowly giving way.

I want the cries in my head to stop. I no longer want to prowl the cacophonous city like one huge exposed nerve, open to infection, disease, electrocution. I no longer want to sit in my house on Sundays, facing the endless stretch of hours during which I try not to notice Zach observing me sadly as I fight not to smoke.

On Friday morning, I open my eyes to the sound of rain drumming against the window panes. I untangle myself from Zach's warmth and climb from under delicious layers of blankets. I raise the bamboo shades. There is not yet enough light in the sky to justify getting my day underway, I decide. So I lower the shades again and sit for a long time before forcing my steps to the bathroom. I splash cold water in my eyes, put in my contact lenses, and the world swims slowly into focus. In the harsh light of the bathroom, I face myself in the mirror. Is that really me staring back, my expression dazed and dispassionate, hair wild and spiked, skin pallid with its sallow undercast, dark circles around my eyes? I concentrate on the strange, naked-seeming face, trying to fathom what mystery Zach manages to coax from it—Zach, with his dark, dramatic looks, the antithesis of my washed-out pallor, my understated, not-quite-symmetrical, just-awakened face.

I often want to ask him: *What do you see in me? What magic have you conjured up?* Mostly I want to ask him: *Why do you stay?* But I refrain. I fear if I pose these questions to him, Zach will begin to pose them to himself. So I beat back the troubling train of thought and turn instead to hug my lover as he wanders into the bathroom from his own reaches of dream. I smile my naked-faced smile—more tremulous than before Sam died—and wrap my arms around his waist. As I lift my face to meet Zach's eyes, sad-wise and somber, last night's lovemaking fires not quite quelled, I feel a deep headiness, as if I am drowning and soaring at the same time, and I abandon myself to the male sorcery of his arms and the lure of his musky male smell.

·   ·   ·

On October thirteenth, the second anniversary of the day I first saw Zach in that Philadelphia parking lot, we decide to paint the house. The sand white walls seem gray from months of witnessing so little good news. We make an excursion to the hardware store on 125th Street and come home with gallons of Dutch Boy paint, brushes, rollers, pans, and a little red step ladder that the man at the hardware store threw in for free.

As we prepare to cover the walls, I glance across the room. Zach is there, constant as always, stirring paint with a wooden stick, then pouring it into a pan. He has moved the furniture, what little there is, to the center of the room and covered the huddle with a sheet. Now he dips a clean roller into the paint—the color on the paint chip was called pink china—and begins sliding the roller up and down the wall. He is wearing only running shorts, and in a little while his hard brown chest is freckled with paint, and the ridges of his arms gleam with the sweat of his repetitive back-and-forth motion.

I am to paint the accents, and so when Zach completes a wall I climb up onto the step ladder and begin to stroke the moldings just below the ceiling, trying to form a smooth margin. My thin brush is soaked with semigloss roseola, a cross between brick, burgundy, and pink, a brave color. But I'm feeling anything but brave. I despair of my ability to sustain this relationship. Zach has tried to console and hearten me; he has been so infinitely kind. I recall the months Sam spent with us as the tumors crept through his body and how, through the worst of it, Zach bore our weight, both mine and Sam's, and never complained. "Lean on me," he told me the evening I found Sam's journals. "That's why I'm here." And in the weeks that followed, Zach found excuses never to leave my side. At night, as my tears soaked his chest, he whispered, "I'm not going to let you go under."

But what if I *want* to go under? These days, I feel more connected to Sam's world of the dead than to Zach's world of the living. Zach's presence in my house requires me to keep swimming, even as the water closes over my head. I know it depresses him to see me like this. I want to release him. I want *him* to release *me*.

I am tired of being accountable to his bedrock belief in me.

Let me drift away from the shore of your faith, I think as I paint the margins. You cannot follow me into the deep. A bleak silence settles between us. It is as if we both know that as he paints the house, Zach is painting himself out of my life. But even this, he will finally make easy.

"You owe me nothing," he tells me that evening, reading me as always. And when we have finished painting all the rooms and moved the furniture back into place, he holds my shoulders gently.

"You don't want me here," he says.

I look down at the floor. I don't answer him. He is quiet for a little while, and then he sighs.

"On Friday, I'll go," he says, letting go of my shoulders.

"Just for a little while," I say.

Zachary makes fast, urgent love to me at daybreak. We do not speak as I dress for work but hold each other for a long time before I leave. When I am gone, Zach washes the paintbrushes in the bathtub and packs his things. Later, he calls my job to say he will leave the key in the mailbox. I thank him and promise I'll be in touch.

I am not prepared for the wave of missing him that sweeps over me when I open the front door that evening.

The apartment looks crisp and new, the hall light coaxing a warm glow from the freshly painted walls. And yet, the rooms as I wander into them, first one and then the other, then back into the first, feel somehow empty, characterless. For so many months I have come home to an apartment full of Zach's presence. Most often, he would be sitting at the kitchen table sipping a beer while he watched a ball game, some simple feast of his simmering on the stove. "Hey, baby!" he would say brightly, opening his arms, and I would find myself gathered to the heartbeat at his breast, breathing his close familiar smell. I catch a briny whiff of him now—a quivering absence in the rose-colored air.

Part Three
1985–1986

"What is a good man but a bad man's teacher?
What is a bad man but a good man's job?"
—Lao-tzu

9
Going Home

ZACH NAVIGATED HIS RENTED FORD TAURUS INTO THE highway traffic, heading south along I-95. He tried to shake the melancholy that stole through him as the spires of the New York City skyline receded in the distance of his rearview mirror. A light rain had begun to spatter his windshield, and up ahead the sky looked soupy and ominous, as if the gray clouds billowing on the horizon would explode into a downpour at any second. It would be a long drive to Philadelphia in the rain, the usual two hours stretching to three or even four. What with the weather and the Friday evening traffic, he wouldn't get in till almost midnight even if he pushed it. His mother would be asleep by then. She wasn't expecting him; he hadn't thought to call and tell her he was coming home. It had been a good few months, in fact, since he'd last spoken with her.

Zach didn't know how long he'd be gone, or even whether he would be coming back to New York. He hadn't quit his job, though. He had had three weeks of vacation and comp time coming to him from the juvenile detention home, and he'd signed up for the whole parcel. He would see where things stood when the three weeks were up, which meant he'd see where Korie stood, since, much as he'd come to enjoy the quixotic surge of life in New York, she was his only real reason to be there. Without Korie, there was no real point to New York for Zach. His family and most of his friends were still in Philadelphia, and though he would happily forgo proximity to them to be with Korie, he had missed them in the year and a half he'd been away. He had been so caught up in the slow drama of Sam's dying, and in the vortex of Korie's grief, that he'd neglected to stay in touch with what was happening in their lives.

His family was fond of Korie. She had spent most of her weekends with Zach in Philadelphia until he'd lost his job at the Carson Agency and moved to New York. And before Sam got sick and came to live with them, Zach and Korie had taken the train or driven down to see his family every few weekends. Florida and Korie had liked each other at once, which had as much to do with an earthiness they shared as with Florida's quiet perception of what the young woman from New York had come to mean to her son. It had been as clear to Florida as the crystal waters of Lake Winslow that Korie had fully captured Zach's heart. She had seen it in the solicitous way he looked out for her comfort, not because Korie demanded or required the attention, but because it delighted Zach to give it. And the way he always had to be touching her. Wherever Korie was in a room, Zach would find his way over to her, even for a few moments, so that he could slip an arm around her shoulders, take her hand in his, or lean down to place a light kiss on the side of her neck. Zach knew that, at first, Korie had been embarrassed by these displays, but as she became more comfortable with Florida, she gave in to her own pleasure in touching him—she leaned up to brush his cheek on passing him in the hallway, sat shoulder to shoulder with him on the front porch steps, jiggled her feet against his under the breakfast table.

So what had happened between them these last few months? Zach wondered as he steered against the pull of a passing tractor trailer. How could such a promising affair have broken down so abruptly? For the first six months in New York, their relationship had been idyllic—Zach hadn't known that he could be so settled and contented with the everyday routine of domestic commitment. Even after Sam moved into the apartment, his presence only served to heighten the intimacy of the bond Zach and Korie shared. Zach knew that Korie had been grateful for the uncomplaining way in which he had allowed her never-divorced husband to become a part of their lives. But really, Sam was dying. What choice had he had? Other than pack up and head on back to Philadelphia. And that would have meant leaving Korie.

He tried to ignore the stab of pain in his chest as he maneuvered his car through the toll booths that led onto the New Jersey Turnpike. The rain was falling relentlessly now, pelting his windshield with huge droplets, defeating his furiously working wipers. The beige upholstery of the interior, which had seemed nondescript when he had first entered it, now felt warm and cocoonlike, a moving bubble of safety in the fierce downpour. It was seven-fifteen in the evening, fully dark out, and Zach fought the urge to pull his car over to the gravel shoulder of the highway and go to sleep. He was tired suddenly, tired of straining to make out the car lights ahead of him in the rain, tired of his ceaseless thoughts. But if he stopped now, it would only prolong the hours alone on the highway, hours thick with the ache of missing a woman he loved hopelessly. So he forced himself to keep going, even though he knew it was dangerous driving.

As he squinted through the opaque walls of spray kicked up by surrounding vehicles, he played back in his mind the last year, thinking he might pinpoint the moment when he might have averted the chasm that had opened between them. All he knew was that after Sam died, Korie had just shut down on him. But the distance had begun to creep into their relationship even before Sam died. It had begun with Korie finding those journals, those pages of looping script that had told her what Zachary had suspected from the moment he took Sam's weight onto his shoulders on that very first day. Zach had seen it in the appraising, almost flirtatious way in which Sam had sized him up. Zach had pretended not to notice the sexual curiosity that, despite his frail state, flickered at the back of Sam's eyes, but he'd been the object of men's advances before, and he'd known at once what it meant.

But Korie hadn't known—at least not consciously—until she found the journals and read them. For her, the discovery of Sam's sexual preference had transformed her grief over his death into a sorrow more intricate than an unambiguous diagnosis of lymphatic cancer might have caused. Sam's dying also became a question mark for Korie, and Zach, too, an event with ramifications they would have to confront.

When had Sam become HIV positive? They might never know the answer, but Zach wanted to believe it had happened after Korie and her husband were no longer lovers. Korie had told Zach that from the day she and Sam separated four years before, they had never again engaged in sexual intercourse. They had sometimes kissed lightly in a fashion more friendly than romantic—no deep, exploring tongue thrusts—and they had even shared the same bed on occasion, like the time they drove to Martha's Vineyard together for the weekend on a whim. But sex had not been a part of the post-connubial relationship.

Even so, Zach could tell that Korie was scared. And she had good reason. As if to prove to Sam how unconditional was her love for him, she had handled his bodily fluids recklessly at the end—emptying his urinal, brushing his teeth, cleaning up his increasingly frequent nosebleeds. Zach himself hadn't been all that careful, for somehow a dying man's immediate need to be held, to be touched and tended to in loving, ministering ways, had eclipsed more personal concerns. But now Sam was dead, and the questions about his illness had assumed belated significance. How long had his HIV infection lay dormant? Even if there had been no sexual intercourse between Sam and Korie in more than four years, Sam might well have harbored the disease for longer than that. The fact was, Korie might already have been a symptom-free carrier when Zach first took her into his bed.

"What if I've infected you?" she had asked Zach frantically one night. "What if I got it from Sam and then gave it to you?"

Curiously, Zach couldn't muster up the appropriate sense of fear. Some deep intuition told him that he and Korie were uninfected. He knew his feelings on the matter were hardly scientific, and yet he trusted them. Still, he supposed he and Korie should get tested, just to be sure.

An uncomfortable thought presented itself. Testing would become more critical, he realized, if they found new partners.

He slapped the steering wheel in frustration. *"Damn!"* he said roughly, unaware he had spoken aloud. "It *wasn't* just me!" The current between them had been so powerful from the start, so absolute, he knew it had to have flowed both ways. So why had she asked him to leave? Not with words, but with her eyes, silently imploring, and her posture, coiled and defensive. And then she had begun to take herself from him in the most literal way, spending night after night at Simona's house, moving through their apartment in a pungent envelope of reefer smoke when she was home. Her plea had been unmistakable. He wondered sometimes if he had misread her meaning, but no, she *had* asked him to leave, just not with words.

It had taken a while for him to get it, to understand that she had begun to chafe under his scrutiny. She smoked first thing in the morning, on waking, then first thing as soon as she got home from work. And though he never said a word to her about it, still, she had felt exposed, criticized by his abstinence, judged by his silence. If only she could have understood that he wasn't judging her. He was worried for her, yes, but that was much different from passing judgment. He knew she smoked so as not to feel the pain that had assaulted her after Sam's death. His worry was born of the knowledge that she was only delaying the inevitable. Sooner or later, she would have to mourn the man who had been her husband, and make peace with his secrets. She would have to find a way to understand that she hadn't *created* Sam's desire for male sex; somehow Korie had internalized the notion that she had *driven* Sam to seek men, that she had been too soft, too fleshy to have held his sexual interest.

If she only knew, Zach thought. If only she would open her eyes. She would see that Sam, *despite* his preference for men, had fallen in love with her, going against his fundamental nature and making love to her for years. It had been obvious to Zach that Sam had been utterly captivated by Korie, by her bold, independent spirit, her fierce loyalty, and, yes, her ripe sexuality. Zach even suspected that Sam, with his closeted desires, his fear of his homosexual urges, had hoped for a while that the sexual stirring he felt for Korie might change him. Because he could get hard for her, he could hide from his true nature. But sooner or later, his sexual and emotional need for men would reassert itself, and he would have to go seeking. Now Korie was caught in the ripple of his deceit, facing her own grief at Sam's inability to love himself, and let her love him, just exactly as he was made.

Zach had arrived at his exit almost without noticing, but now the signs for Camden alerted him that he was close to home. He still couldn't shake Korie from his thoughts, and so he just kept going with the well-worn groove. What was it about this woman? She was certainly attractive, but he had made love to women who were far more beautiful in a conventional sense, and none had crept into his marrow the way Korie had. He supposed he had been intrigued by her willingness to throw herself into their affair, not holding back, skirting the edge of what was safe. From the start, she had been unabashed about expressing how much she desired him; she hadn't feared revealing that she wanted to possess him as much as he had wanted to possess her. She had gone to his house that first night not knowing anything about him, not knowing whether he was a rapist or a con artist or a collector of hearts. She had chosen to live dangerously with him, to ride the furious current of their attraction and give herself up to the edgy excitement of not knowing what came next.

He had been drawn to her like a wanderer to an open flame in the night. The flame had offered him warmth, and a place to lay his head. It had seduced him with its hot bloom. But like an open flame, she had wavered in the shifting winds and finally danced out of his reach. Now he found himself chasing her distant, flickering light, searching blindly for a foothold on the changing ground of her emotions and dreading a return to the darkness he had not known before meeting her that he dwelled in.

•   •   •

The storm had dogged him all the way to Philly, never letting up. But it soon wouldn't matter, because he was three blocks away from where Florida's house stood, an oasis of warm light in the drenching night. Two of Zach's siblings, Annie and Neal, still lived there, even though they sometimes didn't show up for days at a stretch.

The house was really run-down now, and as Zach turned the last corner before Quincy, he resolved to do something about that. He would renovate the kitchen, fancy up the porch, and spackle and paint the whole place. He would give Florida's house a complete makeover in time for Christmas. It was the least he could do for a mother whose welcome he never had to question, even after all these months of preoccupation and silence.

Quincy Street. The familiar outline of the row houses he had grown up with greeted him. Something was immediately odd about the scene though, for even in the rain, even at this late hour, people were running down the street. Florida's house was at the far end of the block and Zach couldn't make it out at first, for the rain still fell in sheets. But as he approached the house, he realized the people he had seen were running towards it, yelling and waving their arms. Now he saw that a thicket of people were gathered outside Florida's house, huddled together in the rain. He noticed other people standing on their porches, their necks craned toward Florida's house.

Zach's mind went blank, but his stomach began to churn. He stopped the Ford Taurus as close to his house as he could get, and jumped out of the car. Instinctively, he began to run, knowing that whatever was in the center of the crowd, he would not want to see. No one even noticed him as he elbowed his way through the throng of people. The roar of their voices filled the air, their words floating unintelligibly around his ears.

There was a clearing at the center of the crowd, and Neal

was locked in a brutal embrace with a man Zach didn't recognize, a huge, burly man, much bigger than Neal, his face contorted into a vicious snarl. Neal's shirt was ripped at the shoulder and bloodstained. One eye was swollen almost shut and rivulets of blood flowed from his nose. Annie was jumping up and down next to them, screaming words Zach couldn't make out. In the same moment, he noticed a group of women kneeling around a prone body, and *knew* rather than saw that it was his mother.

Suddenly Zach was part of the fight, his fists flying into the strange man's ribs, chest, face, his knee ramming into the small of his back, his sneaker tips peppering the man's body as he lost his footing on the slick sidewalk and fell heavily to the ground. Zach didn't care that he wasn't fighting fair, didn't care where his fists or his feet landed. He just wanted the struggle to be over, and the strange man restrained so that he could go over and find out what had happened to Florida. A few of the men from the crowd rushed forward to help Zach restrain the thrashing man, yelling and cursing in a rush of adrenaline as they pinned him to the ground.

"Call the cops!"

"That's Lottie's boy!"

"Frisk his ass! Make sure he ain't carryin'!"

And, weaving under the hysteria, a woman's voice said softly, sadly, "What could you be thinking of, boy?"

One of the older men had referred to the man as Jimmy Jones. Zach knew the name. Jimmy had grown up on Quincy Street, but he'd spent most of the last decade in jail after being picked up as part of some local drug and burglary ring. He was a couple years older than Zach, and when he'd been sent up, he'd been a skinny cokehead, a zoned-out shell of a human. Obviously, he'd been seriously pumping iron those ten years in the pen.

The men were still holding him down, and Zach chanced

letting go of the prostrate Jimmy to restrain Neal, who was still trying to pummel him. Hot tears spilled from Neal's eyes as he panted furiously and punched the air, trying to regain control of himself.

"Cool, bro, cool," Zach urged, gripping him in a bear hug.

"Cool," he answered roughly, "I'll be cool, bro."

Zach released him and ran over to where his mother lay. He saw that she had been injured—she was cradling the ridge of her jaw—but apparently not too badly, for she was conscious and trying to sit up. Her eyes opened wide when she saw Zach.

"Hey, baby," she said weakly. "I didn't know you'd be coming home. Ole fool knocked me flat. Jaw's painin' me."

"What happened, Ma?"

"Oh, baby—" Florida began, but didn't finish. "Help me up," she said instead. "Help me inside."

Annie was kneeling at Zach's elbow now, crying almost hysterically, snot and tears mingling with her whispered oath.

"I'll fucking kill him."

Zach almost didn't hear her, what with all the commotion, but something about the deadly conviction of her words stood in stark contrast to her agitation, so that Zach was forced to pay attention.

"I'm going to kill him," Annie murmured, her sobs beginning to subside. "Mark my words. I swear it." Her eyes, despite the tears, were hard as steel, and as cold. Zach studied her for a moment, noticing for the first time the long red blotches like finger marks on her neck, the rip up the side of her nightshirt, and the fact that beneath the shirt her legs were bare, her feet shoeless. An intimation of what might have transpired came to his mind, but Zach didn't want to believe it, and Annie was in no state to explain anything. He would have to talk to her later, when she was calmer. The sooner they got Florida inside, the sooner he could find out what had happened.

"Take Ma's arm," he told Annie.

Together they lifted her and started for the front steps just as the wail of police sirens rounded the corner. A swarm of blue uniforms spilled over the street, pulling Jimmy Jones roughly to his feet, fanning out to interview the neighborhood folk about what had occurred. Zach watched the scene long enough to see Jimmy Jones handcuffed and bundled into one of the police cars, and a couple of blue uniforms take Neal aside. The circling squad car lights strobed the avenue in yellow and red, painting the wet faces of the few people who were still standing around in the rain. Most of the onlookers had begun drifting back to their homes once the police arrived. One of the cops, a big, brawny black man with a badge that read OFFICER BENEDICT, came over to Zach and Annie as they were helping Florida up the steps. He climbed the steps behind them, and held open the door as they ushered Florida into the living room.

"How're you doing, ma'am? That's a nasty bruise you're sporting."

"She thinks her jaw's broken or something," Annie said.

"Hurts like the devil," Florida confirmed.

Officer Benedict went to the front door and called for one of the officers to radio EMS. "We'll get that bruise taken care of, ma'am," he said, turning back to Florida. "But your jaw's probably not broken or you wouldn't be talking to us." He spoke in a deep, gruff voice, and swung his torso as he walked, his shoulders squared as if to assure everyone that things were under control now that Officer Benedict was here.

"So what happened out there tonight?" he asked, taking out his notebook and readying his pencil. He looked at Zach.

"I couldn't tell you." Zach shrugged. "I just drove here from New York. I arrived in the middle of it."

"I can tell you what happened," Annie said quietly.

·   ·   ·

Jimmy Jones had come back to Philadelphia two months before. He had spent some years in Savannah, Georgia, after his release from jail, and had observed his parole uneventfully there. On his first Sunday home, his older sister Zoe and her lover Mabel had thrown a welcome-back barbecue for him in their yard. Annie had been there, along with just about everybody else in the neighborhood, except for some of the older folks who, after all these years, still considered Zoe and Mabel's lifestyle a sin against the Lord.

Jimmy couldn't wait to see Annie. He had dreamed about her the whole time he had been in prison, and then later in Savannah, recalling her sculpted dancer's body astride his hips, her sweet breasts bouncing above him. He had waited till his parole was up to come home to Philly, because he hadn't wanted her to think of him as a two-bit ex-con. He had plans for Annie, and he wanted to be free and clear when he saw her again.

When Annie walked into Zoe's yard that afternoon wearing baggy painter's pants and a black leotard, Jimmy imagined rather than saw her nipples outlined by the fabric, and he got an instant hard-on. She had had that effect on him before he got sent up, but he had been a hotheaded adolescent then, so it intrigued him to discover that she could still arouse him so easily. She didn't even have to try. Because of the bulge in his pants, he didn't stand up when she told him hello—she was a little indifferent, he thought—but with his look, long and lingering, almost obscene, he had tried to tell her that he still wanted her in all the same ways as when they were teenagers grappling in the back bedroom of his sister Zoe's house.

Annie had been curious to see Jimmy, to gauge how much the intervening years might have changed him. But given what had happened between them just before Jimmy went away, the last thing she wanted from him was any suggestion of sex. She met his eyes briefly and turned away, the resolute set of her back delivering her message loud and clear. Rage flooded him momentarily, but Jimmy fought it down. He had waited ten long years, he told himself. He could wait a few more days.

But Annie stayed away from him after that. She wouldn't take his phone calls, and didn't acknowledge him if she happened to run into him in the neighborhood. He supposed she was still mad at him for the way he had taken her that night so many years before. Ten years, he thought wearily. She should be over that by now. Besides, she knew he'd been all strung out on coke and 'ludes and dust back then. He hadn't truly known what he was doing. The cops had busted him for selling and using dope and a host of theft charges just a week later. But now he was back and Annie wouldn't give him the time of day, wouldn't allow him the chance to make it up to her.

He had written to her from jail, begging her to come see him. But she never came. And she never sent so much as a hello with Zoe.

She was beginning to piss him off. It wasn't that he couldn't get laid. He was a fine-looking, brown-skinned brother, and he'd pumped himself up in the years away. He was finding that a lot of women were drawn to him, turned on by the edge of danger his jailhouse rep gave him. But not Annie—and she was the one that counted.

He decided to wait for her to come home from work one evening. He had heard from Zoe that she had been trained as a rape counselor at Lincoln Hospital. Those women she worked with must have filled her head with some man-hating shit, he thought bitterly as he lounged outside the corner store at Quincy and Bachelor, sipping beer from a bottle in a brown paper bag. Jimmy wondered if Annie had ever told Zoe about that night. He didn't think so. His sister would have blown it all out of proportion—she'd her own problems with men, what with their father stealing into her room nights from the time she was nine. No, if Annie had told Zoe about that night, his sister would have written him off. She wouldn't have stuck by him the way she had all those years he was in jail. Once when she came to visit, she had asked him: "So what happened with you and that Annie Piper? I thought you were in love." She wouldn't have asked him that if she had known what went down.

So Annie had held her tongue. He respected that. He needed to talk to her, tell her he was sorry, so she could stop holding a grudge. Then maybe they could pick up where they left off. He felt a tightening in his genitals, the way he always did when he imagined fucking her. He was half erect by the time Annie turned the corner onto Quincy Street. But she crossed to the other side as soon as she saw him, so that he had to sprint across the street to catch up with her.

"Annie, hey, wait up, girl. Why you dissin' me like this?"

Annie kept walking, ignoring him. He kept up her pace.

"You not still mad at me after so many years? Hey, you know I was buzzed outta my mind."

She stopped suddenly and turned on him.

"That's your excuse? That's supposed to make it all right? You simple motherfucker."

"Watch your mouth, girl."

"I ain't your girl, Jimmy, so stop following me. Stop bothering me. I don't want anything to do with you, you jailbird."

The "jailbird" made Jimmy mad, just as Annie knew it would. He grabbed her arm roughly. She didn't fight him. She just looked at him witheringly and said, "You haven't changed a bit, Jimmy. You'd rape me again if you had half a chance. I'm not giving you that chance."

He let go of her arm, stung.

"Who says I raped you?"

"What would you call it?"

"They done brainwashed you at that clinic, girl. It weren't no rape. Okay, I wasn't real gentle. But you were right there with me. I never forced you into that room. You came 'cause you wanted it, just like I did."

"I came because I was worried about you, Jimmy. You were doing that freebase and shit and it was making you crazy."

"I got off it in the pen. I ain't crazy no more, 'cept about you."

Annie sucked her teeth and turned to walk away from him. He grabbed her arm again. This time, she jerked free of his grip and pushed him backwards.

"Don't you *ever* touch me again, Jimmy Jones!"

Jimmy was pinned to the spot by the venom in her voice. He watched her stride off down the street towards her home, her neck stiff with anger, her round butt bobbing side to side with emphasis as she walked. Even after she turned into her small yard, climbed the front steps and disappeared through the front door, Jimmy stood watching the place where she had been.

Annie could remember the rape as keenly as if it had happened yesterday. She had just turned sixteen. Jimmy was two years older. She had known him from around the neighborhood, and had had a crush on him from the time she was ten. Once, at the Western Avenue playground when she wanted to play basketball with the boys, he had stood up for her when her older brother Ben tried to send her home.

"She can play if she wants," he had told him. "I don't care if she's a girl, she can be on my team."

And Annie could play ball. She had played with her brothers often enough. She was tall for her age and had quick hands, and she could duck and weave effortlessly under the arms of the boys, passing the ball to Jimmy for layup after layup. Jimmy let her play on his team whenever she wanted after that, and Annie loved him for it.

Jimmy hadn't really noticed her in an amorous sense for another few years, though. But when Annie was fourteen, she sprouted small breasts, rounded out in the hips, and developed intriguing angles to her face. Her eyes were large and dark and her lips kewpielike and provocative. She swished past Jimmy every chance she got until finally he invited her over to Zoe's house to listen to some tapes. Not long after that, Jimmy took her virginity in the back bedroom of his sister's house. Annie had really had a thing for Jimmy back then. And Jimmy seemed to fall hard for Annie, too. But the fates weren't lined up behind their relationship, because around the same time they fell in love, Jimmy began using dope.

Annie smoked marijuana with him from time to time, but she had enough sense to know not to get started on the cocaine and amphetamines and crystal meth and 'ludes and all the other stuff Jimmy was getting into. He had even started selling the junk. At first, she thought she could turn Jimmy away from the path he was traveling. She thought she could redeem him, make him see sense, make him stop selling, and maybe even stop using. Jimmy was ruining himself, running with a bad crowd, acting like he knew it all, like he was invulnerable. And he was a mean-ass junkie. Freebase in particular made him vicious. Annie didn't like to be around him then. He would be sweating and agitated, paranoid and grandiose, and once when Annie told him he was fucked up, he even slapped her face.

She knew she should have kept away from him, knew she had no business still messing with him. Zach had begged her to walk away. While everyone else speculated on whether or not she was a lesbian, Zach had been the only one who knew what she was really doing over at Zoe and Mabel's house. She hadn't wanted to tell Florida that Jimmy was her boyfriend. Jimmy was a bad seed as far as Florida was concerned, and she would have worried herself sick had she known her daughter was seeing him.

At first, she thought Zoe could help her reach out to Jimmy. Zoe was as troubled as she was about the scene he had fallen into. Zoe couldn't quite believe the way drugs had transformed him. She still remembered him as the sweet little brother who came into her room when he heard her crying at night, after their father had had his way with her. Jimmy used to sit on the floor next to her bed and hold her hand, and somehow his presence in the darkness had comforted her. He'd been her ally in that house. Even now, when the dope had him all crazy, Zoe could still see her sweet-natured little brother in the depths of his eyes.

Jimmy got careless, full of his own power, and talked his business on the street. Annie began to realize it was just a matter of time before the cops picked him up. She had gone over to Zoe's house to meet him that night, hoping she would be able to make him see how he was destroying himself. Jimmy had turned up high on a cocktail of narcotics. Annie didn't know what he had taken but there was a violent edge to him that scared her. Zoe wasn't home that evening, and Mabel was in the front room with her door closed. They could hear the whir of her sewing machine and knew she was working on the alterations she did for a dress store downtown.

Even after so many years, not a single detail was fuzzy in Annie's memory. Jimmy had tried to kiss her, but he stank of reefer, stale beer, and sweat and she had pulled away from him. He'd grabbed her arms and pulled her back, planting slobbering kisses all over her face, her neck, her breasts. Annie wanted to push him away from her, but she quickly realized that Jimmy was out of control, and so she let him push her onto the bed, let him tear her shorts down the seam, and push himself into her. Tears squeezed from her eyes as he forced himself inside her, ramming himself into her again and again. An eternity passed before he shuddered and collapsed across her. A moment later he was asleep, snoring softly, his body a dead-weight on top of her. Annie didn't try to move him. She just stared past his head at the wall, her chest convulsing with silent sobs.

"The past always repeats itself," Annie warned Officer Benedict, who stood opposite her in Florida's living room, his pen frozen in the air, no longer scribbling in his notebook as she spoke. Florida, one hand holding to her jaw an ice pack that the EMS technician had left, sat silently on the couch, staring round-eyed at her daughter. Neal had come inside by then, and was sitting on the couch next to Florida, his face buried in his large hands. Zach sat on the other side of the room, his eyes steady on Annie as she continued her story.

The evening before, after Annie walked away from him, Jimmy must have gone drinking because when Annie woke up around midnight and found him silhouetted at her window, she could smell the liquor on him from across the room. She opened her mouth to scream, but before she could call forth a sound, Jimmy closed the space between them and clasped his big hands around her neck, choking off her voice. She tried to pull his hands from her throat, but he squeezed tighter and shook her violently. Annie kicked and squirmed, and managed to loosen his fingers just long enough to shriek Neal's name.

Annie knew Neal was in the house. And her mother, too. They had all watched TV together earlier, then Florida had gone upstairs to bed. Neal and Annie had sat for another hour talking about a girl Neal had met that afternoon in the apartment building where he worked as a plasterer. The girl, whose name was Samantha, taught preschool, but her true love was the piano, and she had given Neal an impromptu classical recital as he chipped and spackled and smoothed her walls. Neal had been charmed by her simplicity, her lack of airs, and the way she seemed to appreciate him not as an anonymous laborer, but as a craftsman who took pride in his work. And he had been moved by the pure joy on her face as her fingers danced over the piano keys. She'd invited him back for iced tea and another recital the following afternoon.

Annie had started to tell Neal about Jimmy lying in wait for her that afternoon, but she changed her mind, not wanting to dampen Neal's mood. She had left him stretched out dreamily on the living room couch when she climbed the stairs at something to eleven. Outside, the rain was pouring down, and jagged shafts of lightning ripped the night sky. Annie had taken the time before climbing into bed to make sure her window was closed.

She wasn't sure what woke her at just past midnight, but it must have been the sound of the window lock breaking and Jimmy's feet scudding onto the wooden floor. She prayed with all her might that, despite the thunder and rain, Neal had heard her when she screamed, because now Jimmy's hand was clamped over her nose and mouth. All her energy went into trying to breathe as Jimmy pushed her up against the wall and moved behind her, his clothes soggy and cold through the fabric of her nightshirt. One hand still covering her face, he reached under her shirt to grip the elastic of her drawers, all the while grinding his crotch against her. Annie's face smashed into the wall each time his hips jerked against her as he panted and labored to remove her underpants.

Annie's mind went blank. It was as if she had floated outside her body and was looking on dispassionately from the other side of the room. She felt nothing, and she heard Jimmy's grunts and incoherent curses only dimly, as if filtered by distance. From that peculiar vantage point, she saw a wedge of light spill suddenly into the room, saw Neal's tall, skinny figure streak through the doorway and grab Jimmy's shirt. Jimmy, so intent on his objective, didn't turn at first; he just tried to push Neal off, as if he were a minor nuisance. Neal grabbed him around his torso and threw him away from Annie, who collapsed against the wall. Jimmy lost his footing then and fell backwards, but in one swift motion he was back on his feet and lunging at Neal, his fists flying. Neal ducked away from him just as his sister staggered to her feet. Both brother and sister rushed Jimmy simultaneously and tackled him, but Jimmy, much bigger and stronger than the two of them, whirled drunkenly and swung them to the floor before he stumbled through the door into the hallway and lumbered down the stairs. Neal, leaping over the banister, caught him at the front door, and the two of them tangled and rolled onto the porch and down the front steps into the street. There the fight grew brutal, with Jimmy pounding Neal's face and body viciously and Neal getting in every blow he could. Despite the rain, a crowd quickly converged around them, called out of their homes by the commotion in front of Florida's house.

If it had been anybody's house but Florida's, the people of Quincy Street might have stayed inside their homes, but they wouldn't have been able to live with themselves if it turned out that Florida was in trouble and they hadn't tried to help. She had stood by them so often over the years, sometimes doing nothing more than holding their hands when they cried, sometimes writing letters to city agencies for them, or lending cash to pay doctor bills, bail money, or funeral expenses. Even those who hadn't needed much from Florida still knew that if ever they did fall on hard times, Florida would do all she could for them. And so they rushed out of their homes into the rain and fanned out around Jimmy and Neal. But, recognizing them both as neighborhood boys, they were loath to step between them without knowing what the fight was about.

Florida had no such hesitation. Awakened by the ruckus on the stairs, she stormed out of her house into the rainy October night wearing not even a housecoat over her faded sleeveless cotton nightie. She pushed herself between Neal and Jimmy and tried to pull them apart, her bony arms stretched between them, her fingers splayed on each man's chest. Neal let down his guard, the habit of heeding his mother momentarily asserting itself, and in that instant Jimmy hauled back to whack him, but caught the side of Florida's face instead and sent her flying into the crowd. It was right at that moment that Zach shouldered his way through the huddle of people, just as the men who had been watching rushed forward to collar Jimmy for the way he had knocked the lights out of Florida.

Officer Benedict closed his notebook, his eyes sympathetic as he studied Annie. Upstairs, a police photographer snapped photos of Annie's room, while a fingerprint specialist dusted the window frame. Annie was still seated in the straight-backed chair next to the stairs. Officer Benedict cleared his throat.

"Are you willing to press charges, miss?"

"You bet your ass," Annie muttered, looking away. As she'd told the story of Jimmy's assault, she had grown conscious of the fact that she was wearing just a torn nightshirt. Now, she pulled the shirttails primly over her knees, feeling cheap and dirty at the memory of Jimmy jerking his liquor-soaked body against hers.

"He'll end up right back in jail," the officer commented.

"I hope they lose the damn key," Annie shot back.

Florida watched her silently from the couch, her heart prickled with sadness at the revelation of what her only daughter had endured at Jimmy Jones's hands. As Florida digested the knowledge now, it pained her all the more that Annie had never shared her suffering. But then Zach walked over to his sister and placed his hand gently on her shoulder. Annie raised her eyes to his, and the simple trust on her face told Florida that Annie *had* in fact divulged the secret of what Jimmy had done to her ten years before. Like all the rest of them, then as now, she had shared her most secret pain with Zach.

10
The Carpenter's Shadow

THEY LET JIMMY OUT ON TEN THOUSAND DOLLARS' BAIL right after his arraignment. Zoe and Mabel had agreed to put their tiny house up as collateral, and even Annie knew that despite the violence that lived inside him, Jimmy wouldn't have the heart to cheat his big sister out of the one sanctuary she had found.

So just like that, Jimmy was in the neighborhood again, pending trial for breaking and entering, assault and battery, and tacked on at the end of the charge sheet, attempted rape. Jimmy's story was that Annie had invited him over that night, and the whole thing had been consensual. Her brother Neal had heard him in the bedroom and misunderstood his presence there, and now Annie, not wanting to admit to her family that she had sneaked him into her room—and mad at him for the injuries he had inflicted on both Neal and Florida—was standing by Neal's story.

It didn't make sense, of course, because Annie wouldn't

have had to *sneak* anybody in. She could have invited Jimmy up to her room freely; Florida wouldn't have had a word to say about it. After all, her daughter was twenty-nine years old, a grown woman who could just as well be in her own place. Annie couldn't believe Jimmy's gall as he went around the neighborhood telling and retelling his story, until she was sure he actually believed it.

How could Zoe be taken in for a second by it? Annie wondered. And yet, Zoe evidently believed Jimmy because she was avoiding any chance that she might run into Annie, going four blocks out of her way so as not to pass by Florida's house on her way home from work in the evenings.

Annie called her up one Saturday morning and asked if she could come by and talk about what had happened. Zoe's voice was sad. "Annie, hon," she said, "Jimmy's the only family I got left. He was a good kid once. He's a little rough around the edges since he got out of jail, but you know, he was the sweetest baby brother back when. He saved my life some nights just by being there. I just can't give up on him, Annie. If he's lying, he's going back to jail. But until they prove that, I have to stand by him."

"Zoe," Annie said, "why would I lie about this?"

"Maybe you both just misunderstood each other." Zoe sighed. "I don't know, Annie. What happened between you anyway? I thought you and Jimmy used to be so in love."

On her end of the line, Annie was quiet. In that space, Zoe's mind rolled back through the years, back to her childhood and adolescence in that dark wooden house where every footfall held danger. She couldn't bring herself to think that her father's violence towards his only daughter was being manifested again in Jimmy. How could Jimmy ever do to a woman what he had seen their father do to her?

"Annie . . . ?" she said.

"Oh Zoe," Annie said softly. "It's a sad story and you

wouldn't want to hear it anyway. Jimmy's lucky to have a sister like you. But he's violent, Zoe. Underneath it all, he can be brutal."

"There was a time," Zoe whispered, "when I was lucky to have a brother like him."

"Your brother needs help," Annie said. "You can't help him by being blind."

Zoe quietly put down the phone. What else could she do, she thought. She sat for a long time, staring down at her hands, remembering Annie and Jimmy as teenagers, giggling as they stole into the back bedroom when they thought no one was noticing.

Zach figured he would start with Annie's room. He would fix the broken window lock, paint the walls, sand the floors, and change the very air in there. Fingerprint powder still dusted the window ledge and the edges of the floor so that Jimmy's ghost still hovered in the shadows, and Annie had taken to sleeping nights on the old couch under the stairs.

Zach was painting in Annie's room that Saturday morning when Florida came up the stairs with two cups of coffee.

"Bless you, Ma," he said, putting down his brush and taking a cup from her. "I can use some of this."

They went out onto the landing and sat on the top step, not talking as they sipped the bittersweet liquid. It felt like old times.

"So," Florida said after awhile. "How was New York?"

She didn't miss the flash of pain that touched Zach's features. This boy's heart is breaking, she thought, but he's putting on a show.

"Didn't work out," Zach said briefly. Florida studied him with narrowed eyes but said nothing, so he added: "Korie's ex-husband came back into the picture just long enough to die.

Cancer, the doctor said. Nothing was the same after that. She's having a hard time sorting things out." He studied the bottom of his cup, empty now. "I can't help her," he whispered.

"Give it time," Florida said softly. "Time's the healer."

Zach hoped Florida meant that Korie would find healing, and then find her way back to him, because Zach didn't want to be healed of his feelings for her. But he didn't know how long he could go on like this. At every waking moment, the sheer ache of missing her threatened to overwhelm him, and he had to school himself to rise each morning and function in spite of it.

He heard the key in the front door and he and Florida watched as Neal came in, his face still slightly discolored and puffy from the beating Jimmy had given him a few weeks before. Neal was smiling self-consciously as a slender young woman followed him through the door. He grinned up at his mother, who was dressed in a yellow house dress, and Zach, who was barechested and barefoot, wearing old, cut-off jeans.

"This is Samantha," he said almost shyly. "Samantha, that's my mom and my brother, Zachary."

"You didn't tell me she was so pretty," Florida said graciously, rising and walking down the stairs to greet her.

You also didn't tell us she was white, Zachary thought as he stood also.

Florida took the girl's hands in hers and studied her face.

"How old are you, child?"

"Twenty one, ma'am," she said.

"You don't look a day over sixteen. What did you say you do?"

"She didn't, Ma," Zach interrupted. "Nice to meet you, Samantha. Before the interrogation starts, come have a seat."

"Thank you," Samantha smiled. Her reddish hair was thick and long and curly, and was caught in a fat ponytail. Her skin was winter pale, almost translucent. Her eyes were green and piercing, and she had a sweet, shy smile. It was her smile combined with her small, slender frame that made her seem so young.

Neal ushered her into the living room where she and Florida took seats on the sofa. Zach lounged in the arched doorway of the kitchen.

"I'm a preschool teacher," Samantha told Florida. "But I'm studying classical piano."

"She wants to be a concert pianist," Neal put in. "She can play like you wouldn't believe." Like an angel, he thought, but didn't say.

Samantha looked down at her hands. "I'm not *that* good," she said. "At least, not yet. If it doesn't work out, I guess I could always teach piano."

"Oh, honey," Florida said, "don't sell your dream short like that. Sure you can always teach piano, but you have to *believe* that you'll be playing that piano on concert stages around the world. You have to *see* yourself doing it!"

Neal smiled broadly at Samantha, as if to say, *I told you my mama was something special.* Florida didn't indulge him.

"Neal, boy, aren't you going to offer your young lady something to drink?"

Samantha flushed red at the "your young lady" as Zach stepped forward.

"You sit down, Neal. I'll get it." Turning to Samantha: "What would you like?"

"Anything soft," she said.

"I'll have a Coke," Neal said.

Zach looked at Florida. "Whatever Samantha's having," she said.

As Zach moved around the kitchen, getting out glasses and ice and sodas and pouring their drinks, he didn't feel quite easy. This Samantha seemed a nice enough girl, and he supposed she had to like Neal to be sitting up here in his house, in the midst of his family, in the black part of town. But they were safe enough in this neighborhood. No one here would hurt them simply for walking down a street together, even if they did stare at them a beat too long or mutter under their breath. It wouldn't necessarily be like that in the white part of town.

Zach returned to the living room carrying three tall glasses of orange soda and a Coke on a tray. He served them all, and was about to sit with his own glass in the straight-backed chair near the stairs when Florida said, "Zach, honey, go put on a shirt. This is Samantha's first time in our house."

"Oh, that's all right," Samantha said quickly, looking away. Zach realized that she had been watching him surreptitiously and Florida had seen it. He was so used to being shirtless in his home, it hadn't occurred to him that it might make a young white girl uncomfortable. Maybe she wasn't really used to being around black folks, wasn't used to the sight of so much chocolate, at least not close up. Neal himself was light-skinned, nearer to her own skin color, with reddish brown hair that was curly rather than kinky, and a smooth roundish face splashed with freckles. Zach sensed Samantha trying to figure out the dissimilarity between her new boyfriend and the rest of his family. Once or twice, he had caught her staring at the framed black-and-white photograph on the side table. The picture showed Florida's four kids sitting on the front stoop with some of their friends from the neighborhood. Florida had snapped the picture at a moment when the children were laughing, full of the incorrigible joy they could always seem to muster in those days. But at the center of the group, six-year-old Neal sat on twelve-year-old Zachary's knee. His small face was incongruously pale and solemn amid the radiant black faces of his siblings.

Zach was glad, as he set down his drink and left the room to get a shirt, that Neal seemed oblivious to Samantha's confusion. Neal himself had never known his father, the man who had been his mother's secret lover. Mr. Hendricks's skin had been leathery and brown, no, orange—Zach clearly remembered his boyhood impression that the carpenter traveled in a field of orange light—and his hair had been rough and curly, but he'd been a white man just the same. Yet to Florida, he had simply been the man she grew to love, whose color had been unimportant once she got to know him. To everyone else, Mr. Hendricks had been that white carpenter who worked in their home and moved comfortably among them, playing with the children and running errands for Florida sometimes—to the store for milk or diapers, to the laundromat on the next street to switch clothes to the dryer. After a while, the Piper kids, and even their neighbors, forgot to notice that Mr. Hendricks was white. He was just "Mr. Hendricks."

Such was the nature of affection, Zach thought as he pulled on a sweatshirt and neatly rolled up the frayed ends of his paint-spattered cutoffs. Because Florida's kids had liked Mr. Hendricks, they had never questioned their mother's allegiance to him. Instead, they had taken their cues from her, never letting their minds notice that when their father came home from his long absences, Mr. Hendricks swept up the sawdust from his endless jobs around the house, packed up his tools, and was gone. When their father left again, Mr. Hendricks was back, fixing the stairs, and then fixing rotten floorboards, the ceilings, the porch railing. Always something. Always some reason to spend a few hours each week in their home. And he had treated Florida's kids kindly, playing jacks on the floor with Annie, reading story books to Zachary, indulging Ben's endless queries about his tools and his trade and regaling them all with stories about his island childhood. By the time they were old enough to question the kindly white man's presence in their lives, Mr. Hendricks was dead and gone, leaving Neal among them, looking for all the world like the carpenter.

"We're heading down to Wilmington," Neal was saying as

Zach came back into the living room. "There's a jazz arts festival in town there this afternoon." He glanced over at Zachary. "Hey bro, can I tip with your car?"

Since his return to Philadelphia, Zachary had taken back the old blue Rambler from Neal. "Oh, I get it," Zach joked. "If it wasn't for my car, you wouldn't have brought your girl over. He thinks I won't tell him no in front of you. Well, hell no little brother!"

Neal protested and Zach cuffed him playfully. "No, little brother. You can have it. I'm not going anywhere. You and Samantha have fun"

Zach didn't feel like going back to painting after they left. He felt tired. Something about the way Neal and Samantha had skipped laughing down the front steps had reminded him of the times Korie had visited him in Philadelphia, and they'd stopped by his mother's house and, just like Neal and Samantha, had left giggling with delight, knowing the wondrous hours of love that stretched before them. Well, Zach was happy for his brother, even if Neal's joy in finding Samantha underscored his own loss.

Suddenly, he realized that this very decision to paint Annie's room had been an attempt to recapture his time with Korie, to call back those last days they'd spent together, painting her house. It was as if painting had become for him a kind of symbolic act, a gesture he made when he felt outside a situation and wanted to find a way in. He had felt locked out of Korie's life at the end, helpless in the face of her grief and her addiction, and so they'd fixed up her house. Now, here was his sister, Annie, ambushed by an old nightmare. Zach saw that in trying to renovate her room he was doing the same thing, trying to find a path into her pain, and, maybe, a way to help her out of it.

Mr. Hendricks had taught him that.

The old carpenter had fixed things, was always fixing broken things around their house, because this fixing, Zach understood now, had represented his only continuous access to Florida's life. And Florida always seemed to be happy when Mr. Hendricks was there. She would bring him coffee and cake in the winter, tea and toast with strawberry preserves in the summer, and she'd sit with him talking and laughing and whispering sometimes as he fixed up the house. Then her husband Hanson would come home to sleep off his drinking, and invariably he would bring with him a change in Florida's mood. But when Hanson left once more, Mr. Hendricks's industry had made their mother laugh again, had made her step lightly in the house again, had brought a shine to her eyes and a luster to her hair.

Without ever knowing that he was absorbing such a lesson, Zach had learned that a man might fix things around the house, and that the very act of fixing things might bring the joy back into a woman's heart.

Except, it hadn't quite worked the way with Korie. He couldn't simply patch her heart the way he might patch her walls. And it probably wouldn't work that way for Annie, either, for it hadn't been the *carpentry* that had made their mother laugh, it had been the carpenter himself.

Just as Zach was trying to decide whether to clear away the brushes and paints for the day, or finish the wall he had started, the phone rang. It was Joseph Marsalay, the transplanted Nigerian who was his boss at the Springfield Juvenile Home in the Bronx, telling him that he'd extended his leave for as long as he could, and either he came back to work starting a week from Monday or he resign right then.

Zach had never been one to agonize unduly about giving up a paycheck. When a job ended for him, it was generally the clients whom he had served who made the leaving hard—

clients like Grant and Margie at the Carson Agency, and the troubled teenagers he'd just barely begun to counsel at Springfield. But the truth was, he could get past even that. He trusted that there were others more qualified than he was, and equally as dedicated who would step into his shoes. He supposed the easy refuge of his mother's house and a kind of native belief in the benevolence of the universe, made it possible to hold such a laissez-faire attitude about employment. But this job at the Springfield Juvenile Home had come to mean something more to him than a paycheck. It had become a barometer of his future with Korie. Without it, he could no longer pretend that he was headed back to a cozy domestic arrangement with her in New York.

On the other hand, Korie hadn't called him even once since he came back to Philadelphia.

"All right, Joseph," Zach said after thinking for a moment. "I guess it wouldn't be fair to hang you up any longer. So I resign. I just want you to know you've been great, man."

"Save it," Joseph Marsalay chuckled. "If you ever decide to come back to New York, give me a call. We'll see what's we can do."

"Thanks, man."

He put down the phone with an odd sinking feeling of closure. It had been a month since he'd left New York.

Why hadn't she called?

He wandered over to the window, and looked out onto Quincy Street. At the corner of Mission Avenue, Jimmy Jones was standing in front of Neal, blocking his path to the driver's side of Zach's car. Samantha was already inside the car with her head craned towards the exchange taking place between Neal and Jimmy. Zach was about to dash down the stairs and run towards Mission when he saw Neal elbow past Jimmy, get into the car, and drive off.

Now what had that little scene been about? Zach wondered. He watched as Jimmy kicked at an empty soda bottle lying against the curb. It shattered into pieces, which Jimmy crushed under his boot as he turned and stalked down Quincy, towards Spark's Bar, no doubt to cool his temper with a draft of beer.

Jimmy had been idling outside the grocery store on the corner of Bachelor and Quincy, about to light a cigarette, when Neal and Samantha came laughing down the steps of Florida's house and turned down the street. Before he thought about what he was doing, Jimmy blew out the match, stuffed the loose cigarette in his pocket and began walking in their direction, his steps quickening as an impulse to make Neal pay for messing up his chances with Annie surfaced in him.

He caught up with them near the corner of Mission Avenue. Neal was opening the door of the blue Rambler, the same rusty old bucket he'd seen Zachary chugging around in. Neal held open the door for his girl, who dipped into the front seat as Jimmy approached.

"Neal Hendricks!" Jimmy called out. "I see you done got yourself a white girl. Well, I guess knowin' who your daddy is, it make some kinda sense."

Samantha looked stricken. Her eyes searched Neal's face for some sign of how she should act. Neal straightened up and turned slowly towards Jimmy.

"Neal Piper's the name," he said, his tone almost conversational.

"Nah, it's Neal *Hendricks*, man. Don't tell me you ain't never heard you the bastard child of your mama and that old white dude she was humpin' back then. Let's see? Yep, that's about right. That was right when you was born."

"What are you saying?" Neal's voice was dangerously low, his eyes narrowed to icy green slits.

"Your daddy ain't your daddy, man. Hell, everybody in the whole neighborhood know that 'cept you."

Neal wanted to charge Jimmy and take him down, wanted to pick up the fight from where they'd left off. He wanted to pound his smug sneer into a bloody pulp, to erase him from the concern of Annie, Samantha, Florida. Himself. But he had enough presence of mind to know that he couldn't engage him now. Not with Samantha sitting in the car, tense with fear as to what came next. And he didn't want to introduce Samantha to that side of him, the cold, vengeful core that he had discovered in himself that night Jimmy broke into Annie's room. Jimmy probably didn't think a skinny kid from the block could beat him. But Neal knew something Jimmy probably never would. All it would take for Neal to level him was a careful strategy and the heart to carry it through.

"Get outta my face, you piece a shit," Neal spat now. "You disrespected my sister, my mother, my woman, me. Don't think I'll forget that."

"So what you gonna do, punk?" Jimmy stepped back and balled up his fists, a menacing glint in his eye. "Be some hero to impress your white girl? Pu-leese. I could take you with my eyes closed." He looked towards Samantha. "You're kind of nice, though," he said, pursing his lips.

Neal gazed at Jimmy, considering just how he would make him beg for mercy. He stared at him so long that Jimmy started to fidget in his boots and feel foolish. At last, Neal pushed past him and went around to the driver's door. He opened it, got into the car, revved the engine, and took off, leaving Jimmy standing by the curb.

They drove in silence for many miles, not wanting to underline the ugliness of what had just occurred, pretending not to notice the gulf that had opened between their worlds. There were no smoldering brutes like Jimmy Jones in the genteel world of classical piano that Samantha had been raised in, and she trembled at the violence she'd felt in Jimmy—and in Neal, too. It was her first glimpse of that side of him, but she wasn't at all surprised to discover he possessed a vein of steel. Deep down, she'd known he would handle the situation with Jimmy. And if things had got out of hand, she knew he would have fought as fiercely for her as he had for his sister, Annie, that night of the thunderstorm.

But there was incredible sweetness, too, in this new world she had entered. There was a tenderness in Neal that no other boy had ever shown her, a sensitivity combined with that gritty streetwise quality that secretly thrilled her. She looked across at him, hunched over the steering wheel, his brows furrowed.

"What did he mean?" she asked carefully. "About your daddy?"

Neal shrugged, his eyes peeled on the highway, his energy still bristling.

"I don't know what he was talking about," he said briefly.

"He said your father was white," Samantha persisted.

"My pop is dead," Neal said. "He was a strong black man, black as midnight. He died when I was fourteen. Had a stroke. He and my mom never did live together, not after I was born anyway. But he was a fine father anyway."

"Who do you look like?"

Again Neal shrugged. "Throwback, I guess. I don't look like either one."

Samantha forced herself to let the matter rest; clearly Neal did not want to pursue it. But Samantha knew in her heart of hearts what Neal would not let himself consider, much less admit to her. His father had been a white man, not that midnight black one who had apparently claimed him with no question. No, he was what they used to call a mulatto. These days, the correct term was *biracial*. The word itself didn't matter though. The fact was, Neal was half white; it was as plain as the spatter of freckles across his face.

• • •

The thing Samantha would never understand, Neal thought as he turned off I-95 onto the local road into Wilmington, was that it didn't matter what Jimmy said about who his daddy was. It wouldn't even matter if Jimmy was right. The fact was, his soul was that of a black man, Hanson Piper's son, and no amount of mixture in his blood would change that fact.

He knew his daddy Hanson hadn't been an angel. And there had always been neighbor talk of the man who used to come around their house when Neal was nothing but a runt. He hadn't given it much thought till now. He'd always dismissed the talk as so much gossip, for it seemed Florida had often been the subject of one rumor or another. Besides, the one time he'd asked his mama how come he didn't look like the rest of them, Florida had hugged him to her side and cooed that he wasn't different from the family at all, why he looked just like her mama's daddy, a tall, skinny, high-yella man.

It was true he had continued to feel like the odd child among his siblings. But in third grade, he had met a little albino boy in his class named Alfred, and it all became clear to him. Alfred's brothers and sisters were all as brown as walnuts, but Alfred was starch white, with kinky yellow hair and myopic red-rimmed eyes. The other kids made fun of how he looked, but Neal had befriended him at once. He could see that they had something in common; he could see that, like Alfred, he was an albino. That explained why he looked the way he did, paler than his siblings, with light green eyes and rough red hair. He was so sure of the explanation that he never queried anyone about it, just studied Alfred from across the classroom, played with him during recess, and put the matter from his mind.

And yet, the day he met Samantha, the questions were suddenly roused in him again. Why had he been so drawn to her? It had been her music of course, the way her fingers floated across the keys, barely touching them yet producing an exquisite sound that made his heart soar. But it had been more than that. It had been the very paleness of her skin, the silky frizz of her reddish hair, the slenderness of her form—all of it had reminded him of himself. It had been like looking into a mirror and finding at last a reflection that was familiar, comfortable. Opening himself up to Samantha had felt like finally coming home.

In the weeks after the encounter with Jimmy, Neal found himself less and less able to ignore the accretion of mean dramas that had entered his life: Jimmy's attempted rape of his sister; his implied threat to Samantha; and perhaps most disquieting of all, the news, so roughly delivered, that Hanson was not his father. To Neal, the news had had an unmistakable ring of truth, much as he had denied it to Samantha. To himself, he continued to insist that it made no difference, but then he would find himself wrestling with the thought that his mother, in having another man's child and passing it off as Hanson's, had acted like a common whore. He tried to push the thought away, but it kept popping back to the forefront of his mind, torturing him with the sense that he was being disloyal to the woman who had been there through his every childhood whimper and adolescent scrape.

There were questions Neal would have liked to have answered—mainly, was Jimmy just spewing a cruel lie—but he couldn't bring himself to broach the subject with anyone, not Zachary and certainly not Florida. For him to utter the words would give his worst fears the force of reality, and he wasn't ready to accept that. Sometimes, he was even able to convince himself that Jimmy had it all wrong, and he berated himself for being drawn in by the hateful delusions of a foul-mouthed drunk. But, finally, the plausibility of Jimmy's words had pierced Neal's increasingly desperate denial, and it was then that the malice he felt towards Jimmy hardened into stone.

II

The Rooms

KORIE WALKED DOWN THE SHORT FLIGHT OF STEPS AND stood facing a weathered screen door, its green paint flaking in long strips. Through the torn mesh of the door, she could see into the small, fluorescent-lit room where gray metal chairs were lined up in rows. At the front of the room stood a square Formica table with more chairs around it. The chairs in the room were almost all occupied, and Korie hesitated, calculating where she would sit and how she would move through the rows of people to get there. She braced for the moment she would open the door and all faces would turn to her, their expressions curious and pitying and full of a knowing kind of misery that was eager for her company. One more person to offer a lifeline, the faces would say; one more soul to share a nightmare of addiction and torment that might make their own troubled lives seem reclaimable.

Korie made her face blank as she maneuvered through the room and took the only empty seat in the last row. A man sitting at the head of the table smiled slightly in her direction and continued speaking to the people in the room. "I would have given *my life* for that next shot of rum and that next hit of crack cocaine," he was saying. "It didn't matter that my furniture was on the street, my wife had taken the kids, I'd been fired from my job and my bank account was dry. All I wanted was to find me a bottle and some rock and the rest of the world could go fuck itself . . ." Everyone in the room seemed riveted, taking in the man's words with a soul hunger that Korie at once sank into. It was the same hunger that yawned in her gut when she opened her eyes each morning, the same miserable craving with which she pursued the narcotic promise of amnesia. But for Korie, as for everyone gathered in that room, the payoff had become more and more elusive.

Korie had never been in this particular AA room before. A month after Zach had left, she'd gone to a Narcotics Anonymous meeting over on the East Side, but hadn't identified with the people there. She had sat at the back of the room then, too, and had spent the whole meeting reassuring herself that she wasn't as far gone as this speaker or that one. She was quite clear on the fact that she was an addict, but she reasoned that she was still a functioning citizen; she still held down her job. She told herself that the NA group was more hardcore than she was, made up of ex-cons and bar brawlers and dope dealers and thieves. She didn't belong among them. At least, that was how she had perceived it then. Korie understood now that she hadn't been quite ready to quit getting high. She was still only dabbling in the notion of sobriety.

She had run out of the room at the end of the Narcotics Anonymous meeting and called Simona from a pay phone. It was just past eleven on a Monday evening in November, and Simona had invited her to come over. She had gone there without her usual stash of marijuana—before the NA meeting she had decided to quit smoking it, after all—and when

Simona told her she was fresh out of pot, Korie decided to do a little coke instead.

She found she loved the way coke made her feel. It left her mentally buzzed, her mind racing with sudden solutions and glorious flights of inspiration, rather than moodily introspective and dull the way she had begun to feel after smoking grass. She hadn't realized then what Simona could have told her, what she would have seen for herself had she observed her friend closely enough. Just a few weeks later, though, she would discover that once the body learned to crave it, cocaine was a deceitful high; you couldn't stop chasing it until the powder was gone and then the crash kicked your ass. Korie dreaded the crash; her insides would ball into a jangled mass of hostility, her mind humming with undirected fury, unable to form words from the images whizzing though her brain. Simona held her silently at such times, until on a night when Korie lay trembling in her arms, she offered her a little white pill.

"Valium helps you float down easier," she whispered.

Korie by then was past reason and so she swallowed the tablet without protest and discovered that what Simona promised was indeed true. The jagged edges began to soften as the world eased away from her skin, the weight of it no longer pressing into her, making her feel like her brain would implode. After a while, she ceased to care much about anything. The details of her life seemed far-off and irrelevant and she was able to sleep.

That became their pattern. Coke and marijuana at the start of the evening. Valium and white wine at the end of it. During the mornings at the magazine, Korie felt raw and strung out but she was as obsessive about her work as she had always been, and so no one seemed to notice that, emotionally, she was falling apart. At lunchtime, she escaped from the building and walked alone to Central Park. There she found a particular shale outcrop hidden by leafy trees where she would sit, roll a joint, and smoke it. The day went better after that. Mostly she sat in her office wordsmithing her pieces, setting up interviews and photo shoots for her stories, or browsing through magazines and newspapers. She was actually quite good at conceiving new stories while high, and she'd sit at her computer and type up page-long proposals for each idea, which she then slipped into her editor's mailbox. If her editor, Jack Somers, wondered why she didn't just walk down the hall and put the proposal in his hand, he never said. He seemed to genuinely like the ideas she was pitching, which allowed Korie to comfort herself that her use of narcotics was under control.

Sometimes, though, she would be called for a layout meeting on one of her stories, and she would panic that this time, for sure, she would give herself away. But so far, standing in front of the layout table with the editor in chief, photo editor, art director, and Jack Somers, she had managed to acquit herself sufficiently. She thought she saw Jack Somers regarding her through narrowed eyes once or twice, but then decided she was just being paranoid. Surely if her editor were concerned, he would call her in. And the fact was, Korie was hardly the only druggie on staff. One of the assistant art directors was rumored to lock himself in a men's room stall several times a day, and male staffers who happened to stop in swore they heard him delicately sniffing something inside the stall. Jack Somers himself was famous for occasionally smoking pot in his office after hours, although he was far more partial to whiskey than weed.

Still, Korie knew that just because her colleagues indulged didn't mean she was immune from repercussions should they uncover her own drug use. She was, after all, a lowly reporter, and a black girl to boot. They wouldn't hesitate to throw her onto the garbage heap of stereotypes she was sure they all carried in their liberal white heads. She knew they couldn't handle her or any nonwhite employee being less than unimpeachable in their work and conduct. Any deviation was too threatening; any chinks in the race armor and she would be out the door.

That Christmas and New Year's Day came and went. Korie stayed high, sleeping over at Simona's house most nights. Sometimes, they lay naked together and fondled each other on Simona's narrow bed, and once Korie put her lips on Simona's smooth brown nipples and sucked them contentedly. Simona stroked her forehead for a while, then pushed her head away and went into the living room for another hit of coke.

Korie lay on the bed, her fingers moving down her stomach and finding below her abdomen the tiny mound of her clitoris; she brushed her fingers back and forth across it, her breath quickening. This was another thing she liked about the coke— it made her horny. She lay there masturbating slowly, thinking, not of Simona now, but of Zachary, of his hard brown torso poised above her, his pubic slope disappearing between her legs. She could feel his arms pressing her into him, the pressure of his lips against her throat. She could see his face contorted at the moment of orgasm, his eyes screwed shut, his teeth bared, and she could *feel* rather than hear the low moan rumbling from the depths of him. Suddenly, the force of missing him was like a wave breaking violently inside her, rising up through her chest, choking her, spilling from her eyes. When Simona came back into the room, she was crying softly, her body curled into a tight ball.

Simona sat on the edge of the bed and held out a square mirror, the white powder on it arranged in three neat lines.

"Here, honey," she said. As Korie unfurled her naked body and took the cut straw that lay next to the lines of coke on the mirror, Simona whispered, "I wish you loved me, sweet pea. It would be so simple if you did."

Korie sucked in two lines quickly and gave the mirror back to Simona.

"I *do* love you," she said as the white powder exploded in her head, brightening the gloomy corners of her brain. "You're my girl, Sim."

"No," Simona said, but not sadly. Her voice was merely matter of fact. "I'm just a distraction, baby, and that's fine. But you'll get tired of all this soon and then you'll see how empty your life is." She paused to sniff the last line of coke, then reached down for a little white envelope of pills that lay on the floor next to the bed. She popped one tablet and held the envelope out to Korie. Korie shook her head.

"Not yet," she said.

"I have news for you, girl," Simona continued after a while. "You're not a lesbian. You're just a lonely burnt child who wants so badly to understand Sam. But *he* was the gay one, not you. If it weren't for these drugs, you wouldn't even be here."

"I *do* love you, Simona," Korie repeated. "I've *always* loved you."

"Yeah," Simona grunted, "but not that way."

"Are you a lesbian?" Korie asked her then, even though she thought she knew the answer. "What about all your boyfriends?"

"I'm whatever you want me to be." Simona shrugged. "Oh, Korie, don't be so naive. Everything's not always so cut and dry. I mean, I love women but that doesn't mean I've never loved men. Sometimes it's not the gender that draws you, it's a person's spirit."

"Make love to me, Simona," Korie begged suddenly. Tears were pricking the backs of her corneas again, but she blinked them back as Simona planted a dry kiss on her lips. Korie closed her eyes and parted her lips slightly, the tip of her tongue pushing forward to meet Simona's. They explored each other's mouths almost idly, then Simona pulled back. She looked steadily into Korie's eyes and was silent for a long time, as if trying to decide something. At last, she brushed her lips lightly across Korie's cheek and murmured in her ear: "The truth is, girlfriend, I'm not who you want. We both know that. But we can pretend."

Late in the summer, it began to dawn on Korie that she had to get help—for both her sake and Simona's. The two of them were riding a riptide of addiction, and Korie was dimly aware that she was at least partly the cause of Simona's increasing use of coke. And Simona wasn't handling it so well anymore. She called in sick at work too much, and when she did show up, was surlier than usual with the editors and downright caustic with her fellow reporters. Her stories had also been late to production a few times.

One afternoon, on a day when Simona had called in sick, Korie stood with her fist poised to knock on Jack Somers closed door. But she hesitated, because she could hear Simona's editor inside, talking to Jack about Simona. "Her writing's fallen off," Marcie Steinway was saying. "The crisp insights just aren't there. I can't figure out what's going on with her, but I'm afraid to approach her. She seems so angry most of the time. And when she's not angry, it's like she couldn't care less."

Korie had been about to hand in a file she had just completed, a profile of a young New York violinist who had grown up poor and still performed her concerts in garage sale gowns, seducing every ear who heard her. Suddenly, Korie wasn't so sure about the story. Perhaps she'd better give it another read, make sure it contained her own brand of "crisp insights." She let her hand fall to her side and turned and walked back to her office. She sat at her desk, fighting down a torrent of remorse and fear. She knew if they were talking about Simona's work, Jack and Marcie had to be discussing her own work as well. It was too much of a coincidence, the two of them huddled in there behind closed doors. Korie couldn't afford to lose her job, and neither could Simona. They'd long ago snorted and smoked up their savings, and Korie had already been late with her rent two months in a row. But, as much as the prospect of eviction frightened her, another thought disturbed her more: Simona and Korie, the only two women of color on the magazine's staff, couldn't afford to feed into their white editors' hardwired notions about black folks being nothing but junkies at heart. They weren't just letting themselves down, they were messing things up mightily for the next nonwhite who applied there for a job. As all the implications swirled in Korie's head, she saw how she and Simona had egged each other on, each shielding the other from the truth of her dependency, each indulging the other in the dangerous illusion that she could fool the world.

She didn't go over to Simona's last night. Instead, she went straight home and called her friend to tell her what she'd heard. But Simona's phone rang without an answer. Korie wasn't surprised. She could imagine Simona strung out in her apartment after a day of snorting coke. Most likely, she'd turned off the phone, quoting to herself the writer Dorothy Parker's famous response to a ringing telephone: "What fresh hell is this?"

What fresh hell, indeed.

Korie was too restless to sit in her apartment, but she knew if she went over to Simona's, as every sinew of her being was urging her to do, she would spend this night as she had spent most others in the past several months. No, she wouldn't see Simona tonight. She didn't want to abandon her, but she had to get a handle on her own trouble first, and then maybe she could become a true friend to Simona rather than just a convenient drug buddy. And so, here she was, seated in the back of an AA meeting, listening to the speaker describe a life of unquenchable yearning so familiar it might well be her own.

KORIE

I want so much to disappear, to run to my parents' house, or further, to Ocho Rios, my mother's north coast refuge, to swim and laugh and taste the salt on my skin, and hold my face to the sun and breathe as free as I remember doing when I was a child. I want to find my mother and curl up under her cool, talcum-scented arm and close my eyes against the relentless furl of my life.

On Sunday night, I call Osgood and Alice. I haven't spoken to them in many months. They have called me several times, but they always get my answering machine.

My mother answers the phone.

"Mom," I whisper, suddenly so broken I want to cry.

"Korie?" she says.

I open to the concern in her voice; I dispense with the preliminaries.

"Mommy," I say, "Sam died."

"Oh my Lord!" Alice bursts out, and I hear her calling my father, telling him to pick up the extension. "When?" she says, coming back to me. "How?"

"He was sick for a long time," I answer. I cannot admit just yet that I have kept this news from them for an entire year. "The doctors said it was lymphoma, but it might have been AIDS."

"Why didn't you tell us?" Alice says. "Why didn't you call? Oh, Korie, love, you didn't have to go through all that alone."

Osgood is on the line now.

He says, "Hello, Korie." I can hear the pipe clenched in his teeth. "It's been a while."

"Daddy?"

"Sam died," my mother tells him. "Korie thinks it might have been AIDS."

"How are you doing, Korie?" my father says quietly.

"Okay," I say, and then I start sobbing.

"I want to see you," I whisper. "I want to come home."

"Of course," they say in unison. "Of course."

I take two weeks of vacation from the magazine and fly home. As I walk down the steps from the plane onto the tarmac and into the brilliant Jamaican sunshine, I am aware of my guard slipping, aware of my race lenses falling away. Full, deep breaths fill my lungs, and despite the weight of the sorrow I have been carrying, my shoulders become loose and expansive.

Osgood and Alice are at the airport to meet me. I make them out on the waving gallery: Alice in a cream kaftan is golden and elegant as always; Osgood is wearing a white bush jacket, his hair is grayer than I remember, and the bowl of his pipe is clutched in one seamy hand. He is waving vigorously with the other hand, a broad smile on his brown face, and Alice, too, has her palm in the air, though her expression is more pensive. I wave back, feeling suddenly self-conscious and needy. I am relieved when I get to the customs portico and they can't see me anymore.

I clear customs, get my bag from the luggage carousel, and then I am outside the terminal, in their arms. They both hug me at once, so that I am crushed between them, my face buried in their clothes. All over again, I want to cry, but I choke down the tears. Presently they release me, and we walk, arms linked together, to their car. As my father swings my suitcase into the trunk of the old silver Volvo, I step away from the curb. I feast my eyes on the blue-green hills in the distance and suck in the bright yellow air.

It is good to be home.

Home, I suddenly realize, is not a place you can run to, or a place you can leave. Home is not a geographical concept at all.

All this time I have been seeking a *place* to belong, only to discover that the bounty of home has been securely within me—and within those I love—all along.

I do not drink or smoke reefer for the weeks I am in my parents' house. But I am so raw that I open my father's liquor cabinet more than once, and stare at the clear amber liquid, contemplating a swig. Osgood and Alice tiptoe around me. At first, they mistake my efforts to stay sober for grief over Sam. Alice questions me gently about his sickness, our separation five years ago, his death. I tell her everything. I even tell her about the drugs. And I tell her about Zachary, about his goodness and warmth and how, in spite of it all, I pushed him away. And at night, she repeats my confidences to Osgood. I know she does, because the next morning, he rubs my head in a rough-tender way, and doesn't know what to say.

"Have you been tested?" the doctor in Osgood asked me one day.

I shake my head.

"Come with me to the hospital this morning," he doesn't ask, but commands. "You need to be tested."

A couple of days later we get the news. I am HIV negative. Osgood hands me the tiny sheet of paper that holds my test results, and doesn't mention it again.

I carry the paper on my person for days, in my pocket, against my breast. Sometimes, I take it out and unfold it carefully, and after reading it again, just to sure, I hold it against my cheek and I pray. The little piece of paper is my reprieve, my passport back. Reading it again and again, I think I can feel the whole spectrum of light breaking over me, like so many colors, like so much hope, and I realize finally that Sam is gone, and I miss him terribly, but I am here, and my responsibility now is to continue on.

For the rest of my visit, Alice feeds me fresh fruit and sweet juices and delectable suppers. Osgood holds at bay the parade of well-meaning relatives, sensing I cannot handle their sympathy and curiosity just yet. Most of all, my parents stroke my cheek, pat my shoulder, *touch* me. They tell me with their dark, sad eyes that they love me and want me to be well.

When I go back to New York at the end of the week, I know what I must do.

Hello, my name is Korie and I have fifteen days.

It is so hard to be sober, so humiliating this minute-by-minute struggle not to pick up a drug. The meetings help, though. One day at a time, they say in AA. I find in those rooms the company of people whose emotional landscape looks much like my own. My ravaged heart does not scare them. Indeed, it comforts them—as I am finding that their own painful stories are a comfort to me. Somehow, when I am with these fellow addicts, I am less alone, less capable of self-inflicted injury. It is an unexpected blessing that this roomful of people understand how I am made. They are intimate with the very construct of my soul and are showing me where within it serenity lies.

I was supposed to be in the field today, working with Eugene Weeks, the photographer assigned to the Hudson riverkeeper story. The riverkeeper is a sandy-haired, ruddy-faced zealot by the name of Christopher Hargrove. He patrols the Hudson by boat, apprehending industrial and private polluters and bringing them to justice. A former sixties flower child and recovered alcoholic, he has a frightening sense of mission, which while I was interviewing him left me slightly uneasy and more than a little bit tired. I admire him, though. I envy his sure sense of his place in the world, his lack of doubt about his purpose. Eugene is supposed to photograph him on the river, doing what he does, and as the writer on the story, I'm supposed to go with him. But it is raining out, so our plans get soaked. Eugene can't reschedule for three weeks, which is a problem, because the trees along the banks of the Hudson are in fiery autumn glory right now, and the leaves will have already started falling by then. Now is the moment to capture the jaded radiance of fall, but Eugene has other commitments. My editor is acting like I should be able to twist Eugene's arm, make him shift his schedule around so he can do the shoot sooner. Like if I can't get him to do that, I'm failing at my job. The truth is I couldn't care less whether the leaves disappear from the trees. The Hudson Valley in autumn reminds me of Sam, of college evenings in the fall when we used to scramble through that hole in the chain-link fence and sit together on the river rocks, our spirits impossibly full of faith in the redemptive power of changing foliage.

I think I know why Sam died. I think that he chose it, perhaps by default. He sat at the window of his nineteenth-floor studio and watched the river, watched it ebb and flow like the lonely course of his life. He looked towards his future and saw monotony closing in. His imagination faltered. There was nothing more he could think of that he wanted to do. His life had peaked early, in adolescence, when his white senior year classmates voted a copper-colored black boy from across the tracks "Most Likely to Succeed." That was his success—no other could match that triumph over inbred prejudice. It was the newly integrated South. His grandaunt cleaned houses for the parents of the lily-white students who thought him so likely to hold forth.

He saw all the ironies. Perhaps their vision of his potential was merely in stark contrast to what they'd been raised to expect of his kind. And yet, their expectations stymied him. He never quite got past the sense that he was conducting his life before an audience, and that his accomplishments had to confound their stereotypes rather than fill his own heart. He allowed them to define his goals: an Ivy League college, civil rights law, the right kind of income, the right kind of show. But they weren't his goals, really, and so he stumbled after college, then drifted, ebbed and flowed endlessly, like the river from his window, which seemed, if he sat and watched it long enough, to be standing still.

He found some love in his life. He found me. I love him still, love the very air around me which I imagine he inhabits. And there were also men who loved him, most of them in secret, but they failed to give him back the father who had forsaken him, or the mother who gave him away. Then came the day that he decided he was running in place, that he'd never be richer, stronger, better-looking, that his life would forever fail to satisfy, that his days would continue to be a humdrum struggle to pay the bills, his nights an endless cycle of searching for hardbodied thrills.

He wearied of the search, never understanding that his deliverance from monotony and secrecy was within reach all the time. He chose to get sick. He chose to die. There was nothing else he could think of to do. His life bogged down in details, in emotional storms. "These long lives we lead are a slow form of suicide," he once told me. He chose to speed up the pace.

I realized in a meeting last week that I'm not so angry anymore. I think I can finally forgive Sam—not just for dying, but for lying to me about who he knew himself to be. But there is a hole in the region of my heart, a sort of blank space that moves through the days with me, no longer remarkable, simply a fact of my life.

It has been more than a year since Sam died, and many months since Zachary went away. In the rooms, they talk a lot about making amends. I need to make amends to Zach. I ache to see him. I have called him many times since I first went into the rooms, but I lost my nerve and put down the phone as soon as somebody answered. It was never Zach's voice that answered. Perhaps I would have spoken if I'd heard his voice. I don't even know if he is still at his mother's house. And why would he want to talk to me? He gave me himself—heart, mind, and body—through the darkest of times, and I turned away from him, embracing drugs instead.

When he first went back to Philadelphia, he used to call me all the time. There were always messages on my answering machine when I came home. Long nostalgic messages telling me how he missed me, and how the minute I called him, he'd be at my door. He called me *baby* in that sweet sexy way, and explained that he would never love anyone but me. He said he would wait for me until the day I convinced him that it was useless to hope. Unless I told him that, he said, he would wait and pray for the storm clouds inside me to dissipate, and his love to break through.

After a while, I couldn't even listen to his messages. They made me feel guilty and sad. Guilty for the shabbiness with which I treated him; sad that I was, finally, so unworthy of this man, so powerless in my grief and my addiction to substances that I couldn't be for him what he deserved. All I knew back then was that getting high made me feel better, and Zach got in the way of getting high. His presence always made me feel that I had to be responsible for myself, that I had to be conscious of how I was destroying my life.

In the end, though, it was my parents, not Zachary, who orchestrated my surrender, and they didn't have a clue they were doing it. They brought me to submission without ever knowing the abyss into which their only daughter had stared. But the sheer work ethic drilled into me by Osgood and Alice finally ran up the red flag. The message I had learned from them, from my mother in particular, was that one might live with all the high drama of tragedy and despair, so long as one attended to the business of making a living. And true to this instruction, when my work ethic started to fail, and the slippage became visible to everyone, I finally got scared.

There were other things, too, that helped wear me down. For example, I hated going to the drug house. That's how Simona and I referred to it, neither of us having any energy for imagination when it came to procuring our drugs. It was a dingy, first-floor apartment on 150th Street. The windows were covered with black cloth and everyone coming and going from the building looked at you strangely when you stood in front of that door, waiting for Richie or Leon to open it. Richie and Leon were roommates, business partners, really. Richie was white, Jewish. Leon was black, from Harlem. I'd heard the story so often: Their mothers were friends from the time they were babies, and they grew up sharing a playpen, toys, the answers to high school quizzes. Richie was fat and debauched-looking, with curly brown hair, slitty blue eyes, and pink, eternally wet lips. Leon was thin and wiry, and gave off the air of a wise man, a prophet. But it was a false impression, made possible by the drug-induced gleam in his soulfully narrowed eyes, his wispy goatee and flowing dashikis, and the fact that he didn't try to hit on you when you came there to buy drugs the way Richie did.

Simona introduced me to the drug house soon after she came to the magazine. Before that, I'd resorted to buying pot in bodegas and places fronting as variety stores or video arcades. This was the early 1980s, and there were scores of such reefer joints in Harlem, and even in Morningside Heights, where baby-faced white kids from Columbia University entered without any sense that they were putting themselves in jeopardy. They placed their ten-dollar bills on the high ledge of a tiny bulletproof window in the back of the store, and snatched up the plastic dime bag of Colombian weed or Thai stick that was pushed out in return. But, increasingly, the police had started to bust these dens, so that you might go back to your regular joint a week later and find it boarded up, a yellow plastic crime-scene tape across the door. Of course, two weeks later, the den might be open for business again, which meant somebody, somewhere was being paid off. If I'd really thought about it, I'd have had the good sense to feel vulnerable in those places. But the truth was, the only thing that had mattered back then was whether I got to go home with my Thai or Colombian weed.

Simona was hooked up for drugs better than I was and when she offered to introduce me to Richie and Leon, I jumped at the chance. Now that I had an alternative, I didn't mess with the street scene anymore. But the drug house had its drawbacks, too, and, where I was concerned, Richie was chief among them. He leered and stood too close to me with his drooling lips and greasy hair. On the other hand, once I started buying coke, he always had a free hit or two for me whenever I came. I knew what that was about, though. He thought I might get loose enough to play erotic games. Instead, I played dumb, even as I snorted the fat lines he laid out.

Still, I preferred Leon. Leon liked pot better than coke, and we'd smoke a joint together and wander through philosophical realms, reflecting on such subjects as reincarnation and karma and the prophetic potential of dreams. I always prayed, when I set out for the drug house, that Leon would be the one serving. The way it worked was, first you had to call from the corner of the block, which always made me nervous, because there was always a cop car parked by the phone. I suspected that the police had the house under surveillance, and even imagined that they had some device in their car that could pick up conversations from that pay phone. But, just as in the days when

I'd ducked into storefront reefer dens, I played the odds. Okay, they know where I'm going and what I'm getting there, but they won't bust in today. Besides, Richie and Leon had a plaque from the police softball league hanging on their wall, and more than once I'd encountered their cop friends at the house. I decided later that they must get their stash of drugs from the confiscated stuff that never quite made it to evidence lockers. If that was true, then somebody in blue had them under surveillance, but somebody else who wore blue was acting as godfather. I figured it all evened out. And that the day they busted the drug house would be a day when I wasn't there.

But then Richie backed me into a corner one night when we were alone in the apartment. Leon wasn't home, and no other customers were in the living room, and I sat there almost puking as he tried to slobber on my cheek. I ducked under his arm. I tried to laugh and joke and talk about the boyfriend I had waiting for me at home. But Richie was flying that night. His pale white skin had a sheen of sweat, and little beads of perspiration stood out on his forehead and above his lips. His eyes were glassy, the expression in them a little unhinged, and for the first time I realized the ugly potential of my increasingly frequent visits there.

I did, of course, score the drugs I'd come for before I high-tailed it home. I tried never to go there without Simona after that, although once or twice, when Simona couldn't make it but Leon was there, I'd risked it. If Richie answered when I called, I quietly put down the phone. Inevitably, though, I'd call back in half an hour, an hour, all afternoon, waiting for the time that Leon picked up the phone. And every time I found myself back in that bleak place, laying down crisp bills for tiny Ziploc bags of white powder and green buds, my self-respect dipped a little more.

. . .

Tonight, I rented the movie *Drugstore Cowboy*. I sat there mesmerized as I watched it, thinking how precisely this film captures the junkie mindset. "Most people don't know how they're going to feel from one moment to the next," the Matt Dillon character says at the end, "but the junkie has a pretty good idea." That's the thing about drugs. About life. About those of us who feel buffeted by a surfeit of emotion. Drugs hook us because it seems they offer a little certainty. You do the drug, you know how you're going to feel. I guess only when the uncertainty the drug ends up giving becomes greater than the uncertainty of life itself does it become possible for a junkie to dream of quitting.

For me, cocaine became the supreme bad trip. At the end, the only certainty it offered was that I'd feel bad after doing it. But there were litanies of uncertainty: the degree of inner torment; which demons would rise that night; how little money would be left when the dragon was satisfied.

Zach, my love, I am in the rooms, now—that's what us drunks and druggies call AA. There is no place in the world that I am more at peace with myself than in these dingy rooms. Most of them are located in church basements, and the people who assemble here are an extraordinary assortment of lost and found souls: thirtyish types like me, trying to start over; street people in rags who come in for free coffee and to escape the cold; corporate executives down to their last dime; artists, musicians, teachers, housewives, thieves, rich kids, gang kids, firefighters, lawyers, and actors whose faces you've seen on TV. Every strand of existence in this naked city is here in these rooms. Here, as nowhere else I have been, our distinctions pale in the face of our one overwhelming similarity. I go to the rooms, shivering with pain, in the grip of a profound restlessness, paralyzed by the compulsion I feel to get high, and I find people like myself, working to develop the muscle for sobriety. In the rooms, we teach one another to hunker down and rock with the fear. We put our faith in a Higher Power that some of us call God, and blindly trust that power to help us live with the hunger. The platitudes are pure poetry: *One day at a time. Put your troubles on the altar. Keep coming back.* I cling to them like mantras. They are helping me to stay sober, to not crave oblivion so much.

But it is such a struggle. I am grateful, so profoundly grateful that you do not have to see me like this. The fact is, Zachary, I am an addict. But now I am a *recovering* addict. I have sixty-five days.

12
The Secret Savior

WHEN THEY FOUND JIMMY JONES BARELY ALIVE IN Coramantee Park, the tiny quadrangle of brown grass bordered by anemic trees that lay behind Sparks Bar, everyone he had tangled with since returning to Philadelphia became a suspect. Including Neal Piper. Everyone recalled the viciousness of the fight between the two men the night of the storm when, word had it, Jimmy had tried to rape Neal's sister, Annie. Some neighborhood folk had also been watching the afternoon Jimmy threatened Neal and his new white girlfriend. But Jimmy had been roughed up good, his jaw broken, his teeth knocked out, and his spine unceremoniously smashed by blows to his lower back. No one seriously believed that a soft-spoken mama's boy like Neal could have had anything to do with the savage beating Jimmy had received. Police forensics said that the attacker had continued to work Jimmy over with some kind of blunt instrument, perhaps an iron pipe, even after he was down, crushing his pelvis and aggravating the spinal damage. The spinal injury, it turned out, would leave Jimmy paralyzed from the waist down and in a wheelchair for the rest of his natural life.

The police weren't that aggressive about following up on the case, though. To them, Jimmy was bad news, the source of a mushrooming number of complaints at the neighborhood precinct. But this beating ought to keep him relatively quiet in the future, and as far as the Philadelphia PD was concerned, that was a silver lining. Ironically, even Jimmy had something to gain from his condition: It would no doubt induce some leniency on the part of judge or jury in his pending rape case. Jimmy had refused to cop a plea because with his record, the only deals the state would consider involved substantial jail time. So Jimmy had continued to insist that Annie Piper had invited him to her room that night.

In the months that followed, the case had been granted a series of continuances, but had finally been set for trial in three weeks. Now, it would have to be knocked off the court docket again, because Jimmy wouldn't be out of the hospital by then. Besides, there was a good possibility that the state might relent and offer Jimmy's lawyer a more lenient plea bargain. But if it turned out that the case did go to trial and a jury voted to convict, chances were the judge would look at him in his wheelchair and realize that he was hardly a rape or robbery threat now. If Annie Piper didn't press the issue, he might even get probation.

The odd thing was, Jimmy wouldn't identify his attacker—he insisted there had been only one, and that the assailant had worn a football helmet with a tinted face shield and loose black clothes that blended with the night. The assailant, he said, struck him from behind as he was leaving Sparks Bar at three in the morning. The cops found it curious that no one had seen the suspect lurking outside Sparks. A football helmet worn on the street at three in the morning was an incongruous sight. The cops guessed that Jimmy must have blacked out after that, in the sense that alcoholics lose consciousness, because he had no recall of the events that followed. But, blacked out or not, Jimmy apparently put up a ferocious fight, which the police figured was why he got beat so bad—that, and because whoever had done this to Jimmy had *meant* to neutralize him once and for all.

Some days later, Zach had reason to recall that the evening of Jimmy's beating, Neal had come home around eleven, changed into black jeans, a black sweater, and black sneakers, then went out again. No one in the house had thought anything about it, just as they thought nothing of the fact that Neal hadn't returned home for two nights. They'd assumed he spent the time at Samantha's house, as he had often done in the past months. But Zach did think it just a bit odd that when Neal finally did return home, he was wearing new blue slacks, a long-sleeved white shirt, its store-folded creases still crisp, and brand-new docksiders, not the perfectly good pair of black sneakers he'd left the house wearing two nights before. It wasn't just that the clothes were different—Neal could easily have changed over at Samantha's house. It was more that the clothes were new. And there was something else, too. Neal was limping, his arms wrapped around his torso as if every step caused him excruciating pain.

"Neal, you okay, man? What happened?" Zach had asked, going to him.

"Fell off a damned ladder at the job," he muttered. "Was plastering a ceiling at the top of some stairs and the ladder tipped right over. Landed at the bottom of the steps. Pans, trowels, everything fell right on top of me."

"I'll help you downstairs," Zach offered.

"No, man, I can manage," Neal had answered, holding up

his hand. He went gingerly down the stairs to his room, which was in the basement, and had not come out again for the rest of the evening. The next morning, he was gone from the house before dawn.

Zach didn't say anything to Florida or Annie, but he felt uneasy about the way Neal had appeared. He had only just heard the news about Jimmy, but knew nothing yet of what his assailant had been wearing. Later on, though, when those details made the neighborhood rounds, he began to weigh whether Neal could have had anything to do with the assault. Sure, he could have hurt himself falling from a ladder, but the fact that his face didn't have a bruise on it was a minor miracle given the severity of his other injuries. On the other hand, a football helmet with a face shield would have meant that any bruises sustained in a fight would be on his body and easily hidden by clothing, although the pain of those wounds would be harder to conceal.

Zach's misgivings about Neal sat in his chest and grew to be a painful wedge. He had to admit that the idea of Neal way-laying Jimmy in the dark, attacking from behind, was less at odds with the Neal of recent weeks than it might have been, say, even six months ago. Since then a coldness had settled over Neal, a freezing of emotion that Zach had first noticed some-time after the night that Jimmy had broken into Annie's room. Neal had seemed to become secretive overnight, coming and going without stopping to talk much with his family, spending more and more time over at Samantha's. It also troubled Zach that Neal never again brought Samantha home, as if the one time she visited only served to resolve him not to stir that mix again. Zach couldn't quite fathom why, because Samantha's visit had been cordial enough, and Florida and Samantha had seemed to take a genuine liking to each other. Yes, Zach had had doubts about the interracial aspects of things, but he'd figured Neal knew what he was getting into and was prepared to handle it. He hadn't guessed, however, that Neal's chief way of handling it would be to withdraw from his family.

Zach recalled now that the day of Samantha's visit, Neal had asked to borrow his car. He remembered that he'd gone back to Annie's room to paint when they left, and had stopped to watch from the window as Neal exchanged a few words with Jimmy by the car. With Samantha watching from the passenger seat, the encounter had appeared to grow tense, the two men squaring their stances and planting their feet as if getting ready to rush each other. But then Neal abruptly pushed past Jimmy, got into the driver's seat, and drove away.

What had passed between Neal and Jimmy in those minutes? Zach wondered, not for the first time. He had asked Neal about it the next day when he brought back the car, but Neal just shrugged and said, "Petty shit." His tone had been so dismissive that Zach hadn't bothered to pursue it, but now he had a nagging sense that he should have.

Annie, too, had begun to wonder whether Neal had had anything to do with Jimmy's beating, but like Zachary, she kept her apprehensions to herself at first. She was anxious to confront Neal with her questions, but Neal hardly came home anymore. Come to think of it, she hadn't seen him since the week they found Jimmy in the park. Annie didn't know what to feel about her deepening intuition that Neal had done it, didn't know whether to be relieved Jimmy was no longer a threat, or saddened by the psychic damage that had apparently been wrought within her baby brother.

She thought of Zoe then, grieving for the lost potential of her own younger brother. Annie recalled that Jimmy had once been as mild and kind-hearted as most people still imagined Neal Piper to be. Weighing her memories, the bitter and the sweet, Annie didn't feel so absolute about things anymore, for it seemed that the geography of her world was shifting. Neal moving out of focus at the same moment that Jimmy, strangely, snapped into focus in the image of the once-tender boy he had long ago been.

Zoe helped Jimmy sit up in bed to eat breakfast. It was only his second week home from the hospital and they were still adjusting to the demands of his paralysis. Zoe had set a tray of scrambled eggs and bacon, coffee, and toast on the dresser next to his bed. In one corner of the room stood a vinyl-and-chrome wheelchair, borrowed from the hospital until Jimmy could afford to purchase one of his own. Jimmy stared at it as Zoe righted him, propping him carefully against the headboard. It had been three months since the beating, and he hadn't had a street drug or a drink since the night that they took his battered body to the hospital. As Zoe turned to retrieve the breakfast tray from the dresser, he smiled to himself, a tight bitter smile, at the irony: It had taken losing the function of his lower body for him to gain clarity of mind. He hadn't been this clear in more than a decade—not even in prison, where there was always an inmate with a fully stocked pharmacopoeia of illegal substances hidden in his cell. Jimmy reflected that this was the first time since his first joint at sixteen that he had been stone-cold sober. It seemed that the world had exploded into a startling array of possibilities, and that the hours in a single day had somehow multiplied. The only problem was, he couldn't do a thing with all that possibility and time now. He was locked inside an all but useless body, dependent on the kindness of his sister and her longtime love.

He looked up at Zoe, who was holding a cup of coffee to his lips.

"I can get this," he said, taking the cup from her. She sat next to him on the bed, the breakfast tray on her lap. He looked into her dark brown eyes, so weary and resigned, and almost choked on a sudden wave of regret. Life had been hard for Zoe—first their father, and now him. You'd think he would have learned something from that sonofabitch sneaking into Zoe's room night after night. You'd think he might have tried to do better. He felt as if he had been semiconscious all these years, his recollections liquid and surreal, as if played out under the surface of water, and now he was waking up from the nightmare. His brain could hardly fathom the pain he had caused his sister, Zoe. And he was only just beginning to comprehend how he had also wounded the spirit of another woman he had professed to love.

Annie, Jimmy thought, the ache in his chest growing acute. He put the coffee cup back in its saucer and obediently opened his mouth for a forkful of eggs.

"Sis, you don't need to feed me," he said through the mouthful, "I can do that myself."

"Quiet," Zoe instructed, raising another forkful.

Jimmy tried not to think, but an image of Annie the day she had come to the hospital kept floating out of the fog. She had stood tentatively by the door, uncertain whether he was awake, not sure she should even be there. Jimmy hadn't known what to say to her. He was still groggy from the morphine they were giving him, and for a long while he thought she was only a delicious hallucination. But no, she stayed where she was, solid and real, an expression on her face that he couldn't read. Then, she had walked towards the bed, Jimmy's eyes following her and widening with the realization that she was not a figment of the air; she would not disappear.

"How are you feeling?" Annie had asked him, her voice gruff.

Jimmy tried to shrug.

"Well," Annie said, "you look like hell."

Jimmy wanted to smile, but the effort to move the muscles

of his shattered jaw made him wince. He just stared at Annie, thinking that even with all that had happened, the way things had gone, she was still the one woman who could make his heart skip. She had stayed a few more minutes, standing off to the side when a nurse came in to take his temperature, then helping as the nurse changed the bandages on his head. He remembered that Annie worked in a hospital, but couldn't think which one.

His torso and lower body were still in a plaster cast then, but already Jimmy knew his legs would be useless, that there would be no healing his splintered spine. So strange, he thought now, that he should feel so little anger. All he could feel was an unrelenting remorse for the life that had brought him to this. It seized him each morning in the moment that he awakened and not for a single second of the endless day did it let him go.

He watched Zoe gathering up the breakfast things, getting ready to take the tray back to the kitchen. Mabel stuck her close-shaven head in the door.

"I'm going, hon."

Zoe walked over and kissed her lightly on the lips. Mabel closed her eyes involuntarily for a second, then opened them and looked across at Jimmy.

"How's the crip?" she said with a lightness that sounded forced.

"Hangin' in," Jimmy answered.

Certainly, it could have been worse. Zoe could have abandoned him, or Mabel could have put her foot down and demanded that Jimmy be cared for by an institution of the state. But they had taken him home from the hospital, filed the necessary paperwork to get his disability payments started, and just set about incorporating the inconvenience of him into their lives. He didn't really know why Zoe had stood by him so staunchly, but there were moments when Jimmy thought he caught relief in her eyes—relief that the responsibility for his well-being, at least in a physical sense, had finally been wrested from his hands.

Zoe had arranged for a physical therapist from the hospital to work with Jimmy twice a week. And she arranged for a psychotherapist to visit him weekly as well. She had also persuaded Jimmy's doctors to put him on antabuse, a medication that she had read would help control his craving for alcohol. With Zoe monitoring his visitors, making sure that no one slipped him any liquor or nonprescribed drugs, Jimmy was left with nothing but raw memory. Talking to the therapist helped. So did the books and pamphlets she brought him to read—literature about living sober and making amends and the legacies of parental abuse.

As the weeks and then the months passed, he began to see how, at a certain point, he had become so eaten up by hatred and anger towards his father, he had *become* that hate and rage. And the world had suffered because of it, but none more than Annie Piper. In some ways, Jimmy decided now, his paralysis had been both a retribution and a gift. It had forever removed his ability to inflict physical harm on others, while forcing him to sit and examine in solitude the tragic miscalculations of his heart.

"I'm dropping the charges," Annie announced, walking into Florida's kitchen in March. Zach and Florida were seated at the kitchen table, sharing their morning cup of coffee before Zach left for work and Florida set about her daily chores. Since returning to Philadelphia, Zach had found a job with an agency that provided shelter for the city's burgeoning homeless population; Zach was responsible for the smooth functioning of one of the agency's group homes.

Both he and Florida looked up at Annie.

"Why?" Florida asked, but she already knew the answer.

Annie shrugged elaborately, her hands plunged into the pockets of her gray wool dress. "Oh God. He's harmless now. He's pathetic. I couldn't stand to look at him in court. I think I actually feel sorry for him."

"My children and their tender hearts," Florida murmured. She pushed back her chair and walked to the sink where she poured the last of her coffee down the drain. Then she rinsed her cup and put it in the drying rack.

"Not all your children have tender hearts," Annie said, a sudden flare in her voice.

Florida put her back to the sink and regarded her daughter. Annie stared at her, head cocked. Zach spoke first.

"What do you mean?" he asked quietly.

"Oh come on, I know you know, Zach." Annie's tone was aggressive. "I'm just wondering if Ma knows."

"Knows what?" Florida asked.

"Annie—"

"Shit, Zach!" Annie burst out. "It's better that she knows what her baby's become!"

Zach jumped to his feet. "He was trying to protect you!" he shouted.

"What are you two talking about?" Florida cried.

"He was getting his own revenge!" Annie yelled back. "He couldn't stand that Jimmy was walking around after whipping him in front of everyone. But he got sneaky with it! At least Jimmy was in your face!"

"Check you out," Zach said with disbelief. "You sound like you're turning on your own brother. He tried to help you, Annie. If it wasn't for him, Jimmy would have raped your ass."

"Annie! Zach! Enough!" Florida commanded.

Annie flopped into a chair, a sob escaping from her throat.

"But it *killed* him," she said in a small voice, the sobs gathering and breaking closer together. Florida moved across the room to Annie and stood stroking her hair.

"Baby," she whispered, "what are you saying?"

"It turned him into a walking dead man," Annie sobbed. "I wish I *had* let Jimmy rape me. I could have got through it. I would have survived. But Neal, I wish he'd never got involved. It just *destroyed* him, Mama."

"Hush, hush," Florida said, drawing Annie roughly into her arms. "You don't really believe what you're saying."

"I do," Annie cried. "Ma, open your eyes!"

Zach stood rooted to the spot, fear twisting through him. He couldn't pretend anymore. He couldn't hide anymore what he knew to be true. Neal had almost killed a man. Only God had spared Jimmy's life—and spared Neal the stain of murder on his soul. But it was a fine line between the brutality of Neal's assault on Jimmy and murder, and now Annie had chalked that line in plain sight of them all.

Zach turned and walked out of the kitchen without a word. He picked up his coat and headed through the front door for work, aware that the emptiness inside him had begun to assume frightening proportions. It was at moments like this that Zach missed Korie most fiercely, missed the ease with which he could share himself with her, rummaging through his thoughts without need of defenses. He could hardly believe more than a year had passed since last he had seen her, a year in which so much had torn at the fabric of his life. He supposed it was better that he had been with his family in Philadelphia during that time, but what good had he really been to them? Annie seemed to have pulled herself together well enough after the night Jimmy climbed through her window; Zach supposed that the support she received from the rape counselors she worked with were helping bring her through. But Neal was another matter. At a critical moment,

Zach thought, Neal had needed him, or needed *someone* to talk to, but Zach had been oblivious, distracted by his longing for Korie. He had assumed that when the dust settled from the fight with Jimmy, Neal had simply gone on with his life. If he had seemed distant, or increasingly absent from the house on Quincy Street, Zach had thought that only the natural course of new love. Later on, though, when Neal shut himself up like a tomb, he should have paid closer attention. But by then, Zach was as entombed as Neal by his own pain, lost in his yearning for Korie and full of self-recrimination at having left her so easily.

The thing he couldn't seem to get over was the fact that Korie had never once tried to get in touch. Zach had called her often at the start, but always got her answering machine. Then not even a machine picked up. Her phone just rang and rang. He called her at the office and left messages on her voice mail there, moody ramblings expressing his love for her and the sting of missing her. He felt quite literally that he had been *born* to love her, and if he couldn't fulfill that, he told her, then his entire life would become one of merely going through the motions. And so he would wait. But Korie hadn't responded to a single message, so that Zach at last began to feel foolish and wondered if she'd ever loved him at all.

Still, he had lived a monk's life since coming home. He found he didn't have the heart for other women. And there was that other matter, the lingering question of whether he and Korie had been exposed to the AIDS virus. One day, when Korie's silence cut particularly deep, Zach had walked into a clinic in a fit of anger and demanded to have himself tested. The results when they came were negative, as he had somehow known they would be, but that hadn't been the point of the test. He had meant it to be a watershed, a decisive action that would mark his resolve to forget about Korie and move on with his life.

Annie tried to set him up with women she knew, and for a brief period after getting tested he had dated this one or that. But nothing ever seemed to spark in him. He went out drinking with his boys sometimes, but more and more he preferred to stay home with Florida, browsing through magazines or losing himself in cheap thrillers as his mother flipped through sitcoms and police dramas with the remote control. Sometimes, Florida joined him in watching a ball game. In this manner, Zach's life dwindled to a monotonous routine, but he wasn't bored, exactly. It was more that he wasn't truly alive.

A pall settled over the house on Quincy Street. Night after night, Florida, Zach, and Annie all sat together in the living room, wordlessly watching TV, waiting for Neal to come home. None of them broached the subject of whether or not they should go to the police. The truth was, none of them could imagine taking such an action. They told themselves that they wanted to put the questions to Neal first. But a week passed, then another, and still Neal did not show up. It had been months, in fact, since Neal had been home for even a pit stop. They had all assumed that he'd moved in with Samantha, but now that they wanted so desperately to reach him, to stand before him and look into his eyes, they realized that none of them knew Samantha's number or even her last name.

At last, when she saw that their laissez-faire approach would yield no answers—in fact, the questions had multiplied so that now they lay like a miasma in the house—Florida called Neal's job. The news was unexpected. The foreman of the painting and plastering crew sounded mildly surprised by Florida's call. He told her Neal had just up and quit one morning with no explanation and hadn't been seen since. It had been about, oh, three, four months, now. Yes, the foreman recollected, Neal had been staying for a while with a young lady in one of the buildings, but no, he couldn't say what her name was and wouldn't have been able to pass it along even if he did know. It was the kind of thing, he explained, that could cost him his job. He did add, however, that he thought the young lady in question had vacated her apartment a few months ago. Three months ago to be exact.

"Lady," he said finally. "That boy is your son. Now, you oughta know better'n me where he done got to."

"Thank you," Florida said quietly, and put down the phone.

Numbly, she turned to Zach and Annie, who were sitting shoulder to shoulder on the bottom stair, looking for all the world as they had when they were children waiting for Florida to come home. Her mind flashed for an instant to where she had been on those long afternoons when her children missed her. For a moment, she felt again the sensation of long, warm arms around her, saw the large, gap teeth, the laughing green eyes, the orange aura that enveloped her like slanting sunlight. Rick—Mr. Hendricks, as her children had known him—was long dead, and yet, in her moments of greatest agitation, Florida imagined she could still feel his comfort moving around her.

"Ma," Zachary said.

"He's gone," Florida answered flatly. "Quit his job." She seemed dazed, as if the words she spoke had no meaning.

"Gone where?" Annie pressed.

Florida shrugged and sank into the nearest chair. "Don't know where," she murmured. "Into thin air."

They were all silent for a long time. Then Annie had an idea. "Maybe Neal went to Atlanta, to Ben," she tried. Sudden hope infused her. "Maybe he figured his big brother could get him onto a construction crew there. We should call Ben."

Florida shook her head, and Zach knew she was right. Neal's whereabouts were far more complicated.

"All the same," Annie insisted, "we should call, just to be

sure. Besides," she added with new conviction, "it's only right we let Ben know what's happening to his family."

"But let's not call him today," Florida said wearily. She still seemed numb and far away. More quietly, she continued: "I say we let one member of this family rest easy today."

To Zachary, watching from the foot of the stairs, Florida looked suddenly old, all sixty-two years of her life settling into her features at once and pushing her shoulders lower than they had been a moment before. Zach looked down at his hands, not wanting to see the resignation and defeat dim Florida's eyes. There was nothing he could say that would offer any comfort, and if he couldn't bring the light back into Florida's eyes, then he didn't know what else to do.

It occurred to him then that of all those who had sought his comfort through the years—his brothers and sisters, neighbors and friends—Florida had been the one whose interior life had always made him feel the most in jeopardy, and whose core of suffering he'd never been able to touch. Oh, she had turned to him for consolation sometimes, sharing the truth about Mr. Hendricks and the love that had claimed them, confiding the secret of Neal's conception. She had even led Zach to believe that he could provide the refuge that she so sorely craved, that his filial understanding and acceptance of her secret could make her whole. But then, she had moved out of the circle of his arms into the same imperfect landscape of her life. And, deep inside her, nothing had changed.

In a way, his mother had always been his big failure. As a young boy, Zach had sensed, in the wordless manner of a child, her deep disillusionment with her marriage and had fantasized about healing her relationship with the husband who had so disappointed her. It had become a potent childhood fiction, and Zach had spent many solitary hours imagining how he would turn the bitter fire between his parents into something cool and sweet. While his older sister and brother went off with each other to play, he had sat alone with his army of green plastic soldiers, manipulating the figures and causing war to break out so that he could negotiate a peace. In the background, Florida and Hanson yelled and pushed and shoved, though they never seriously injured each other. Then they'd drink beer together and yell some more. Zach had stayed down in the basement during these fights, trying not to hear the blame and resentment his parents hurled at each other.

Now that he thought about it, it wasn't surprising that he had fallen so hard for Korie. The scent of her had set off all kinds of chemical reactions in him, and he couldn't ever get over the silkiness of her skin, or stop marveling at how perfectly she fit in his arms. But it had been even more elemental than that. She had blown into his life like an immaculate wind, free of conditions and demands, and with not a single tie to his past. She'd chosen to embrace him just exactly as she'd found him, simply folding whatever new aspect he might present into her pliable understanding of him.

Only later, he realized now, when he had felt compelled to save her from her grief, and liberate her from the pain of Sam's secret, had they run into trouble. In wanting so fiercely to spare her, to heal her deepest suffering as he had never been able to heal Florida's, he had denied her the space to mourn Sam in her own way. And so she had sought to escape him, metaphorically at first, through drugs, and then physically, when she asked him to leave.

Zach saw, suddenly, that he couldn't spare Florida or Annie or Neal their hurts and disappointments any more than he could spare Korie hers. He began to feel that every secret he had kept, every deceit he had accommodated had been a disservice to the one who had confided in him. Not that he should have betrayed their confidences, but perhaps he might have encouraged those who came to him to give up their secrets, to release them from their guilty realm so as to dissipate their potency. Instead, by hoarding their pain—by pacifying Florida's guilt at not having told Neal who his real father was; by acquiescing to Annie when she begged him not to reveal that Jimmy had raped her; by never encouraging Sam to share the truth about his sexual nature—he had helped to transform these secrets into a personal shame.

And now, it was all unraveling. Threads he had spent his whole life trying to keep securely bound, secrets he had built his self-worth by keeping, were coming loose.

Zach rose from the step on which he sat. His legs felt wooden.

"I'm going out," he said.

Florida and Annie didn't seem to hear him, but it didn't matter. There was someone he had to see, a hunch he had to track down. He thought he might already knew the answer but hoped all the same to be proven wrong.

Zoe wasn't home, but Mabel ushered Zachary in to see Jimmy. Zoe had cautioned her against allowing Jimmy's former low-life friends in to visit him, but Mabel figured Zach Piper had to be okay. They'd known him practically all his life, and she recollected that back when she and Zoe were first getting together, he had been one of the few neighborhood kids who hadn't snickered when they walked holding hands down the street. He'd always been respectful in his greeting of them, and hadn't ever really paid much mind to the whispers that had eddied like a stinging desert wind around them.

"Thanks, Mabel," Zach said, unzipping the black wool jacket he had thrown on over his sweatshirt. This was Neal's jacket, a little tight across the shoulders, and Zach didn't know what had prompted him to reach for it in the hall closet rather than his own brown leather windbreaker.

"I'll get that for you." Mabel took the jacket from his hands, then touched his arm. "How's the family?"

"Oh, doing okay." Zach glanced over at Jimmy, who was sitting in his wheelchair, a book with black leather binding and stenciled gold lettering in his hands. He'd closed the book carefully as Zach walked in, and now he stuffed it between his hip and the chrome side panel of his wheelchair. He looked up at Zach. The spine of the book remained partly visible, and Zach saw the letters THE HOLY B. He realized with a shock that Jimmy had been reading the Bible! He didn't comment; he didn't know why he should be so surprised. A lot of folks beat a path to religion in hard times. Sometimes, the conversion might even be sincere, but most of the time, especially with ex-cons, it ended up being just a convenient show. On the other hand, Zach reflected, Jimmy hadn't been expecting him, hadn't been expecting anyone as he sat with the Holy Bible open on his ruined legs.

After Mabel left them, Zach stood awkwardly in the middle of the room, uncertain how he should begin. Jimmy waited for him to speak, his eyes curiously placid, a smooth lake. The eyes caught Zach by surprise. He wasn't used to that expression in Jimmy's eyes, that unassuming openness to what Zachary might share. A line of poetry popped into Zach's head, something he'd learned in ninth grade, when Mr. Howlan had tried to interest his literature class in the English Romantic poets. Wordsworth, Zach remembered. The line was from a poem by William Wordsworth: *A deep distress hath humanized my soul.* Zach couldn't recall the name of the poem it came from, and he doubted he could think of another line of Romantic poetry that had stayed with him like that one. But somehow this fragment had resonated in him. He supposed he had been struck by the idea that there might be a rationale for pain. As far as Zach could tell, pain was an inevitable fact of life, and so it might as well be educative, purposeful.

Jimmy, he thought now, seemed *humanized*—reconciled to his condition and yet not neutralized by it. Somehow, the violence that always sputtered in his eyes had been tamed, so that now, sitting before Zach in his wheelchair, a Bible tucked against his useless hip, he seemed almost pious.

Still, Zach thought he should lead up to things carefully.

"How're things, man?" He reached across to clasp and shake Jimmy's big hand, the palm already spongy with inactivity.

"Hey, I'm here." Jimmy regarded Zach for another moment, then said, "So what's on your mind?"

Zach decided to plunge right in.

"I need to ask you about a conversation that happened between you and my brother Neal." Jimmy said nothing, so Zach pressed on. "The day Neal brought his new girl to the neighborhood—you remember, the white girl—you followed them from Jake's Grocery to the car."

"Yeah. So?"

"I need to know, man, what you said to Neal."

Jimmy looked towards the window, which opened onto a bleak landscape of brick row houses set closely together in tiny yards, their short stoops giving onto broken concrete sidewalks with grass sprouting through. The dreariness of the scene was eased somewhat by the sheer white curtains Zoe had hung at his window; their delicate fabric rustled softly in a crisp breeze. Gazing out the window, Jimmy brought his thick fingers to his temples and rubbed the skin there in hard circular motions.

"Why?" he asked at last.

Zach didn't want to give away too much. He didn't know what Jimmy knew, or what he would do with any new information he might discover.

"Neal's disappeared," he said briefly. "He's been gone since that same afternoon when you followed them to the car." It was only a slight exaggeration, Zach reasoned, and a useful one.

Jimmy sighed. "I told him he was your mama's bastard child," he said. "I told him that he wasn't his daddy's kid, that the white man who used to come around when we was kids, the carpenter, *that* was his daddy."

Zach let out a slow breath. Somehow he had known that *this* was the thing that had been working in Neal.

He asked, "What did Neal say?"

"He didn't believe me."

"What else?" Zach insisted. "What else did you say? I was watching from the upstairs window. There was more than that. The whole exchange seemed fucking intense from where I stood."

"Hey, man. I told him I could take his white girl. Something like that. I don't know. I leered at his girl—just to get his steam up, you know." Jimmy chuckled then, but there was no humor in the sound. "Got his steam up, all right. His steam put me right here in this chair."

Zach could hardly believe what he'd heard. *Jimmy knew!* Jimmy knew Neal was the one who had attacked him! Zach moved across the room and reached a not quite steady hand down to find Jimmy's bed. He sat a few feet from Jimmy, almost primly on the edge of the bed, careful not to rumple the sunshine yellow chenille bedspread.

"What did you say?" he whispered. He was stalling, trying to figure out the best way to proceed.

"Neal did this to me," Jimmy said, his voice supernaturally calm. "I didn't remember it at first, but later on, in the hospital, it started to come back to me. I saw his face just before he knocked me out cold. I woke up as he was dragging me into the park and really got conscious when he started whaling on me with that crowbar. He had the football helmet on then, but I knew it was him. He didn't put the helmet on till we were in the park. That's why no one saw anything strange. He was just another brother walking down the block. As I recall, no one was out at that hour anyhow."

Zach asked, "Why didn't you tell the police?"

"Hell," Jimmy shrugged. "Maybe I deserved it. Besides, Annie came to see me in the hospital."

"And you told her?"

"No," Jimmy answered. "And I'll never tell her, neither. And *you* don't tell her." A hint of the old threat crept into his voice, but in the next second it was gone. Jimmy went on: "See, man, for me, it's always been your sister, Annie. I never wanted anyone else, just her. Even in jail, all I could think about was her. But I really fucked things up where she was concerned. Fucked 'em up big time. And then she came to see me in the hospital after the beating and she seemed, well, sorry for me, and I thought, if she can see me as human enough to feel sorry for, well maybe, just maybe, there's hope."

"I see," Zach said icily. "If Annie doesn't fall into line, you'll tell the police about Neal."

"No, man, no. That's not what I mean." Jimmy sounded tired. "I *know* what I did to Annie. I know it might be impossible for her to ever forgive me. I ain't stupid, Zach. I know." He glanced again towards the brick-and-concrete landscape beyond his window, the lake of his eyes now full of sadness. When he spoke again, his voice was quiet. "I just didn't want to hurt her anymore. To put Neal in jail would hurt her. Especially when this whole nightmare might never have happened if it hadn't been for me.

"Like I said," he finished, "I pushed Neal to what he did. Could be I deserved what I got. Actually," he laughed, "my sister finds this whole situation a big relief."

"This is so deep," Zach muttered, shaking his head.

He sat with Jimmy without speaking for a long while after that. Together, they watched the gray morning light brighten into noontime, and listened to the sounds of pots and cutlery clattering in the distance of the house as Mabel moved around the kitchen preparing lunch. They didn't speak any more about Neal or the blows that had crippled Jimmy, because there seemed nothing more to say. At one point, Jimmy asked how Annie was holding up, and Zach, still distracted, merely nodded his head. He was thinking how God, after all, was not absent in this comedy, and that sometimes secrets got kept for noble reasons, too. The fact was, whatever Jimmy's reasons, Zach was grateful to him for his silence about Neal. Still, Zach knew that his brother wouldn't escape the consequences of his brutal premeditated act entirely: He knew that wherever Neal was, his conscience would punish him more than any court of law ever could—it had already taken him from his family. As Zach continued to sit there with Jimmy, the thoughts kept streaming through his head. Presently, he realized with a kind of wonder that little Jimmy Jones, the easygoing boy he had grown up with on the Western Avenue basketball courts, the lanky youth he had good-naturedly talked trash with in a hundred pickup games, had, after all, been cowering under the violence the whole time. Now that the violence within Jimmy had forcibly been stilled, perhaps the frightened boy inside him might finally grow into a man.

Epilogue
1987

*"Ten thousand flowers in spring, the moon in autumn,
a cool breeze in summer, snow in winter.
If your mind isn't clouded by unnecessary things,
this is the best season of your life."*

—Wu-men

Rest

SPRING WAS LABORING TO BREAK THROUGH THE LAST stubborn chill of winter. Korie could tell by the birdsong in the park, the clouds of pink and yellow blossoms haloing the trees, the luminous green of new grass. It was almost Easter in New York, and tulip buds poked through the freshly turned flower beds on the edge of Park Drive. Korie breathed the brilliant earth-scented air as she hurried through Central Park, on her way to Payne Whitney, the psychiatric wing of Cornell Medical Center on the East Side. She was eager to see Simona and didn't want to be late, but she'd been unable to hail a cab in Midtown and had been forced to walk.

It was a good distance from her job. The hospital was all the way over on the East River. As Korie approached it, the air quickened, chilled by the icy crust on the river and compacted by tall stone buildings that made wind tunnels of the streets. Korie leaned into the cold, eager to cover the last few steps that separated her from her friend. On impulse, she ducked into a card shop a block away from the hospital and picked out a small brown bear, a stuffed red heart in its arms. The white lettering on the heart said I'LL BE THERE. Corny perhaps, but she hoped Simona would get her meaning. She didn't know in what condition she would find her friend. She hadn't seen her for two weeks, not since the night she and an ambulance full of paramedics had brought her to the hospital's emergency room, terrified that they might be too late. Simona had been trembling wildly, the irises of her eyes flying up in her head, her mouth slack and muttering. Earlier that evening, Korie had found her sprawled as if crucified on the brick red Oriental carpet on her living room floor. Her arms were stretched at right angles to her body and her long legs were as straight and rigid as boards.

Korie had gone to Simona's apartment after calling there for days on end and getting no answer. She had been alarmed, because Simona hadn't shown up at work for more than a week, but she hadn't called in sick. No one, not even Korie, had heard from her. Korie had gone to her apartment twice that week, but Simona hadn't answered the buzzer. The second time, Korie was desperate enough to try conning the building's super. She persuaded him that she lived in the apartment with Simona and had forgotten her key. The super wasn't difficult to convince; he had seen Korie in the building often enough, practically every evening for almost a year, and so he easily bought her ruse that she lived there. Besides, she stood before him a clear-eyed, clean-cut young woman—fact was, she looked a damn sight better than the last time he'd seen her— and the super didn't see where she could do any harm. It was her wild-haired, raccoon-eyed roommate he was worried about.

When he'd unlocked the door, Korie had thanked him sweetly, then slipped inside and shut the door before he could peer into the apartment. A moment later, standing over

Simona, looking down into her glazed, unseeing eyes, Korie's breath caught in her throat. *Oh, God,* she prayed, *not again.* The thought came involuntarily, and with it a flash of Sam lying unconscious in her hallway. Cold fear turned in her stomach and she had trouble focusing for a second. Her brain played tricks: She kept seeing Sam's frail body superimposed on Simona's, both of them thin and wasted, their waning lives a slow suicide. She didn't notice the drops of blood on Simona's carpet at first, for they blended with the red in the design. But the blue break-collar shirt Simona wore was speckled with dried blood, and caked trails of it led from her nostrils to her mouth, which was slightly agape. Korie bent closer and saw that her teeth, too, were bloody, her gums oozing red.

"Jesus Christ!" Korie had screamed. Much later, they would laugh about that, because Simona had, in fact, been lying on her carpet trying to simulate Jesus on the cross. Her notion was to pierce his sensibility at the moment of crucifixion, and thus tap within herself the power of deliverance. She had wanted that evening to be delivered of the torment of her enslavement to cocaine. She was never sure afterwards how the crucifixion idea came to her, but at the time, it had seemed perfectly reasonable.

And then, there was Korie's face swimming down to her own, screaming. Korie seemed to be behind a thick pane of ice, so that her scream seemed muted, distant. Simona tried to move her limbs, but found she couldn't. Her body felt frozen in place. She tried to speak, but the words wouldn't rise out of her throat. Only then, facing Korie's terror, did she begin to grow frightened. Korie disappeared for a long while after that—in fact, it was only a few seconds—then reappeared, dragging the Aztec print comforter from her bed. She wrapped Simona's stiffened body in it, rolling her over and over until she was snug in the pillowy cloth. Then she pulled Simona into her arms.

"Don't do this, Sim," she cried, slapping her cheeks. "Don't you do this to me! Wake up, wake up, wake up!"

She lay her back down on the carpet gently and went to find the phone. It was unplugged, of course. Korie followed the cord and located it under the kitchen sink. She quickly reconnected the line and dialled 911: "I need an ambulance immediately!" she yelled into the phone, and gave Simona's address. Then she raced through the apartment, gathering up little white envelopes now empty of pills and a plethora of tiny Ziploc bags, cloudy with tracings of white powder. She grabbed up a plastic bag that still held buds of fragrant marijuana—Korie's drug of choice, but now she didn't even pause over it. She scooped up Bambú papers, cut straws, and the rolled-up dollar bills Simona sometimes used to snort cocaine. She flushed them all down the toilet, even the dollar bills. Then she wet-sponged white dust from all the surfaces she could think of, stashing the five or six empty wine bottles she came across under the sink. At last, she unlocked the front door and went back to holding Simona. It seemed that she sat with her arms around her friend for an eternity before the ambulance came. Simona's boardlike body had begun to thaw by then, so that when the paramedics arrived she was curled within the comforter, bony knees at her chest, her cheek shivering against Korie's breast.

They took her to Cornell because that was the hospital with which Simona's doctor was affiliated. And Simona didn't live far from Cornell. But her physician, it turned out, was away on vacation, and a rotation of weary residents attended her instead. Eventually, after the residents had succeeded in stabilizing her, a psychiatrist arrived. Korie was relieved that she was a black woman, a brusque, no-nonsense Trinidadian named Dr. Redwood. She admitted Simona to Payne Whitney, the psychiatric residential treatment program at Cornell. She estimated that Simona would be there for six weeks undergoing drug detox and counseling. She wouldn't be allowed any visitors for the first two weeks, she explained to Korie, but after that, she was welcome to see her friend during visiting hours from one to five on Tuesdays.

That first week, Korie had to clear the admittance with Simona's insurance, which necessitated signatures from her employer, which meant explaining to Marcie Steinway exactly where it was that Simona had landed. She had had a nervous breakdown, she told the editor, and would be forced to take a medical leave of at least two months. Simona's editor regarded Korie with a cool silence that told her she wasn't fooled, but she accepted the explanation without comment, and signed the papers. The fact was, she was rooting for Simona; she had found her a gifted reporter before her troubles got out of hand. Besides, Marcie Steinway had lived through the flower child decade of the sixties, and she had seen enough to know that one could grow beyond the easy escape of drugs and return to a productive life. So she would give Simona time and privacy, and when she returned to the magazine, she would behave as if this whole unfortunate episode had never happened—provided, of course, Simona's work was back up to par.

After that, there was no one else to call, no one to notify that Simona had crashed emotionally. Suddenly, Korie was jolted by the reality of how alone Simona was in the world. She saw how she had tried to reinterpret her aloneness, casting it as freedom rather than what it truly was: a lonely, orphaned existence. In fact, Simona had resented her isolation, but when in adolescence she'd tried to break out of it, she'd discovered that the habit of aloneness had become too ingrained. Then she'd gone to Berkeley, and somebody offered her a toke of marijuana. Later, somebody else gave her mushrooms, and soon enough, a man she was dating introduced her to coke.

Drugs, Simona decided, dissolved the forced separation she felt from the world around her. Or, if they didn't *dissolve* the boundaries exactly, they reordered her thinking just enough so that she didn't really care about them.

Korie began to think that maybe she could help Simona make peace with her losses, and create a new family from scratch. She realized that she might have brought Simona into her own family. Osgood and Alice would have folded her in without question, if Korie hadn't been so busy keeping her distance from them. What had she been trying to prove? She could hardly remember now. Well, she would change all that. She would call her parents, tell them what had happened to Simona, tell them how it was for her, and ask if she could bring her to their house in Jamaica for a while, after she got out of rehab.

As Korie went about taking care of the details of Simona's hospitalization that first week, she was plagued by a persistent and uncomfortable sense of déjà vu. She had taken care of similar details for Sam as he lay dying, and now she had to keep pushing back the image of him blanching into nothingness while she stood helpless vigil at his bedside. She reminded herself that this time would be different. Addiction was a sickness of the soul, not the body. The soul could recover. Simona would not die.

Simona's room was on the fourth floor of the white brick building that formed the hospital's east wing. Korie stepped out of the elevator, and walked down the hall with its flat, colorless carpeting to where the nurse at the information desk had directed her. Room 403. She stopped at the door and looked in tentatively, not wanting to startle her friend. Inside, Simona sat at a scarred desk, writing. She was dressed in a short, plain brown skirt and a too-big beige sweater, her feet clad in blue paper slippers. Her short black hair curled into wet ringlets, as if freshly washed and her face, when she finally looked up, appeared barren and scrubbed. She looked impossibly young, painted in a watery kind of light.

"Hey, sweet pea," Simona said in a soft husky voice, delight transforming her face.

Korie came into the room, her arms outstretched. She didn't have any words just then, so she hugged Simona tightly. Simona put her arms up and stroked the flattened wave of Korie's hair, which she'd had cut close to her head in the past week.

"Shaved off your hair."

Korie nodded mutely, her eyes filling with tears.

"It's okay, it's okay, hon," Simona whispered. "I'm going to be fine."

Korie pulled back then, and stared into Simona's face, bathing herself in the nascent radiance of it.

"I was so scared," she said.

"I know," Simona answered. "I'm sorry."

"No, no, no, I'm sorry," Korie said, her words suddenly tumbling. "I helped you go deeper into cocaine, I egged you on, thinking only of myself. And then I walked away from you, trying to save my own ass."

"What else could you have done?" Simona said. "Thank God you walked away, Korie, or you wouldn't have been able to help me that night. I might have laid my tired body on that carpet in my living room and stayed right there until the super came to investigate the stink."

Korie shuddered and moved out of Simona's embrace. Simona reached out and touched her shoulder.

"You must never think," she said seriously, "that you caused any part of this. That's plain stupid. I did what I wanted to. Of my own volition."

Korie nodded, looking around the room because she couldn't right then look into Simona's eyes. The room, she noticed, was spartanly furnished: a cot in one corner; an ancient-looking dresser; a mirror on the wall above a sink; a desk by the window. The window didn't open, but it looked out onto the river and the tree-shaded wooden promenade that bordered it. The scene was tranquil and expansive, and seemed to connect the occupant of this room to the patient promise of the outer world.

"Here," Korie said, remembering the stuffed bear. Simona smiled and put it to her heart for a moment, then carefully placed the stuffed creature next to the notebook in which she had been writing.

"I'm writing my mother," she said. "Just one of the people I'll never see again, but who I'm learning I still have to forgive. . . ." Her voice trailed off, and her expression seemed vulnerable and scared. But then she squared her shoulders and reassembled her composure.

"They said I could go walking with you," she said, cheering visibly. "I guess they trust you. You brought me in, after all."

"Trust me?" Korie asked, puzzled.

"To make sure I don't wig out out there. To make sure I don't make a beeline for the candy. You know, the drug house."

Korie shuddered, even though Simona's voice was perfectly matter-of-fact. As she spoke, Simona bent to take off her paper slippers, then reached under the bed and pulled out her patent leather boots. She slipped her bare feet into them, then went to the closet and pulled out the navy pea coat that Korie had put over her shoulders the night they brought her to the hospital.

"Come on," she said, shrugging into her coat. "I can hardly wait to breathe some of that sweet New York air!"

"Korie?" Simona said as they walked arm in arm down the East River promenade.

"Hmm?" Korie answered absently.

"This is something," Simona said. "All this air, this big wide world, that clear blue sky—so much bigger than the dark rooms of my apartment. Why didn't I get out more?"

"You will now," Korie said. "To AA meetings, for example."

"To meetings," Simona nodded.

They walked a bit more in silence, letting the cold air fill their lungs. They each sensed that the boundaries of their friendship were growing wider, and this thrilled them. They knew that no matter what came next, no matter how steep the road ahead, they each had a traveling companion, someone who had shared in the seductive, nightmarish pursuit of oblivion, and who understood, therefore, the need for daylight.

"What are the meetings like?" Simona asked.

"You'll love them, Sim. Amazing stories, life stories beyond imagining. Heartbreaking, horrifying, triumphant stories. And they're all true. The reporter in you will be fascinated."

Simona looked at her dubiously. They kept walking.

"Korie," she said at last.

Something new in her tone made Korie stop and turn to face her. She unlinked her arm from Simona's so she could stand before her and look into her eyes. "What's up?" she said.

Simona said, "You did wrong by Zachary. Which wouldn't bother me in the least, except you're still pining for him. He's the one, Korie. The one God put on earth for you. You realize that, don't you?"

Korie looked down at her scuffed cowboy boots, her chapped hands with their bitten nails. She didn't answer.

"You have to go find him," Simona insisted. "Go to Philly. Look him in the face. Say the things you need to say to him." She paused and looked away from Korie, squinting into the sun. "He loves you, too, Korie. He hasn't stopped. I heard his messages on your answering machine."

Korie sighed and walked a little distance from her friend. If only it were that simple, she thought. Simona held out her hand. "This way, Korie," she said. "I have to get back."

With the comradely air of two who have survived an ordeal that only they can describe, they strolled back to Payne Whitney together. Halfway there, as they stood waiting for a traffic signal to change so that they could cross the highway, it suddenly struck Korie that it *could* be that simple—she just had to choose it. She had to believe that the stars were aligned in support of her, that her Higher Power was working on her behalf. She had to trust that Zachary would have the capacity and the willingness to understand. She would explain it all to him, the spiraling into addiction and the slow climb back. She would ask him to forgive her year and some of silence, and try to make him see that not for a single moment had she stopped loving him. Perhaps he would turn away from her, and tell her it was too late. But it was also possible that he would embrace her. How magnificently he had loved her once!

Right then, as if reading her thoughts, Simona whispered, "We deserve to be happy, Korie. Oh God, we do." She spoke so softly, and with such reverence, that for a moment Korie believed she had imagined it.

In May, a letter came for Florida. Sorting through the spring catalogs and bills and junk mailings that had been pushed through the door slot, she recognized Neal's handwriting immediately. She picked up the plain white envelope with his crunched scrawl and walked to the armchair. Sitting, she put the envelope on her lap and just looked at it for a long time. Her heart pounded in her chest, and she realized that she was afraid of what might be contained in the letter, afraid that after reading it, her youngest son might be lost to her forever.

She smoothed the surface of the envelope with her fingers, even though it was not rumpled. She held it before her and watched it tremble in her hands. At last, she slit it across the top and unfolded a single sheet of white paper. The letter was dated March 3, 1987—more than two months ago. Neal must have walked around with it in his pocket for several weeks before mailing it. There was no return address.

Dear Mama,

I know I left without saying good-bye, but so much went down before I left that I just had to get away from Philadelphia and start fresh. Samantha (that white girl I brought by the house that day) decided to come with me. It's clear to both of us that her folks will never accept me, but we love each other and we want to get married. I think it's important not to let love just slip away from you. But the way I see it, that's something you could tell me.

It looks like we're going to have a baby in September. We got the news a month ago, and I thought I should let you know you're getting a granbaby.

I think maybe Zach has figured out the reason I left. I saw him the day I came home to pack up my clothes. Zach always did know things about us before we knew them ourselves! I think you told Zach the truth about that white man they say is my real father, that carpenter you named me after. You always did tell Zach everything, but this time, Mama, I was the one of your children that needed to know! I was the one you should have looked in the eye and told the truth to. Why didn't you do that? Did you think I wouldn't understand? Well, you should have tried me. It would have been better to hear it from you than on the street, the way I finally did.

Well anyway, Samantha says that's water under the bridge, and I guess she has a point. We're doing all right really. I got a job on a plastering crew here and Samantha is teaching kindergarten. She's planning to go back to school and finish studying music after the baby comes. Me? Maybe I'll go to trade school and study carpentry, since it seems I have carpentry in my blood.

I feel more free here than I did back home, and people don't stare at me and Samantha as much. Here, maybe we can live in peace, and I can be daddy to my own child rather than let another man raise him.

Tell Zach I'm sorry I didn't say good-bye that day. You and Annie and the others, too. I miss you all, Mama. Will send pictures of your granbaby.

Your son Neal.

P.S. You should have told me, Ma.

Florida picked up the envelope again and studied the postmark. Topanga Canyon, CA. Somewhere in California, a place she had never heard of. It didn't matter. Neal was never coming home. She knew that; there were echoes in the letter that told her. So Neal knew she had lied to him about Hanson being his father, and though it seemed he'd been casting for a way to forgive her, he hadn't yet achieved that. Perhaps he never would. Florida couldn't say she blamed him for being bitter. What had she been thinking of, sneaking around with Rick, hiding his identity from the son he had so wanted to love? What had she been trying to preserve with Hanson? She supposed the fact that they'd had three children together had been the reason she'd given herself for staying, and yet, when finally the split with Hanson had come, her children had adjusted, visiting their father in his rented apartment and moving back and forth between the two of them with more ease, in fact, than had been possible when the two of them were still living wrathfully under the same roof.

Why hadn't she tried to make a life with Rick? Why had that never seemed possible to her? She admitted now that the fact that he'd been white had prevented her from considering anything other than the part-time, not-quite-clandestine affair that had continued until his death.

P.S. You should have told me, Ma.

The first part of Neal's letter was painstakingly formed, as if Neal had carefully drawn the lines. That last line, though, was rudely scratched, heavy strokes slashed across the page with an angry fist.

Yes, I should have told you, son. But by the time I realized it, your daddy, your white daddy, was long dead.

Florida refolded the single sheet of paper and sighed. Well, she wouldn't cry about it now. Fact was, Neal had had two men who were proud to call him son. Some of these boys out here didn't even have one. So she took comfort from that, and from the fact that Neal had apparently gleaned a powerful lesson from her well-meaning lie. *He* wasn't about to walk away from the one he loved, even if the rest of the world might cast upon them a jaundiced eye.

Florida looked up as Zach came in through the front door. He didn't see her at first, sitting there in the corner. As he shrugged off his jacket and slung it over the ladder-backed chair next to the stairs, she found herself thinking that for a change there was something that Neal could teach his brother.

"Zach," she said from her chair. "Your brother wrote."

Zach frowned. "Why didn't he just call?"

"Not Ben," Florida said. "Your brother Neal."

"No kidding," Zach breathed, coming over to his mother and bending to kiss her cool, dry cheek. "What did he say?"

"Read it for yourself," she said, handing him the letter. "And when you're done, you read it again. But this time read what he's saying between the lines."

Korie had been driving for almost two hours, and she still hadn't managed to leave the New Jersey Turnpike behind. The Friday afternoon traffic was like molasses, with construction delays from the Newark Airport exit all the way through. Cars inched along bumper to bumper for endless stretches, as traffic merged from three lanes to two, then from two lanes to one. Korie was low on patience; she wanted to scream. Instead, she rolled the window down, allowing the cool May air to circulate through the car, a rented one, a blue Chrysler. She had specifically requested a blue Chrysler for this trip, though the only model available was hopelessly out of date. So much the better. She wanted the same kind of car that she had been driving three-and-a-half years ago when she'd first set eyes on Zachary.

She had embarked on this trip on impulse. She hadn't woken up that Friday morning and decided to drive to Philadelphia. She had merely decided to take the day off from work. Then she'd attended an early morning AA meeting with Simona, who had been released from Payne Whitney but wasn't due to return to the magazine for another three weeks.

The meeting was what they called a "step meeting," and the step the room had chosen to focus on that morning was the one about making amends. Korie glanced up at the framed wall-size poster listing the twelve steps of AA. She quickly skimmed to the ninth step, which suggested that recovering addicts "make direct amends" to all persons they had harmed during their active phases of drinking and drugging.

Korie had always felt uncomfortable when meetings turned to this subject, but on this morning, she realized that a portion of the burden she'd felt had been lifted. Whenever she had considered the need to make amends, she had always thought first of Zachary and then of Simona. But now, Simona was here with her in the rooms, no longer strung out in a dark apartment, hurtling towards destruction. All though her rehab, Simona had insisted that she had nothing to forgive Korie for. No amends were necessary because she had not ever held

Korie responsible for her problems with drugs. And besides, she'd pointed out, Korie had literally saved her life.

It was true that, for Simona, staying sober was a struggle. Some days, she ached so badly, all she could do was sit through meeting after meeting, not daring for hours at a stretch to leave the safety of the rooms. On such days, Korie would try to tend Simona's ragged spirit with as much care as Zach had once tended hers. She could see more clearly now what Zach had tried to give her, and so, on the nights that Simona felt particularly vulnerable, Korie would escort her home, feed her dinner and put her to bed. As she tucked Simona's Aztec-print comforter around her, Korie would murmur the most tender words she could think of, words Zach had once, so very long ago, whispered to her: "I'm not going to let you go under, Sim." Simona would smile as Korie said this, knowing that her words were a promise and a prayer for them both.

Simona had forty-five days clean now, and in two weeks she would fly to Jamaica with Korie to spend six days in Osgood and Alice's beach cottage in Ocho Rios before reporting back to work. That morning, as the meeting's leader read the ninth step chapter from the "Big Book"—the AA bible—Korie watched her friend from across the room and realized that she had been freed of guilt where Simona was concerned.

That left Zachary.

Not for the first time, Korie recalled an exchange she'd had with her father just before she'd left Jamaica on her last visit home. She had been in the family study browsing through a magazine, and Osgood had come in to put some documents in his desk drawer. Seeing Korie curled up on the sofa he paused for a moment, then came to stand before her.

"This young social worker your mother told me about," he said, "did the two of you have plans?"

"No," Korie sighed.

Osgood cleared his throat, took his pipe from his lips, and peered at his daughter. "Your mother seemed to think you'd had plans. You were living together, after all."

"We haven't talked in a year," Korie said briefly. It was her second week of trying to stay sober, and conversation was an effort.

Osgood wasn't finished, though. He made a sound like a snort, and went over to his desk drawer. He pulled out a pouch of fresh cherry tobacco and began tamping the moist leaves into the rosewood bowl of his pipe. Not looking at Korie, he commented, "This young man was good to you, Korie. Better than you were to him."

Korie pushed the magazine away. She studied the terrazzo-tiled floor.

"An American, is he?"

"Yes, Daddy."

"Where did he go to school?"

"Howard."

"In Washington, D.C.," Osgood nodded. "Your Uncle Ashton went there." He stopped speaking to light his pipe, but he stayed silent for so long that Korie finally looked up at him. Osgood puffed on his pipe and blew the smoke out and waited until it cleared. "This young man Zachary," he said at last, "I'd like to meet him someday." With that, he put the pouch of tobacco back in its drawer and strolled casually from the room.

When the AA meeting let out at ten-thirty, Korie caught up with Simona and explained that she'd decided to rent a car and drive to Philadelphia that afternoon.

"All right!" Simona had answered. She even grinned and punched Korie's arm at the news, but her eyes stayed bleak. Korie, observing her closely, almost changed her mind about leaving, but right then a plumpish woman in her late forties, whose thin golden scars curled like ivy around her wrists, walked up to them and asked if they wanted to go and get coffee. Korie knew the woman. Her name was Marina, and she'd celebrated four years of sobriety the month before. She was well known in the rooms as a sponsor, someone who would take fragile newcomers under her wing. Korie liked Marina. Her first days in the rooms, the older woman had pressed a torn scrap of paper into her hands. "My phone number," she'd said gently. "Call if you start hearing voices."

Korie had declined Marina's offer of coffee that morning, but was relieved when Simona accepted. Simona turned back to Korie and embraced her quickly. "Whatever happens down there in Philly, remember who loves you," she said gruffly. Then, not looking back, she sauntered down the street towards the Greek coffee shop, her hand on Marina's arm.

At home, Korie packed some clothes and picked up her credit card. She changed from jeans, T-shirt, and sneakers into a black linen skirt, cropped white cotton tank top, and her wear-everywhere red cowboy boots. Then she shrugged on her jean jacket and hopped a cab to the car rental place at 78th Street and Broadway. There, she had rented the baby blue Chrysler and, her heart pounding with excitement, slipped behind the wheel, fired the ignition, and headed for Philadelphia.

Now, just past exit six on the New Jersey Turnpike, the traffic was still bumper to bumper, and Korie fought down the tide of nervousness and impatience that had filled her from the moment she'd set out on this road trip. God, she could hardly wait to see him now. After so many months, she could barely endure an hour, a minute, a second more. She could almost see him already, looking much as he had that very first time in the

Carson Agency parking lot. Their attraction to each other had been instantaneous, like something already known, an ancient affinity renewed. Why had she waited so long to make amends to this man whom she had loved from the day she met him? She prayed, as she had been praying all that afternoon, that when she finally reached Philadelphia and stood before him, he would not be too bitter, or worse, indifferent, to let her back into his life. Her imagination zeroed in on the place on his chest where she would rest her head, the shallow valley that ran between his nicely shaped pectorals with their small, inviting brown nipples. Oh, God, she prayed again, please let him understand. She had held her need for him at bay for so long, and at such cost, so that now that she'd finally admitted it, the absence of him was dizzying, like a sudden lack of light and air.

She wasn't even sure she would find him at his mother's house. But Florida would know where he was; she just prayed that it wasn't too far away. Suddenly, she felt foolish. What if he'd hooked up with someone else? What if he'd found himself a more worthy love? The possibility pierced her. She began to think that she should have called him at his mother's house before leaving, but she'd been afraid that he wouldn't hear her out over the phone. She had calculated that it would be harder in the flesh to turn her away.

She tried to reason now: She would drive to his mother's house and knock on the door. If Zach were living with someone new, he would have moved away from Quincy Street, right? In which case, Florida would enlighten her, and Korie would thank her, then turn around and drive back to New York. She wouldn't embarrass him if he'd moved on. She wouldn't make a scene. But the more she thought about Zach's arms around another woman, the more she wanted to put her head on the steering wheel and cry for all she had lost when she'd let him go. Okay, so she was feeling a little emotional.

One day at a time, she reminded herself. And when that gets too much, take it one *minute* at a time.

Up ahead, a rest stop sign came into view: BOB'S BIG BOY, MCDONALD'S, BOOTS COFFEE, it advertised. God, she could use a cup of coffee. Impulsively, she flicked on her indicator and maneuvered to the left, positioning herself for the exit. Yes, she would exit the fray of her thoughts for a while. She would stretch her legs, drink some coffee, use the bathroom, try to make her heart calm down.

The rest stop parking lot was full when she pulled into it, and she had to circle three times before she spotted a gray Mazda backing out. She pulled into the space it had vacated and switched off her ignition. Her hands were trembling, so she sat for a moment, trying to gather herself. Then she got out of the car, slammed the door, and walked with a defiant jaunt towards the glass front of the sprawling building. People jostled her on all sides, coming and going with their brown paper bags and Styrofoam containers of fast food. Children raced up and down the sidewalk, their harried parents calling after them. Lovers strolled hand in hand. Her heart dipped a little at the sight of them, but it smiled, too. Perhaps she would have that again. Perhaps if she stretched forth her arms, love might enter them again. This was how she was thinking as she grasped the handle of the glass entrance door and pulled it open, and almost bumped into a pair of endless blue-jeaned legs.

She knew the contour of those legs. Slightly bowed, muscled at the thighs, slender all the way down. The intimacy with which she knew those long hard legs paralyzed her. She didn't dare lift her eyes, so she focused on the shoes, brown desert boots in need of a cleaning, disappearing under the cuffs of the jeans. She didn't recognize the boots. Irrelevantly, it occurred to her that in the year and some since she'd seen him, the boots had had time to wear out, time for the outer corners of the heels to wear down in that characteristic way she remembered.

She was aware of a crowd gathering behind her, waiting for her to step around the blue jeans and walk through the door, but her feet wouldn't budge. The air around her felt charged, electrified. Slicing through its crackle, he spoke her name.

"Korie?"

Low-voiced, disbelieving, a question mark at the end of it. Then large brown hands with knotted knuckles clasped her shoulders and eased her gently through the door, and a warm flannel-clad arm slid 'round her shoulders and guided her into the hot, busy lobby of the rest stop. Korie felt as if she were moving in a dream, her feet not quite touching the floor. She let her head rest against his shoulder and breathed deeply of his smell.

At last they stopped moving and Korie looked around and saw that he had guided her through the mall-like interior of the rest stop, past the fast food counters with their lines of impatient customers, past the crowded entrances to restaurants and gift shops, past the rest rooms and the florist and the magazine stand, into an alcove behind a bank of pay phones. No one but the blonde, apple-cheeked teenager whispering into the last pay phone in the row could see them. The teenager gave her back to them, cupped the receiver closer to her lips, and continued her hushed conversation.

Zach turned Korie towards him, put a finger under her chin, and raised her face to his. She allowed herself to meet his eyes then, and found an ocean of tenderness there.

"Zachary," she said, so much gratitude filling her.

She noticed he had grown a glossy black mustache and short goatee, and developed three faint lines across his brow. She wanted to reach out and trace those lines, and put her lips to each one. He saw that she had cut short her wild springy hair. Involuntarily, his lower regions pitched and coiled as, unbidden, he felt again the sponginess of that hair in his hands, against his face, in his mouth as he made love to her.

He closed his eyes and moaned and crushed her body against his. He buried his face in her neck, and moved his hands down to her buttocks, pulling her hard into him, bending his knees, his hips straining against hers. Their mouths tasted each other hungrily; their urgent hands ranged over each other's bodies, touching all the secret places, gathering evidence that this was not a dream. It had been so long. He couldn't get enough, he couldn't let go. He could only draw back to gaze at her and then bury his face in her skin again, knowing that if he tried to speak he might weep from happiness.

They were still in that alcove some time later, Zach sitting on the floor, Korie sitting sideways between his legs. The teenager had left, and each person who came after her to use the last phone had taken one look at Korie and Zachary and chosen another phone.

They were only just beginning to trust their voices. There was so much to catch up on, so much to forgive.

"Where are you headed?" Korie asked at last.

"New York, to find you."

Korie laughed out loud and shook her head, a feeling of wild exhilaration overtaking her.

Now that she let herself consider it, Korie realized that meeting Zach this way, finding him again at a random rest stop along a ribbon of asphalt that connected their two worlds, *had* to be something more than foolish luck. In that moment, Korie understood that this was not a chance encounter, understood that just like that first meeting so many years before in the Carson Agency parking lot, this one had been perfectly designed. She put her palm against Zach's face, marveling that there were no coincidences, merely the quiet vectors of fate, drawing her towards this man with a force as insistent as memory, as absolute as love.

Korie didn't tell Zach that she was on a mission identical to his. She sensed that he already knew.

"But why now?" she asked him softly.

Zach sighed, a rueful little smile on his lips. "It just, finally, got to be too much," he said. "I suddenly felt as if I couldn't get through one more day without looking into your face. And I have to thank my mother. She helped me see that."

It had been the day that she got Neal's letter. Florida had made him sit next to her and read it, all the while studying him sternly.

"Zachary," she had said when he'd finished, "you're a ghost in this house, and I don't want a ghost living in my house anymore. I've had enough of ghosts. It's time for you to wake up. Stop living for everyone else! Start living for yourself! What do *you* want? Whom do *you* choose? Maybe it's time to go and find her, Zachary, and see what this life of yours is all about."

The funny thing, Zach told Korie now, was that his mother had sounded truly angry, like she wanted to shake the sense into him. Afterwards, he'd understood that she was also exasperated with herself. "I've lost one son thanks to my own lack of imagination," she had snapped. "I thought I had to live that way for everyone else, for your father, for you children, for the world. I was so wrong, Zachary, and I'm not going to let you sacrifice your life on the same altar."

"Lost one son?" Korie asked, immediately aware that something momentous had happened in Zach's family.

"Neal," Zach said briefly. "He went away." He paused and gazed at Korie like a man who had been starving and who now faced such a banquet he didn't know where to begin. "Oh Korie," he said, taking her into his arms again. "It's a long story. I have the rest of my life to tell it."

As he folded her to his chest, her head came to rest in that shallow valley that she remembered, and she turned her face into him, and pressed her mouth against the warm musky skin just below his throat. She knew they would have to move from this alcove soon, and decide whether they were headed to Philadelphia or New York. But not yet, Korie thought, not yet. Right now, she wanted only to linger in this half-exposed alcove and bask in the miracle of Zachary's arms.

ABOUT THE AUTHOR

Rosemarie Robotham, former staff reporter for *Life* magazine, is an editor-at-large at *Essence* magazine. Her short fiction has appeared in John Henrik Clarke's *Black American Short Stories: One Hundred Years of the Best*. She is the coauthor of *Spirits of the Passage: The Transatlantic Slave Trade in the Seventeenth Century*, and editor of the literary anthology, *The Bluelight Corner: Black Women Writing on Passion, Sex, and Romantic Love*. She lives in New York City with her husband and two children.